SAKHAROV THE BEAR

JOHN ELLSWORTH

COPYRIGHT

Chapter 1

R ussell Xiang

WE'RE BOUNCING around Red Square on Christmas Eve. The Kremlin is off to our right, spread beneath stars that have exploded into the cloudless night sky. Beneath the wheels of our Lada, the frozen snow is rutted where the trucks have it channeled. The bouncing traffic's endless points of light sweep across the sky, buildings and abutments and burnout oncoming eyes. Drivers confuse headlights with after-effects whereupon they over-steer and glide sideways along the roadway. Putin could charge admission.

Outside the windows of our little car the air is freezing while up ahead the red taillights of our quarry's Volvo send Morse Code signals through their rusted wiring. We can see the lone occupant frantically wiping his windshield with a white cloth. His name is Henrik Nurayov and my guess is that his breath has glazed the windshield because the defroster in his car is shorting out just like his taillights.

They are victims of the Russian rust that eventually causes everything to quit working, including the people. We would hate to lose poor Henrik to a violent motor vehicle accident, blinded as he appears to be. If anybody gets to kill him tonight, it should be us. But on the other hand, it would get us home in time for nightcaps were he to crash. At last, Henrik creates enough of a porthole to continue his journey without veering into a car loaded with angels.

Henrik is a British subject in the employ of MI6. Never mind MI6's loyalty oaths and all that, says Henrik. Instead, he collects Russian rubles in exchange for the wiring schematics of Her Majesty's aircraft carriers the *Queen Elizabeth* and the *Prince of Wales*, currently under construction. Or perhaps he'll receive payment for a flash drive loaded with the Prime Minister's nuclear codes to deliver a preemptive strike on Moscow. If it can be downloaded, Henrik has it for sale.

Tonight Henrik is a little off his usual route home. We know because we have been following him for a week waiting for him to make a move. He heads for the parking lots serving St. Basil's Cathedral, where he will pick up a succulent treat: a ten-year-old refugee boy from Syria.

Our job tonight—my driver and I—is to infiltrate Henrik's home and steal back all manner of computers, laptops, drives, gadgetry, and papers that could possibly have some value to Her Majesty's enemies. Henrik believes in free enterprise except when it shouldn't be free, which is when it should be paid for, which is always. It is around that syllogism that he has amassed a fortune, money which Henrik stores in the First World banks of Third World countries like the Caymans. Henrik never saw a bank sitting in the middle of banana trees that he wouldn't stuff with money from his traitorous ways. He was very democratic that way, giving all nations a chance to bid on Her Majesty's secrets.

And why are we from Moscow Station assisting our UK friends? Because we've been ordered to. CIA orders are never questioned. We're more like the military than the military.

Henrik's Volvo jostles across the washboard to the parking lot alongside St. Basil's. The brake lights flare and hazard lights take over. Children are everywhere along the block wall, standing in ones and twos and threes, some in cheery laughter and games, some blank-faced and despondent; others shiver, coatless, against the cold that would turn us all into statuary tonight. It is one of these—a coatless one —that Henrik waves at, indicating the child should come and speak into Henrik's lowered window. The chosen one points to himself, Henrik nods violently, and the child rushes around to Henrik's side. We can see the boy wipe a long smear of snot from his upper lip with the sleeve of his cotton shirt. Henrik ignores this, reaching outside his window without hesitation to inspect the child's testicles. Gently he weighs the sac in his palm, decides the boy is suitably pre-pubescent, whereupon Henrik, ever the consumer, smiles as if at a waiter tendering the sweetest lamb in all of Athens. The boy, whose nuts have just been jiggled, moves a step nearer the car. Suddenly he bends down and kisses Henrik squarely on the mouth. As he does this, two children rap on my driver's window—we are pulled up behind Henrik as if we, too, are shopping for the holiday—and Petrov, my driver, shoos them away. They kick the trunk of our Lada Vesta as they pass behind us onto the sidewalk. We don't notice.

The coatless chosen passes proudly around to the passenger door of Henrik's Volvo and slides inside. His head instantly disappears from view as the Volvo's hazard lights vanish and it crunches away from the curb, bored with the sidewalk chum. We follow behind but then, just as Petrov thinks Henrik has made us, she swings around him and moves us ahead with the traffic in the fast lane. There is no need to follow our man at this point: we know he is headed home because he has nowhere else to exercise his sexual hunger on the chosen except at his home.

We angle off through the traffic for a good twenty minutes. At last we leave behind the city limits and more of the sky comes into view.

Home is a crouching, single-family dwelling along a dark, sharply crowned road north of Moscow. Along its edges are irrigation ditches, and the look on Petrov's face tells me that if we were to slide off the road into one of those we would likely freeze to death after we have run out of gasoline, still undiscovered in this lonely place. So while Petrov takes care, her eyes glued to the road, my own eyes search out Henrik's surrounding acreage. I'm looking for any vehicle or form comprising a new addition to the property since our spy satellite beamed down its pictures late this afternoon. It is a difficult task, mine, because the pictures were an overhead view while mine is a view of the elevation. Still, somehow the mind makes the translation of the one to the other, and I'm happily satisfied to see there is nothing new under the sky. At least nothing on the outside; what or who might be lurking inside, that is anyone's guess. Which is why Petrov and I carry PSS Silent Pistols, the proud sidearm of the Spetsnaz. With our firepower we will overwhelm any person bent upon keeping us from Henrik. We will have our man and be done with it tonight. Make no mistake about that, I think to myself, and the phrase becomes a refrain in my mind. In my state of exhaustion—

we have been up three days—my mind produces images of Russian dancers in a line gliding gracefully to the lyric *Make no mistake*. The tune is Russian, I imagine, and I'm suddenly cognizant that I might be imagining this whole entire moment. I suck in a lungful of air and swallow it hard down inside my chest, where it creates a bubble that asserts itself against my diaphragm. Yes, I have hallucinated oftentimes tonight; it must all stop now before I shoot someone who isn't there and hit someone who is. My greatest fear.

I belch and my pulse returns to normal, the crazy time subsided.

My name is Russell Xiang. Petrov and the others at Moscow Station call me Rusty. I don't mind; Station is one-half American. But some of our tribe are recruited from the trash heap of KGB discards. Where they were dross to the Russians, they are gold to the Americans. Those of us who came here from America, we were well-received in Moscow, paid well, given new identities and sent out to collect information in that most traditional way of all spycraft: combing the late-night bars and clubs in search of lesbian and gay bureaucrats. These are the desperate ones, the angels who will sell Putin's secrets for warm arms and cuddles. I have held them in my arms, these desperate ones, and I have whispered sweet nothings while my bedroom video recorded us. We were never ones to ruin anyone, either. Neither did we ever expose anyone. But we certainly mined them for their gold while we ignored their dross.

We pull by the house and back into a lane overgrown with the barest of nut trees. Their branches weave a basket overhead, partially blotting out the starlight and it is from this shelter that we will watch for Henrik's Volvo. We aren't there five minutes until we see headlights approaching and ever so slowly the dashboard light of the vehicle resolves into the silhouette of two human heads side-by-side as if sitting knee-to-knee in the front seat.

"Two heads now," says Anna Petrov. "Rubles have been earned."

Without signaling, Henrik maneuvers into a looping right turn and speeds up his driveway to the circle drive in front.

"What's the hurry?" asks Petrov; we both laugh. All of our work should be so easy as this. Henrik's lust is steering the car and pressing the gas. He parks and the inside light flares and we know, Petrov and I, that Henrik can't make it inside the house and into the hot tub fast enough with his juvenile. The entire scene fills me with nausea and a sense of disgust for the man, which violates my cardinal rule that I harbor no feelings for my quarry, good or bad. I maintain this equilibrium so that I will make no errors in my work that might be born of emotion. Emotions kill. That should be the first line in every recruit's spy book.

We decide to give it ten minutes. At that point, Henrik and the chosen will be at the peak of their transaction with their attention sidetracked; Petrov and I will move in on them then. We wait now, without talking, watching the beginnings of snow as the sky is clouding over and flakes are sifting sideways all around our little car. It is serene here, almost, and I find myself wishing that I could just be with Petrov like this throughout the night except maybe even closer together in the car. She knows nothing of my feelings for her and would never guess: back Stateside I'm now a married man. Petrov would never suspect that a man like me would allow himself to embrace feelings for a work part-ner. I'm known as cold and methodical and able to kill without even a flinch at the instant the death blow is struck. Moreover, I'm known as the best field agent the Station has in Russia—particularly in Moscow—which requires the highest degree of self-control and lack of whimsy in one's personal life as is possible. There are other parts of me my comrades know nothing about, parts that could lead to a needle in my arm with a paralyzing agent streaming toward my heart. But those parts are never shown—ever. Those secrets will die with me. Those same secrets, ironically, could also be the death of me.

She nudges me. "Ten minutes," she whispers across the frozen air.

Without a word, I open the passenger door and stand up. She follows. There is no dome light; we are too seasoned for that. Wearing our goose down coats with hoods, we trudge off down the middle of the frozen road. Then we are turning up Henrik's drive and making our way from shadow to shadow as we come up on our quarry. The heavy gun inside its holster is tight up under my arm; Petrov carries hers likewise. Together my partner and I have expended tens of thousands of rounds through our service weapons at the range in Zarkovnia. We are expert marksmen, both of us, capable of field stripping our weapons then reassembling them in forty seconds, blindfolded. We are, in a word, ready for war as we slip around behind the house. There is but one light on inside, and I'm quite sure it is a night light in the master bedroom. That's right, I have been here before, as Henrik's guest, when the Station and MI6 were still talking. Anymore, not so much, as relations have been abraded. Blame it on Henrik.

We glide along the back of the house, pausing at the sliding door. I try it first. It is locked. Petrov produces two suction cups with handles and fits them tight against the glass, pressing down a hasp affair that seals the vacuum against the glass. Using an industrial glass cutter, I turn and carve out a man-sized hole in the glass, large enough for both of us to step through together. Petrov manipulates one suction handle and I the other as we lift the excised glass up and out and lay it roughly in the snow. A blast of warm air coming from inside causes the curtains to flutter, momentarily providing a quick look inside. There is no one in the room, though my field of vision is limited. I tap Petrov on the shoulder and we step through into Henrik's kill zone. Momentarily it will be our kill zone—if we are lucky, if we are fast, if Henrik isn't luckier and faster.

Just as we step inside and pause to get our bearings, a calm, commanding voice booms forth.

"Don't take another step. There are all manner of guns pointed at you right now."

The light that was on earlier is doused. We are completely in the dark and helpless, our guns still holstered —for whatever difference that makes: there are no targets.

"Withdraw your weapons and hold them by the muzzle as if you're passing them along. Because you are."

We follow the direction. No sooner have I extended my weapon than it is plucked from my hand.

Then the lights come alive and we are stunned by harsh spots being directed at our eyes. Now we are really blind.

"Rusty, old bloke, did you really think we didn't see you behind us?"

It is Henrik. I raise my hand to shade my eyes and I can just make him out in front of me. A heavy gun is held in his hand, its muzzle pointed at my head. Beside me I can sense Petrov doing the same, searching through the light for any kind of opening, any kind of advantage. She sees what I see, I'm sure: we are in the company of five men plus Henrik, all heavily armed, all prepared to shoot us, I have no doubt. They are Russians, I know by their ill-fitting suits and lackluster haircuts. One thing is for certain: they are not MI6 operators like Henrik. No, this little affair tonight is being held not under the auspices of British Intelligence. We have stepped onto the set of Russia Behind the Curtain. Which means we will die here tonight before we're done.

Henrik gets right to it. "How much do you know of Ehrlyich IT?" he asks us both.

In all honesty, I have no idea what he's talking about. And I tell him so.

"We know nothing about Ehrlyich. We don't know who he or she is and that's not why we're here."

I can hear the sarcasm almost before Henrik speaks: "You dropped in to check on my juvenile visitor? Is that what you're going to use to squirm out of this? Pity that, both of you. Bloody hell, how dare you insult me!"

"I wasn't going to say that at all," I reply. "We came here to rob you. We had no idea you were anywhere near."

Henrik laughs long and hard. "Please, spare me. You followed me here, you wanker. You damn sure knew I was here."

"On my honor, one American spy to one British opera-tor, we weren't behind you tonight, Henrik. Whoever you saw back there, it wasn't us."

I still can't see clearly because we are blinded by the spots, but I can hear the clearing of a throat, a mild cough, an emphysematous inhalation of air: they are allowing me to formulate, in my mind, the location of those spread around us waiting to shoot us.

"Your honor. I see," Henrik says. Then his voice becomes strong. "You two, take these two interlopers out to the pig pen and shoot them. Leave them for the pigs to devour. By morning there won't be even a bone left over for us to clean up."

"You will turn around and walk ahead of us," commands a new voice. "You will not turn around. If you do, you will be shot on the spot. We are going forty meters straight back until we come to a feedlot. You will unhook the gate and walk inside and wait."

"And then you will shoot us?" I ask.

"Then we will shoot you," says a second voice, a female. "And we will leave you to the pigs."

Already I know a deal has been struck between Petrov and me. She will attack the female; I will take the male—if the chance comes around, which it probably won't. These people are professionals. They're not known for giving chances.

We turn as ordered and step back through the hole we made in the sliding door. The wind has picked up and the snow is coming down in fat flakes that catch on my eyelashes; they would be a welcome touch from a caring universe at any other time. But tonight I tell myself that I don't want to die in a snowstorm; I want to die an old man, at home in my own bed, my children gathered around and my wife reading from *Psalms*.

Forty steps more and we are abreast of the pig pen. You smell it long before you can make out its confines by the ambient light from the house. Never a welcome perfume in anyone's night.

"Halt!" cries the man. Petrov and I freeze mid-step. We know better than to disobey but we also know he wants us to use our last energy getting ourselves inside the pen. It would be a great labor for him to have to wrangle us inside and, clearly, he isn't about doing that.

"Open the gate and step inside."

I slip in the snow, catch myself, and reach out for the gate.

"There's a loop over the gate post. Lift it up and away."

I do as instructed and pull at the gate. It slides toward me on the frozen ground.

"You first," the female orders Petrov. I know the moment has come as soon as she says it.

Petrov takes one step toward the opening in the livestock pen, feints with her body, then flings the back of her hand like a hammer across the nose of the woman with the gun. In that same instant I bring my foot around and catch the gentleman behind me across his left skull. He crumples to his knees, stunned, but his gun is still gripped in his right hand. Then—thankfully—he loses his balance and swings his gun hand down onto the frozen ground to catch himself from pitching face-first onto the ice. In that exact instant I finish him with no less than a soccer kick to the head and, as I connect, I hear the sharp crack of his vertebrae as his head snaps sideways, all but lopped off. In these same milliseconds, Petrov has jammed her elbow into the female's throat and the woman has crumpled to her knees, gripping her throat and gasping to draw air over her crushed larynx. She dies like that moments later, a startled look spread across her face as one who has received a telegram advising of one's own death. We quickly retrieve their guns and, without speaking, fire one shot each into their skulls. Henrik will hear the shots and know that we are dead and presently in the jaws of the feedlot's residents.

We waste no time. The odds aren't good: four armed expert killers against two CIA agents. Admittedly, we could also have been classed as expert killers, but there were only two of us. Half the firepower of our quarry and his guards. So be it.

Back to our car we trek, where we open the trunk and retrieve our shotguns. We work the pumps, making sure we are chambered. We remove our goose down and shrug into our body armor. Then back on with the goosedown so we don't freeze on the hike back down to Henrik's. When we are dressed and armed, I turn and have a look at Henrik's layout from our vantage point. It is clear he is feeling safe and secure; several lights are on inside the house and I think I can make out the strains of Ella Fitzgerald floating across the night air. It is no secret the Russians love American jazz, especially Billie Holiday and Ella Fitzgerald, so maybe they are even more relaxed down there than we hope. Petrov slaps me across the back and, without words, we begin our return.

Stars are low and glowing all around; the snow has blown through and this time we can hear the clank of the pigs rooting against their feeders in the feedlot as we come up close to Henrik's dacha. We creep around the western corner of the house, where we are startled by a flock of cuckoos flushing out from under the eaves. I would have thought these would be wintering in the deserts but evidently they have found warmth emanating through the ceiling and have decided to winter in Moscow, as unlikely as that sounds. They circle, return, and dive inside the attic through a small hole beneath the eave. I suck in a deep breath and can feel Petrov bump up against me. She reaches around and gives me a thumbs-up—we're quite sure no one has heard the flush, given the music playing inside and given that our targets are probably, by now, enjoying their vodka and finger foods.

Just as we are about to tiptoe around the corner to the back, a lone figure steps through the hole in the sliding glass door and moves several feet out into the dark. We can hear him cry out in Russian, searching for the duet that took Petrov and me out back for the killing. There is no reply and so the figure calls out again. I'm faced with a sudden quandary: do I take him now or allow him to return inside and perhaps re-emerge with all four targets as they launch a search party? What if he—they—don't re-emerge? What if we are again faced with the prospect of storming the house, two against four? I step back, deciding to wait and see. I make hand signals which Petrov immediately understands, and I kneel down on the ice while Petrov leans around me from above. Now we have two guns at the ready should our targets come into view.

I hear a loud cry from inside, then, and hear something crashing—a plate hurled against a wall, perhaps. It is a note of anguish, I'm quite certain. Seconds later, we are rewarded for our patience. Four men have come out, dropping immediately into a star defensive position where they are standing back to back while their eyes adjust and while they wait to determine if there is an immediate threat in the area. Petrov and I shrink back and hold our breath. We allow them to wait us out. Several minutes tick by. Slowly, then, the men step apart, turn, and put their heads together in a whisper. It is clear they are going to fan out as they move in a single line out toward the feedlot. Petrov and I are pros at this kind of thing. We know it's now or never, that the targeting will never again be this good and this lucky. The gods have smiled down on us and we don't hesitate.

Petrov fires first, immediately followed by the blast of my own shotgun, and two men are knocked down like straw figures. One of them moans and scissors himself in a circle on the icy ground, his legs involuntarily trying to escape. The other two are running and I take the one heading to our left while Petrov takes the one heading right. Two more blasts, then two more, and the figures are knocked to the ground. But Petrov and I don't immediately go running to our targets for any necessary mercy shots. We don't because there may still be others inside. We initially were exposed to six hosts waiting to gun us down as we stepped through the glass. But who's to say there weren't others inside, engaged in this or that while we were being intercepted? No guarantees at this point, so we wait and whisper before deciding we'll need to enter the house and search it down. Somewhere close by I hear a car motor rumble to life. We're preoccupied and cannot stop to see. I go in first.

Petrov waits for me outside, hidden in the shadows. If I'm killed, she will still have the opportunity to take out my killers and remove my body so our presence remains a mystery to the Russians. It is critical for world peace that Moscow Station not be connected to the night's events. So Petrov rides shotgun, in a sense, with her shotgun.

Into the house I step, this time into a room blazing with light. My instincts tell me I'm alone in the house and I search throughout. Several minutes later, I give Petrov the all-clear. We are somewhat secure—but some neighbor by now has probably called in the gunfire and very likely the authorities are on their way. So our time on-scene is very limited. Then I hear the second Russian we shot. He's still scissoring on the ground, I see when I look back outside. So I heave to and step out and march up to him. He looks at me, his eyes reflecting starlight and they tell me they know this is their last night. With one hand I raise my gun and blow away his head. "Peace out," I say, not harshly but sorrowfully. I have never enjoyed killing anything.

Returning inside, our real search begins. We are looking for anything and everything that Henrik might have had that he shouldn't have had. We are specifically searching for paper and computer files he might have been readying for sale—or have already sold—to the enemies of NATO. Petrov bends to Henrik's computer and begins analyzing files. I perform the physical search of the premises. I don't have far to go. For inside what appears to be his university yearbook from 1992, Henrik has hidden away a bill of lading. The items that were shipped by Henrik are jarring. The printout reads:

> *Browning Machine Gun Cal .50*
> *Squad Automatic Weapon M249*
> *Kalashnikov AK47*
> *F2000 Assault Rifle*
> *M60 7.62 mm Machine Gun*
> *FIM 92 Stinger Missile*
> *M72 Rocket Launcher*
> *Sarin, GB Chemical*
>
> *Bill of lading: Ehrlyich International Shipping,*
>   *Moscow, Russia*
> *Shipping containers: NB322V-1993x - NB322V-*
>   *1223x*
> */s/ HN*

"Here is what we came for," I tell Petrov, holding the paper over her shoulder down in front of her eyes. She scans down its length then turns her face to me.

"Jesus, Mary, and Joseph," she whispers.

"I know. Our little friend was having quite an adventure."

"Who is Ehrlyich International?"

"I might have heard the name. Shipper, evidently."

I look again. It is a bill of lading. The items have been sold and shipped already. But to whom? What NATO enemy has purchased enough wartime matériel to take over the State of New York from its National Guard? Or Middle

Eastern city? Is some Saudi emirate going down? I'm sure I don't know. But I know people who will.

One thing I do, because I know my employer and know what it might do, is I adjust the bill of lading. The part at the bottom that lists the shipping containers—NB322V-1993x - NB322V-1223x—I rip off that part. Then I commit those numbers to memory. Then I set a match to the smaller portion and watch the shipping container numbers go up in smoke. Now only I know the container numbers for I have memorized them. They are my ticket back to my home and my family. I always acquire a ticket like this when I'm at work.

I locate a folder on Henrik's desk that appears stuffed with the flotsam and jetsam of everyday life, slip my bill of lading inside on the top, and hoist the folder up under my arm. Bingo.

"Give me five," says Petrov. "I'm nearly finished uploading his hard drive."

"When we hear sirens, you're on your own if you don't pick up and leave with me immediately."

She brushes a curl of dark hair from her forehead where her hood has pushed it forward.

"I'm guessing I'll be going out the door ahead of you," she smiles. Then she holds up her hand and we fist-bump. "We have what we came for."

She means we've taken down Henrik's cache of bad deeds. Moscow Station will be elated by our work while they will be stunned at our find. There's enough military dreck on my bill of lading to send everyone scurrying to locate the weapons that departed Russia for God-only-knows-where. Our work is only just beginning. And I, who until tonight was about to return to New York in just twelve more days, suddenly find myself hemmed in from all sides.

The mission to locate the small war about to happen and especially the arms that will make it so, will fall to me as I'm senior. And to Petrov.

She turns and looks at me. She nods.

I nod back.

It has only just begun for us.

Then we hear a siren cutting across the wind, blown several miles ahead of the GRU. Petrov removes the satchel charge from her backpack and places it under Henrik's desk and engages the timed fuse.

Outside again, Petrov raises her hand. She switches on her small flashlight.

"Let's double-check," she says.

We begin turning over bodies and checking faces against the "most wanted" cards we have brought along. The cards picture the CIA's high-value targets. I switch on my light and follow Petrov from body to body, comparing the cards to the dead faces. Or what's left of them. After the fourth man is turned over, Petrov looks up at me.

"Well?"

I shake my head.

"He's not here."

"Then where—"

"Knowing Henrik? Probably out the front while we were coming around to the back. I heard an engine start up. We'll know if his Volvo's gone."

"He left everything behind."

"Except for himself. He never leaves himself behind. Or the young boy. I'm sure he was dragged along by Henrik."

"Of course he was."

"What we've made off with could just as easily be disinformation."

"Meaning none of the stuff on the bill of lading actually

even exists. It was just left behind to derail us from what he's really been up to."

We both know the drill. She's only verbalizing what we have known since we received the assignment.

I shrug. "Might very well be."

"So what do we do?"

Sirens of the approaching police are much nearer now. Maybe five kilometers at most.

"It's time," I tell her, and break into a run for the road. Petrov, who has proven she can outrun us all, passes me at full gallop.

I watch her backside as she pulls head of me, arms pumping, head down, shotgun slapping her in the back. Even at that terrible, post-homicidal dash for our lives, I can't keep from looking. Those tights she's wearing are everything. And as hard as I try, I cannot catch up to her where, if I could, I would caress that undulating ass. But then, fear always brings out the worst in a man.

Our little car is gaining traction and we are a hundred meters past the dacha when the charge goes off.

Henrik's lair of romance is no more.

Chapter 2

Try as he might, Igor Tarayev couldn't stop the tears from coming when he heard his son was dead. Henrik had made it to FSB headquarters, where he gave Tarayev the bad news about his son. FSB was the successor to the old KGB and was every bit as fierce and nasty as the Soviet military arm had been. But Tarayev, while he was the Moscow chief of the FSB, was also human. So he wept and shook and blew his nose over and over. Then he looked across his desk at Henrik. "Tell me," he said.

Henrik's face was twisted in pain. "Your son, this brave comrade, led the search team that ventured outside. As a captain of the guard he performed exactly how you would expect. He was fearless, passing through the door first, leading his men. And he was also the first one gunned down. The criminals who did this were hidden in the dark and Andreyavitch never had a chance. I saw the whole thing."

"You were where?" asked Tarayev. "Why weren't you with him?"

"You already know the answer. I had my documents and

computer files to protect. I shouldn't have to tell you that," said Henrik, scowling. He didn't like being taken to task for something he might have or could have done differently. "Do not forget, comrade, your son was there to guard me. Not the other way around."

Tarayev was a bull of man whose ears curled and whose blunt nose was cramped with protruding gray hairs. He was Henrik's FSB case officer while Henrik betrayed MI6 by working with the Russians. Tarayev had set the station's zero tolerance policy for failures in the field and his policy covered spies such as Henrik, too. As Henrik related the night's events, Tarayev's face turned cherry red. Henrik thought the man might have a stroke and told him so.

"Comrade, you're overreacting at the one who was put in jeopardy by your guardsmen. I was the one who was let down," he said in a measured tone. He was nobody's fool; the FSB needed him much more than he needed them. And he was reminding Tarayev of that important fact. "Were it not for my own quick thinking I would have been captured and tortured. Even now they would be hearing about you and the coming strike against Washington. But as it turned out, I made my escape and your secret was protected. So when you ask why I wasn't there with him you are forgetting all this. It just wasn't my role to guard your boy. I'm terribly aggrieved by his loss but I'm not responsible, comrade."

Tarayev sat back in his desk chair. He studied Henrik, the MI6 operative sitting across from him. At that moment he would have liked nothing better than to draw his service weapon and blast the child rapist between the eyes and have him dragged away. But he didn't. One thing was true: the FSB needed him much more than he needed them. There would be holy hell to pay if he followed his impulse and shot him dead. So he didn't. Instead, he turned elsewhere for his payback.

"Our man at Moscow Station will have names of those responsible within the hour. We will then move against them and I expect you to lead that attack, Henrik."

"Absolutely, my friend. I want nothing more than to strike back against these cowards. I want nothing more than to put a bullet in each one myself. I'm ready when you are ready to give me your plan."

"My plan is to hit everyone involved from the station chief on down. But with one important exception. Those who did the actual shooting at my son, they will be taken into custody and thrown into Lefortovo prison. Then we will deal with them slowly and exquisitely. We might even give them a trial as a warning to others. That is my plan."

"And it's a good plan. I would suggest that you allow me to create the details for this strike."

"I wouldn't have it any other way," said the FSB officer. "You know these people better than anyone we have. But one thing. I want this finished tonight. These animals will not see the sunrise, Henrik."

"Of course they won't. I make my solemn promise."

"And I want photographs of their dead bodies if they cannot be taken into custody. Don't fail me in this, comrade."

"You may count on me to do it right. Your son was my friend too. It will be my honor to avenge his death. Plus I will bring you the gunmen. I'm already thinking of how it might happen."

"Excellent, Henrik. I'm counting on you. Now, what artifacts might the cowards have found when you fled the dacha?"

"I left nothing behind," Henrik lied. "What was left was

disinformation. I've been around this block before, comrade."

"Excellent. But you're sure they found nothing useful?"

"Positive."

Tarayev searched Henrik's face with his own eyes. He believed he could see into a man's very soul, that he was gifted with a power of sight that enabled him to read minds. As he examined the traitor he realized that the man was perfectly protected when it came to covering up, that his eyes, his demeanor, were going to reveal nothing. The man was a pure professional. Tarayev had no choice, then, but to accept what he was being told. He didn't believe him, certainly, but he knew he had to proceed with the attack on Washington as if Henrik had left nothing behind when he fled. At least for the time being.

"All right, then."

Henrik allowed himself to fully exhale and settle back in his chair. It had been close, this conversation, this station chief's rage. But Henrik had managed to re-direct him against the real evildoers, taking the focus off of himself. He knew he had been deft and he knew he had been lucky. Many had gone before with this man, who had never been heard from again. Henrik knew that whatever else he did tonight, he could not fail. Not if he wanted to see the sunrise himself.

"Then we're done here," said Tarayev. "Leave me now. We will give you names and photographs of the killers within the hour. Be close by, Henrik."

"Done and done."

Chapter 3

R ussell Xiang

WHILE PETROV and I were tossing Henrik's office in our search for documents and computer files, the reality was never far from my mind about who Henrik really was. Granted, he worked for MI6, but Henrik was also the son of a wealthy international financier. So wealthy that his father had invested five billion dollars in the U.S. in the last few years. Hotels, retirement communities, inner city hospitals —he'd built them all. It won't surprise me, then, if the Station's way of dealing with Henrik is quite different from what I would like.

Moscow Station is hidden inside the United States Embassy in Moscow. The embassy complex is located in the Presnensky District in the city center of Moscow. Our floor is long and extremely crowded, like a boxcar. It is the target of constant electronic assaults from the Russians as they steal our secrets. Here are the ways the Russians have stolen secret information from us just since I have been stationed in Moscow these past weeks: bugging phone lines and bugging phones; miniature cameras hidden inside our copy machines; electronic circuits encased in concrete walls; laser beams broadcast from parked trucks into our windows that can eavesdrop; electronic eavesdropping of the electromagnetic fields that all computers generate; computer bugs and typewriter bugs that broadcast keystrokes to the outside world, as well as never-ending attempts to bribe the Marines who clean our offices. Do we know about all this? Of course, but in this age of disinformation we leave most of it in place. If there's a political angle to work, we call in the newspapers and TV and make a huge commotion to embarrass our hosts. Oh, and there's another side to all this: it's a *quid pro quo* relationship: they do it to us, we do it right back at them. And of course they misinform us just like we do them. Which, in the end, means that all stolen data and conversations and files anymore are never believed to be genuine.

Which brings me to the bill of lading we have taken from Henrik's office outside of town. A bill of lading is ordinarily a document given by a shipping company to a seller for goods received to be shipped. As Petrov and I discussed earlier tonight, the bill of lading could be 100% phony. It could have been kept inside that yearbook for months—years, really—awaiting the advent of spies in that office. Or, it could be 100% legitimate and we just happened to find it while I was grabbing books from the bookcase and shaking them to disgorge hidden papers. So there's always the possibility that the munitions, guns, and chemicals contained on that list were actually shipped and are hidden away in America right now, waiting to be utilized when selected cities are targeted by our enemies. Why move a whole army into a country when you can just take out its government and military installations and poison its water supply—all in less than two hours nationwide? Armies are passé. Little wars are the latest accommodation East to West. And, by the way, West to East. Our brain trust and military minds have likewise established fighting units throughout Russia equipped with the same or even more powerful munitions, guns, and chemicals. Chemicals? All bets are off if the U.S. is ever attacked at home. We will do and use anything to survive.

But there's another side to this. What if the shipments haven't arrived in the U.S. yet? What if the shipping container numbers I have memorized are all the U.S. has to lead it to the weapons of war? That makes me indispensable. Whatever else happens, Moscow Station will have to get me home to America if things suddenly go to hell over here.

So now we are in downtown Moscow on a freezing December night, holding a piece of paper up to the light to decide if it's real or not. Not actually up to the light, of course, I'm speaking metaphorically. Suffice it to say our laboratory is much farther down the road with our find, running many more sophisticated tests than mere porosity, ink manufacturers, and tool marks.

Moscow Station Chief Edward R. Henshaw rolls out of bed with the first buzz of his phone. The buzz is reserved for exigencies that require his presence at the station without delay. He knows its sound by heart and by training. Chief Henshaw is a rawboned sixty-year-old who boxed light-heavyweight at Annapolis, a man who married his Gamma

Phi sweetheart, and the father of three grown children—all Stateside and sometimes available to him only as barely recognizable contacts on his phone. He dresses in wool slacks and a polypro shirt underneath a wool sweater. As he unlocks the front door of his apartment inside the Embassy enclave, he slips into a Northface shell for protection against the snow, which is dropping from the sky in clumps at 12:44 a.m.

PETROV RETURNS to the room where we will debrief, holding two coffees before her. Between us we have knocked back two apiece since returning to our home base a little over an hour ago; we are frozen throughout and our toes and fingers are just beginning to thaw. On arrival, we separated into our restrooms where we cleaned what mud and blood we could from our boots and washed away the night's grief from our hands. For people like us, there is never enough soap or water to fully bring us clean. And we talk about that, Petrov and I, about the abiding sense of betrayal we carry around inside of us as we lash out at people who once trusted us enough to let us close. They are our customary targets: people we meet while undercover, people we know only slightly from galas and balls around Eastern Europe, and people we know only from kill sheets or sometimes even just artists' renderings.

She sets the coffee down in front of me. Then she sits down next to me and stretches her arms out wide while yawning. She playfully backhands me in the face as she stretches. I turn my face away and seize her forearm with my left hand. Like our Chief, we all wear polypro underthings and tonight Petrov is no different. When I seize her arm the material is cool and glossy to the touch, just as I imagine her skin. She isn't a woman who reveals much about herself; our relationship up until tonight has been one of secret operatives who often are paired up and who just as often are acting alone, but there is a kind of meritocracy between us that shifts back and forth depending on who has struck gold or eluded the FSB or made a kill that night. Tonight we are equals in that, since we have each taken down three men. I release her arm and push it away.

"Must you?" I ask.

"I must," she replies. "Rusty, old man, you did good tonight. Plus, we scored an important document."

I shrug. "Maybe, maybe not."

"Oh no," she says, "I just talked to Eddie Scales from Science. He says the document is genuine, the items on the list have been reported missing from various military bases and stores, and it all appears to be on the up and up."

"We've hit a home-run, then. We should go celebrate."

"Yes, a drink wouldn't hurt anything."

"Is your husband waiting up?"

"Rodney never waits up. He has his classes at oh-seven-hundred, remember. I'm oftentimes just loading into bed as he's leaving."

"His loss."

She looks away then, refusing to lower herself by acknowledging my meaning. I pull back. Maybe I have just given up one hint too many.

We are silently staring into space and keeping our distance when a guard comes charging into the debriefing room.

"We've been looking for you!" he breathlessly shouts. "The Chief has been shot!"

We leap up and follow the man, breaking into a jog

behind him. We are on the third floor of the embassy, on the enclave side, looking down on the walled-in courtyards below. A cadre of armed Marines surround a fallen body and we can make out the facial features of Chief Henshaw lying on his back in the snow, one leg crumpled behind him, arms out-flung, with half his head missing where the bullet found him and expanded upon impact. A large red patch is off to the side and I know that down in that blood, mixed among it, are pieces of skull and brain matter where the missing head parts have come to rest. Several Marines are pointing and peering off to the north, across the street to the north end of the embassy. A building rises up there where they are pointing, and the pantomime tells us they believe they know where the kill-shot originated from. Or thereabouts.

Petrov runs for the elevator and I follow but grab her hand from behind.

"You can't go out there!" I shout. "You could be shot too. This is payback for our work tonight. You and I come up on video as the two agents who left here together in the Lada. Maybe the Lada was seen by Henrik as he went by, and they know who we are. Henrik definitely saw us at the dacha! We are in play, Petrov! Do you understand?"

She removes her hand from the down arrow at the elevator and turns around to me.

"Yes. They've made us. And we're in danger."

"So where are you rushing off to?"

"I—I was going to go to Rodney, to warn him."

"If they want Rodney, he is already dead. They're way out in front right now."

Tears wash across her eyes and she sucks in a sharp breath. "Oh my God. Poor Rodney!"

"Yes, this isn't about the fact we made off with Henrik's records. Someone is really pissed. Someone high up."

She is stuck. She cannot call her husband on her cell phone as all calls emanating from the embassy are monitored by the Russians. Tipping them off to her husband—if they don't already know about him—would almost certainly get him killed.

We both know I'm right. Our days are filled with theft/counter-theft machinations and there is never a thought of retaliation by physical means. But tonight a bridge has been crossed. War has been declared on Moscow Station by the Russians because we have done something unacceptable. I can only assume that in our ambush of the Russian guards we managed to kill someone of note. We managed to kill someone who had friends in high places. I have no idea who that might be and I have no idea if my assumption is right. But I have a strong instinct about these things and I'm worried we might have crossed over. An internecine war could and maybe already has erupted among spies Eastern and Western, spies nobody actually cares about in a larger sense. While the powers that be turn their backs on us, we are left in place to kill and be killed.

My thoughts are pulled up short when Asuncion Robles arrives on the elevator.

"Good. You two should be out of here and on your way someplace safe," says our second-in-command.

"And where might that be, Señor Robles," Petrov says almost as a mockery. "Where do we run off to where Russians cannot find us in Russia?"

"I'm thinking of the green house."

"Not a chance," Petrov exclaims. "I'm going home to look in on Rodney."

"No," Robles says in his controlled manner. "No, you are

not, Anna Petrov. You and Rusty are going to leave underground and hide yourselves in the green house."

Unbeknownst to the Russians, our people have dug a tunnel leading from the embassy to the sewer system running below the streets surrounding our enclave. I say they don't know; that is probably more hopeful than it is accurate. They probably know all about it and have cameras monitoring those warrens and subterranean walkways. But I'm too tired to argue. Besides, it would do no good. Robles doesn't like me and won't put up with my objections for even a minute. We will do as he says and Petrov knows this too.

Robles brushes on past us and says over his shoulder, "My office. Ten minutes. Be collected up and ready to leave."

Chapter 4

R ussell Xiang

ASUNCION ROBLES HAS SENT us down to the tunnels. Our
armed guards are taking us to the exit, where we will board
a bus and ride several miles, get off, and walk two blocks to
the green house. The green house is the Station's safe house
where operators can hide while the FSB turns the town
upside-down looking for them. Why is it believed safe?
Because it is a large guest house behind the residence of
Rudina Alaevsky, who sits on the Duma, the lower house in
the Russian Federal Assembly. It is the more powerful
legislative house, the Duma. All bills, even those proposed
by the Federation Council, must first be considered by the
Duma. Which means her political reach is nationwide and
local politicos and constabularies are frightened of her.
Alaevsky has been bribed by the Americans, of course, and
the FSB would never dare to suspect she might be housing

the enemy. The Station remits to her Swiss account ten thousand dollars per month. In return we have our safety.

We emerge from the tunnels and head for the bus stop. It will be an eleven-minute wait for the next bus and we are freezing as soon as we climb aboveground. Petrov sits down on the bench and I stand beside her. Around us, in varying degrees of proximity, our guards pose as if busy at other tasks. They will watch over us all the way to Assembly-woman Alaevsky's house.

"Did you ever think you would be hiding out in sub-zero weather, in Moscow, waiting for a bus that will have no heat as its system will be broken?"

I smile at Petrov. She has changed her clothes from earlier and is now wearing jeans and a sweater and a hooded goosedown coat that reaches her knees. The coat is black and is not meant as a fashion statement. Her words are her attempt at humor in an uncomfortable situation. Always one with a try at levity, that's Petrov.

"No, I never thought I'd be waiting for a bus in sub-zero weather. I thought it would be sub-zero weather in an ice storm. Where's the ice?"

She giggles. "You're standing on it, Rusty. It's all around. This entire country is nothing but a solid block of ice. By the way, we've never been to the safe house. Will there be decent food and warm beds, I wonder?"

"Well, I've heard stories. I've heard that it's very comfort-able and well-stocked. I hope I'm right."

She kicks her feet back and forth, as a child on a swing, and appears totally innocent at that moment. I'm pierced by her beauty and I'm happy we are together and that we'll be spending time together, secluded, our time unmonitored by anyone including our spouses.

My own wife is in Washington, D.C., where she is

expecting our second child. I'm very happy about this but sad that I'm unable to share in the preparations. Antonia has sent me ultrasound images of our baby—a little boy— and that helps, but it isn't, of course, satisfying in any sense. Even with that blessed event going on in my life as I know it stateside, I find that I'm attracted to Anna Petrov, my friend and partner, in the absence of my wife. Maybe I'm just weak, I don't know. But there is something about the embrace of another human—especially an attractive one like Petrov— that pursues me and would see me roam.

We are quiet for four or five minutes until finally the bus approaches. Two of the four armed guards sidle up and casually stand with us, as the bus whooshes when it brakes and its front door slaps open. We climb aboard. Petrov and I sit near the front; the guards are someplace behind. The seats are narrow and I find myself pushed up against Petrov's thigh and torso, a not unpleasant seating arrange- ment. She feels me pressing against her but makes no attempt to move away. Maybe she has the same longing for the touch of another.

At the next corner the bus slows again and rocks to a stop. The front door again flies open and this time three sturdy-looking men in heavy wool topcoats and trooper hats climb aboard. In an instant I know they are Russian FSB agents. I shut my eyes and feign sleep as I sense the men drawing near, pausing beside us, and then moving on back until they are seated just behind us. Great, I'm thinking, they know who we are and they will drag us off at the next stop.

Except they don't. Because I realize I can smell alcohol and that they are passing around a bottle and sharing a drink in the middle of the night. They wouldn't be doing that if they believed they had located two spies—at least that is my take on it. Or else they are play-acting to convince our guards they have simply stumbled aboard the same bus. Which is it? Up under my left arm my gun is heavy and warm from my body heat. Slowly I reach up with my right hand and unzip my Northface coat down to sternum level to give me access to my weapon should I suddenly need it.

Petrov suddenly stiffens beside me and I turn to look. One of the Russians has reached forward and is tapping her on the shoulder.

"Hey, beauty, do you have the time?" he asks in Russian.

Petrov doesn't acknowledge him. So he tries again, this time punching her in the shoulder. "Hey, did you hear me, bitch? I want to know if you have the time?"

I turn in my seat and give the man a look. A grim look. His eyes shift to me.

"Turn around, fool," he says to me.

But I don't. I continue staring at him.

"Did you hear me, fool? I said turn around. That's an order!"

Again I ignore him.

Then I speak. "Don't touch my wife, please. She has no interest in you. Go on about your evening now, please."

It is a fair request. The man leans back, his eyes still locked on mine, then he looks away. I realize that the man next to him has pushed him back with his elbow, telling him he should disengage. The second man smiles at me.

"My friend has had a little too much to drink tonight. Please excuse his rudeness."

I'm about to say thank you, when the first man suddenly leans forward again and drops his hand on Petrov's shoulder, which he begins kneading through her coat. I bring my elbow up and knock his hand away.

"Don't," I warn him.

"Says you?" the man asks. "Don't you see there are three of us?"

"I don't give a damn if there are twenty of you. You are being impolite and I don't like it."

Whereupon the man reaches down to his hips, unsnaps his holster, and brings his pistol up to my eye-level. He points it directly at me.

"Polite? How's this for polite?"

He waggles the muzzle of the gun and sneers at me. As I feared might happen, two of our guards have come forward and have drawn their own weapons.

"Not good, friend," says Samiov, the leader of our guards. "Suggest putting that back in its holster." He nudges the ear of the first Russian with his gun. The first Russian starts to turn, realizes that there is a gun pointed at his head, and lowers his own gun, replacing it in its holster.

"Smart man," says Samiov. "Now get off the bus. Yes, step to the front and get off our bus. Up you go now."

The three Russians standup as one and shuffle forward, our guards crowding them and forcing them down the steps to the door.

"Pull over now," Samiov tells the driver in Russian. "These gentlemen have overstayed their welcome on your bus."

The driver obeys, braking and then throwing open the door. The three FSB men scramble down the steps and step over to the curb. The door swings shut and we are moving again.

"Did they know?" I whisper to Samiov as he returns to us.

"They knew," he says. "They would have followed you to the green house and mounted an attack after we were gone."

I shoot a look out the back window of the bus. The

threesome can be seen coming up to the bus stop at the corner, where they stand, stamping their feet in the cold and speaking animatedly. There won't be another bus by for fourteen minutes, according to the schedules along Presbinaya Avenue. It is good. Petrov and I settle back in our seat.

"That was stupid," I say to Samiov. They had us and they gave us up."

"Alcohol," says our lead guard.

"Thank you," Petrov whispers to Samiov and his crew.

The guard smiles. I realize I have never seen him smile in all the time I have known him and been in his presence.

"It's our job," he whispers to Petrov. "Just doing our job."

And at that moment, I can see it in his eyes. He, too, is attracted to Petrov.

The poor woman. Surrounded by men, men, and more men who would like to inhale her.

And there am I, at the front of the pack, howling the loudest.

I remove my right hand from inside my jacket for the first time since the men became belligerent. My gun remains in its holster.

I didn't need it after all.

Chapter 5

R ussell Xiang

IT IS our second night in the green house, the second night Petrov and I have sat at opposite ends of a soft leather couch and watched Russian state TV. Hearing the broadcast, you'd think we were enjoying the comforts and offerings of the world's most robust economy with the lowest unemployment and highest wages anywhere. But to walk the streets of Russia you would quickly know otherwise. People are going without, people are hungry and cold, while the overclass is, in fact, living in that world created on state TV.

But do I really care? Out of the corner of my eye I'm watching Anna Petrov as she shifts position, sitting more on her lower back on the cushions, one foot pressed against the coffee table with the other leg up over her knee, munching Papas corn chips and drinking a Russian Coca-Cola. She yawns and shoots me a look and a smile.

A coded number calls the phone I was issued. I answer.

Challenge and password exchanged, we can talk.

"Moscow Station, laboratory."

"Yes?" I ask, already knowing why the CIA lab is calling me.

"Was the bill of lading already torn when you found it?"

"Why do you ask?" I ask.

Long silence. Muffled words, hand over phone.

Then, "The paper tear is new. Did you tear the paper?"

"Yes."

"Why?"

"That information on the bottom of the bill of lading is my ticket home."

"The information ripped away was the numbers of the shipping containers, am I right?"

"Yes."

"Why did you tear off those numbers? They are critical to our ability to intercept these shipments."

"Consider our position here at the green house. Our cover is blown. Knowing our government, there is at least a fifty-fifty chance it will deny us. It will deny we are connected to it. So where does that leave Petrov and me? Are you taking us home now?"

"You know that's a question I can't answer, only your manager can."

"Give my manager this message, then. Petrov and I have been talking. Our cover has been blown and retaliation already began last night when they killed Henshaw. We believe something is terribly wrong for the Russians to go after our station chief. We believe we caused that thing to go wrong and we believe we are targets. That being the case, we want the Company to make sure we get out of Russia safely and get home to the States safely. Only then will I give up the container numbers. Are you writing this down?"

"I am." He repeats my comments almost word-for-word.

"Good night, then," I tell him. Then I hang up.

"Was I good?" I ask Petrov.

"Couldn't have been better."

Then we are silent. Then, "You know we are at great risk."

"I know," she says. "But now I need sleep. We'll talk tomorrow."

"You're off to bed?"

She nods. "It's half-past nine. I'm off to bed after the news."

I return her nod. Despite all the good things between my wife and I, I want nothing more right now than to slide down the couch and take Petrov's hand in mine. But how foolish would that be? Station would be angry with me; Petrov would hate me; I would hate myself for being so weak. So I remain glued in place, appearing to watch TV while secretly eating my heart out. Damn and be damned!

Which is when we first hear it. Someone running outside.

Then we see a figure flash by on the porch just outside the French doors leading out to the deck that overlooks a city park. There is a barbecue out there, covered in snow across its domed top; four chairs drawn up around a table that is too high for them; and a chaise lounge fully extended and flat that is likewise latticed with snow. These things are there and in place, I see when I cross and open the door, but there is a new addition: footprints in the snow. Crossing right to left behind our green house. I turn to retrieve my gun from the fireplace mantle and, as I move, a bar swung from beyond the door catches me across the forehead and I go down.

COMING TO. Alone and in a dark, cold place.

There is no light, period, and I realize my clothes are wet and I'm out-of-control with the shivers. I have wet myself. I call out to Petrov, but there is no answer. I sit up. I have been lying on concrete. As I sit up my head bumps against a solid object and I reach up. It seems the ceiling is so low that I cannot sit up. I lean and reach out with my hand, trying to touch the floor. I cannot easily touch it, so I swing my legs over a ledge and let myself down in the dark. Down, down I go until finally, when my hips are over the edge, my feet touch a solid floor. Now I'm standing in the dark and I take inventory of my body. There is a screaming ache across the front of my head where the bar caught me at the green house. Where have I been taken? And where is Anna Petrov?

"Hey!" I call out in Russian. "Help me!"

There is no answer, nor did I expect one. That would have been too much, for help to come running.

Doing what I do, my training is to expect the unexpected and to not over-react to anything. Which is what I'm forcing myself to do right now: remain calm, slow my pulse rate, even-out my breathing. I turn and attempt to climb back onto my ledge but cannot raise my leg high enough to swing it up onto the concrete shelf. Reaching out across the black I try to find a handhold to pull myself back up but there is none. Nothing to grab onto.

"Hey!" I call out again, but this time in English. "Help me if you will!"

My legs are shaking, I realize, and I let myself crumple down into a squat. Which is when I feel my tongue playing over my front teeth and I realize the two top teeth have been broken off. I inhale a gulp of air over them, testing their nerve endings and, thank God, I'm not shot full of pain by exposed nerves. I don't remember being struck across the mouth. But whoever did it thankfully didn't break off enough tooth to expose nerves. Otherwise I would be fighting more than just fear and alarm upon coming awake in this dark place.

So I take inventory of my surroundings. Arms outstretched, I walk across—I'm guessing it's across—the room until I come to the far wall. My walk is short, only three steps. Then I trace my way from right to left until I come to the back wall of the room. It is small enough, four steps this time, that I can only refer to this place as a cell. Three steps again to my left and then back up to my concrete bed. Following beyond that further left I come back across and find there is a metal door closed tight with only the smallest seam of yellow light.

I guess that I'm at the Moscow Jail. Also known as Lefortovo Prison. That would be the logical place for the FSB to take me. Guessing again, Petrov will be imprisoned here too. They no doubt have perceived that we are a team; they no doubt have determined that we were the shooters at Henrik's dacha.

Squatting, my legs begin to tremble and I let myself topple over onto my side. There is no other position available to me. I wrap my arms around my upper body and close my eyes.

I'm not afraid. Our training exposed us to much harsher conditions at Camp Peary and the Farm than what I'm experiencing here. I will simply and quietly wait until they decide to approach me. They might torture, they might even kill me. I might become a star on the wall at Langley.

But I'm not afraid.

Chapter 6

President Hubert S. Sinclair hated taking that first piss in the morning. The enlarged and boggy prostate became even more cantankerous overnight, refusing to allow a good stream of urine to flow and fill the toilet bowl in the president's private bathroom, just off his private bedroom. He was glad he no longer shared a bedroom with the First Lady; as he stood at the toilet and tried to force the urine stream to strengthen he leaned his left arm against the wall above the toilet and turn his face sideways and grunted and moaned. Dorothy—the First Lady—would have heard his *toilette* noises and immediately been all over him to call in the doctor without delay. And President Sinclair hated doctors almost as much as he hated his enlarged prostate. They had ordered him to give up jogging after his knee replacement and if they found out the prostate was acting up again—who could say? Who could say what they would come up with next? Prostatectomy? Wouldn't that leave him unable to perform in bed? He shuddered at the thought and shook his penis with his free hand, squeezing the last drop of production into the toilet bowl and then flushing.

News of the Moscow arrests had hit Langley before dawn and was escalated to cabinet bureaucrats and escalated again, this time to the Oval Office. Delicate arms reduction talks were underway with the Russians. The U.S. absolutely could not allow itself to be connected to the murder of an FSB chief's son. All connections to Xiang and Petrov would have to be disavowed.

The President, after voiding, returned to his private office adjoining his bedroom. He took his seat while still in his pajamas and ordered coffee and toast from his steward. Then he called his contact's cell phone, avoiding the Langley switchboard where the man worked. The man's name was Anatoly Palatov. His cover was a phony Ph.D. from Stanford in Russian languages. He did, in fact, know some Russian, but that was after working two tours at Moscow Station, not from sitting in a university classroom. His duties at Langley were few and were clouded with mystery. It was known he was tight with the White House but not much else could be said about him.

"Anatoly," said the President as if talking to an old friend —which he wasn't—"about this Moscow arrest of your agent."

"Russell Xiang. Anna Petrov. Good people."

"Good or not, I can't allow this thing to be connected to us."

"I understand, Mr. President."

"So here's what I need you to do."

"Sir?"

"Deny, deny, deny! Disavow any connection between them and the United States."

"Leave them dangling, sir?"

"You're getting it now, Anatoly."

"Yes, sir."

"Here's part two of your task. I've been briefed on the shipping containers carrying weapons to the U.S. I know all about that and the bill of lading seized by Xiang and Petrov. So here's what we're going to do.

"Sir?"

"I'm told that Russell Xiang's wife works as a prosecutor for the U.S. Attorney here in D.C. She has the legal smarts to hire an attorney to defend her husband in the Moscow courts."

"Certainly agree with that, sir."

"Good. So I want to know who this person is that she hires to defend Russell. You will determine his identity and advise him that this government will do everything it can to help free Russell Xiang and Anna Petrov."

"How far will we go?'

"Anything the lawyer needs, we will provide. Anything. We must get Xiang out of there if we are going to obtain shipping container numbers. That's what's been explained to me. Days like this, I hate this job, Anatoly."

"Yes, sir."

"Get back to me every step of the way. You have my direct line and you have my ear, Palatov."

"Yes, sir."

"And here's another thing. What was Xiang working on?"

"He was leading a team at Langley. His posting to Moscow was TDY only. He wouldn't have been there another week in the normal course of things."

"I appreciate that. So here's what I need you to do. How big is Xiang's team?"

"Three men and one woman."

"Are they anybodies?"

"Sir?"

"You know, are they connected—any senators or

congressmen in their families? Any war hero daddies? That kind of thing."

"No, sir."

"Good. Then I want them taken out."

"Sir?"

"I cannot afford to have people running loose who might connect Xiang to the United States CIA. Loose lips sink ships, Palatov. As true now as it ever was."

"Sir, the CIA doesn't just go around killing off its own employees. I don't know where you got that—"

"Goddam it, Anatoly Palatov! Are you not hearing me? The lives of millions of people are at risk. Nuclear disarmament cannot be sidetracked because of one stupid CIA officer. Don't your people know they're expendable? What kind of camp are you running over there?"

"Sir, I can't—"

"Mr. Palatov, we are not negotiating here. This is a matter of greatest national security and I'm giving you an order. Do you have any questions about the order?"

"No, sir."

"Do you understand my order?"

"Yes, sir. Eliminate Xiang's team."

"So we're clear?"

"Yes, sir."

"Look, Palatov. We can even improve our play here. When you hit these people, make it look like the goddam Russians."

"Make it look like the Russians did the hit?"

"That's my guy, yes! Now we've got something we can toss back at them. This is pure inspiration, Palatov."

"Sir, if—if you say so."

"Get it done, Palatov. Without delay."

"Yes, sir."

"One more thing. Plan on coming by the White House on New Years Eve. We'll be singing songs and drinking Dom. Your wife will love it."

"I'm not married, sir."

"Then bring a date, you—Anatoly. Don't let me down, son."

"I won't, sir."

"Good man."

The President hung up the phone. His hands were shaking and he wrung them together and tried to bring them under control.

By the time he received his toast and took his first bite, the shaking had gone away.

Xiang and Petrov were abandoned, as far as the public and the Russians knew. But behind the scenes his administration would do everything it could to see them released and returned to the states. He drew a deep breath and slowly chewed his toast. Now if he could only make it all happen before the weapons crossed into the United States. If he failed, the most horrific attack on American soil would occur and it would come back on him.

Failure wasn't an option.

Chapter 7

The President's order to locate the weapons in the shipping containers in no more than twenty-four hours was taken on by the FBI and DHS. It involved pulling out all the stops to locate the weapons containers at American seaports before they were waved through. It was a huge task, probably impossible, but there were jobs at stake—that was the bottom line. It had to appear that the government had taken all possible steps to locate the shipping containers. The President ordered the FBI and DHS to throw every last asset at the problem.

Special Agents Timkins and Ng of the FBI were tasked to head up a large force of agents in L.A. First up was gaining an understanding of the shipping industry. According to the FBI computers, there were over twenty container terminals in the United States classified as maritime. They knew the interception had to be at the maritime container terminal when the arms came through.

But how to narrow it down?

In talking with Homeland Security, the agents got up to speed on searches and scans of incoming containers for nuclear materials. Incredibly, they found that less than 100% of containers were scanned for nuclear contents. Moreover, the statistic for container searches—where the government agents actually opened containers and searched inside—was all but non-existent. Physical searches were minuscule compared to the risk involved, which had huge potential for sneaking in the kinds of weapons terrorists wanted. So Timkins and Ng immediately knew they would outright fail without the container numbers. There was no choice: they had to have the shipping numbers assigned to each container that would be carrying the Russian war making matériel.

However, only Russell Xiang had those numbers.

Timkins and Ng wasted no time reporting that locating the shipping containers by inspection would be like finding one needle in ten thousand haystacks. Still, they were told to proceed anyway. What they weren't told was that theirs was a political mission. There was zero expectation of finding the weapons.

It was only important that they try.

Then, when the attack came, the President could show all that he had done to head it off.

Chapter 8

Antonia Xiang was married to Rusty and she believed he was in Russia, though she had no proof. "But a wife senses these things," she said to her closest friend from work. Antonia was a staff attorney at the U.S. Attorney's Office in Washington. She worked within walking distance of the White House. While her married name was Chinese, and while her husband was of Chinese descent, Antonia was not Chinese. She was a Wisconsin girl, born and raised —a true cheesehead who still had a secret crush on Bret Favre.

On Tuesday she was home from work with their son, whose sore throat had brought on a temperature and who, in the last few minutes, was crying out that his muscles ached. Antonia switched off the vacuum cleaner and was about to go check on him when the phone rang. Her heart leapt. It could always be Rusty!

But the number was not calling from Russia. It was not a 7 prefix.

"Hello?"

"Mrs. Xiang, this is Mr. Slosser."

She knew she was supposed to know who it was. And she did. Rusty's boss.

"Yes, I remember you from the Christmas party, Mr. Slosser."

"Good. Well, the reason I'm calling, we've had a bit of an upset in Moscow and Rusty has been arrested."

"Arrested! What for?"

"We don't exactly know yet. He was working at the Embassy, preparing new brochures for the visitors. Somehow he got entangled with the Moscow police and now he's in jail."

"Did he call you about this?"

"No, but our sources—"

"What sources? Who are we talking about here, Mr. Slosser?"

"Our switchboard received a call. Unfortunately, the operator didn't take down the calling number. But the message was that Russell Xiang was arrested. He's in Lefortovo Prison here in Moscow."

"That doesn't sound like a speeding ticket, Mr. Slosser."

She was not easily alarmed at arrests and that's why, she would later tell her friend, she was not wetting her pants. Her job at the U.S. Attorney's office was to put bad guys in jail. She would go along with Mr. Slosser and find out what she could, then she would decide what to do.

"Oh, I didn't say it was a speeding ticket. Truth is, we don't know why he's being detained. Probably some kind of mistake. It happens, you know."

"Mr. Slosser, I know a little about Rusty's work. I know he doesn't do Embassy work—"

She was about to go on and tell him she knew Rusty

worked for the CIA but the bastard had hung up on her. She called his number back and got a "not in service" recording. *Not in service, my ass*, she thought. *What makes the sons of bitches at the CIA think they can't come clean with members of the U.S. Attorney's Office? I know how CIA officers and FBI special agents trade back and forth all the time. So why can't their superiors? Question for the world at large: come in, please. This little housewife in Maryland wants to know.*

Oh well.

So now what?

Then Russell junior called to her again. This time he did sound worse. And he was coughing. So she went into his bedroom.

WHEN HE HUNG up the phone, Slosser fixed the two FBI agents in his gaze. "You hear all that?"

They unplugged earpieces and said yes.

"Your job is to watch who she goes to. We need all conversations, all travel, all meetings. We have to know who she chooses to defend her husband. Understood?"

"Understood."

"Notify me as soon as you have a name for me. The person she chooses belongs to me."

"Understood," they said in unison.

TEN MINUTES LATER, Antonia had OJ in her son, cough syrup from the last go-around dosed out, nose blown and Vicks on the chest—all her mother's old remedies, none of which actually worked but they made the patient think he was doing better. Plus plenty of hugs. Russell was only six, so he hadn't yet started to pull away from his mother like she had heard would happen.

She had two choices facing her now. One, she could drop what she was doing and try to call someone in Russia and learn more about Rusty, or, two, she could go into the kitchen and pour two fingers of scotch and see if she could find where she hid her cigarettes after the last time. With a heavy sigh, she decided to make some calls and then have the scotch. Two birds, one stone, and all that.

"Who do you call when your husband is arrested in Russia?" she asked her friend at the U.S. Attorney's Office that afternoon by phone.

"I give up."

"Well, believe it or not, there are tons of American law firms operating out of Russia. Some of their people even do criminal law. Just Google *Russian Lawyers* and be ready to start dialing."

"Goodness," said Laura.

"So tell me, Laura. Does our office maintain any contact with prosecutors in Moscow? Or police?"

"Um—not that I'm aware. I've never heard of that."

"I wonder if any Russian law firms have English speakers?"

"Surely they will."

"All I can do is try. Poor Rusty!"

"Poor Rusty. Call now, Antonia. It'll make you feel better."

She took her friend's advice and made several calls. She found out right away that most of the Russian firms wanted to deal with American businesses looking to do business in Russia. Of course, that was where the big bucks were. So she kept dialing. Finally, she found a small firm with Russian names and dialed 7 plus the number. The guy had to be call-forwarded, she decided, because he answered even though it was probably the middle of the night there. They talked and she explained her problem. His English was good enough. He said he'd make some calls the next day and call her back. She asked him how she could pay him and he said, much to her surprise, "Visa? MasterCard?"

The next morning he called her back. He had some news. Russell Xiang was being held in Lefortovo Prison in Moscow. "Is this your loved one?" Mr. Andaleyev asked her. Antonia told him the name was right. He asked what else he could do for her and she asked him whether he handled criminal cases. There was a long pause. Finally he said, whispering, "We do not mix with the Ministry of Justice here. Too dangerous."

"You mean you won't go to the prison and find out why my husband is locked up?"

"No. Too dangerous."

"You could call the prosecutor and ask them, correct?"

"Too dangerous."

"What *are* you able to do."

"Nothing more. Don't worry about payment. Goodbye."

And with that he hung up.

So now what the hell do I do? Antonia thought. I can't just hop on a jet and leave my son to fly off to Russia. That doesn't work. Besides which, I don't speak the goddam language so I would get nowhere. I'm really pissed at Mr. Slosser that he didn't offer to help me with this. But that's the CIA. They are quick to ask you to go in harm's way and even quicker to throw you under the bus. Rusty knew this going in. I guess I did, too, but just never admitted it to myself.

Now what? she was wondering, when Russell junior called out and begged her for an Xbox. *Great,* she thought, *your father is locked up in a Russian jail and you want to shoot Russian soldiers in a video game?*

I need to talk to someone.

Then Antonia remembered, *Rusty's father. Just the guy.*

Chapter 9

The next morning, Antonia got a sitter—sick child—then called Henry Xiang, reporting on Rusty. Henry was immediately on it. He said to check her office's connections in Russia. He was hoping for some kind of relationship between the U.S. Attorney's Office in Washington and its counterpart in Moscow. Something like that could go a long way toward getting Rusty out of prison. She drew a deep breath as she backed out of the garage at their condo. It was everything she could do to hold it together, but she was giving it all she had. *One step at a time,* she told herself, *and it will be all right.*

Inside the Robert F. Kennedy Building, upstairs in her office, Antonia had just pulled off her shoulder bag and poured her first tea when Maggie Maison, the administrative assistant to Jeb Niswanger, the Special Teams head, knocked once and entered her office without invitation. "Jeb wants you on eleven. Stat."

Jeb was just the man she wanted to see about the Rusty problem. The timing was perfect. Antonia pushed aside the steaming mug, dipped the tea bag up and down twice more for good measure, and grabbed the tablet she would need for any notes. Jeb's meetings were commonplace for Antonia and usually amounted to nothing more than a policy change or new policy announcement. Niswanger was tasked with keeping all prosecutors in line with departmental policy. There would probably be thirty others in attendance with her. She would buttonhole him after the meeting and pick his brain about Rusty. She just had a feeling that there would be some connection, some backdoor way into the Russian prosecutors' offices.

But when she entered the conference room she was taken by surprise to find present only Jeb and the U.S. Attorney herself, Barbara Anne Belizza. There were no recording devices and no one to take notes, as was the usual practice of Niswanger and his staff, especially during those rare occasions when the U.S. Attorney herself—the boss—sat in on the event. A mere Assistant U.S. Attorney, Antonia didn't sit until directed to by Niswanger, who was sitting one-off from the head of the table at the USA's right hand. Antonia was directed to the fourth chair down from the USA's left hand. She took her place and switched on her tablet.

"Thanks for coming," said Belizza. "We know this is an unusual meeting for you, Antonia, coming in to find just me and Mr. Niswanger waiting for you, but what we have on our plate today is also unusual."

Antonia felt her pulse quicken. Was she about to be tasked with a top secret job? She hoped so; she loved being on the inside of what went down with the U.S. Attorney's office. Especially those major crime prosecutions that would occupy the front pages of the *Post* while the cases crawled through the judicial system. She typed the day's date on a new page and waited.

"Unusual, but I'm up to it," she replied with a smile. "How can I help? Oh, and then I need to ask you a question." She looked up from her tablet. Neither Niswanger nor Belizza was smiling.

Belizza answered, "We're going to need to put you on administrative leave and order you to stay away from the office for several months."

Antonia was shocked. Her face paled and a crease appeared between her eyebrows.

"Did I do something wrong? Did I—"

Belizza shook her head. "No, no, it's nothing like that. Jeb, why don't you fill Ms. Xiang in?"

Jeb Niswanger nodded. His thick eyeglasses slid partially down his nose as he did so.

"Very well. Look, Antonia, we've known each other for what, seven years?"

"Eight."

"Exactly. And during that time we've developed a certain level of trust between us, wouldn't you say?"

"I would, yes."

"But now a new prosecution is going to take place. A prosecution brought by this office against—against—well, against your husband."

Antonia half-rose up out of her chair. But then she slowly lowered herself back down. "Wait, did you just say our office is prosecuting my husband?"

"I did," said Niswanger. "Your husband has been holding himself out to the Russians as a CIA agent. He is not any such thing, of course."

She was floored. She'd never heard anything so ridiculous. "What is this, a parallel universe? Of course Rusty works for the CIA. He has for ten years now!"

"He might have been telling you that, but it's not true. He

was involved in a murder in Moscow, the Russians arrested him and are putting him on trial. We've been tasked by the President with prosecuting him for holding himself out to the Russian government as an agent of this country. He will be tried in absentia or, if he returns, he will be tried upon return here."

"This is insane! Something is very very wrong here. You people are helping the President throw Rusty under the bus!"

Niswanger looked at Belizza for help. "Ms. Belizza?"

"Right. All we can say right now is that another agency has been looking into your husband's activities. Your husband has been indicted as of this morning."

Antonia felt her heart racing. Her forehead became damp with the sweat of fear. She abruptly sat back in her chair and caught her breath.

"Indicted? When does he get told about this? He's in Russia as of yesterday."

"Yes, he's in the Moscow City Jail.

"City Jail," Antonia whispered to herself. Then, "I must go. I must get in to see him immediately."

"Hold on," said Niswanger, raising a hand and indicating she should stay seated. "Hold on, Antonia. Let's think this through. You're a member of the staff that is prosecuting your husband in the States. You are being put on admin leave while the prosecution works its way through court. In the meantime, you are not a defense attorney and you can't just go right inside the jail in Moscow and flash your bar card and expect to see your husband. Also, as a member of this staff, you could be said to have a conflict of interest where Mr. Xiang is concerned. While you're on administrative leave to avoid the appearance of impropriety, you're still staff and that means that ethically and legally you cannot communicate with the prisoner. At least not without his lawyer present and some kind of waiver signed and approved by this office. It gets into a very gray area. But the point remains: you cannot just go running to his side right now. It isn't legal."

"Legal be damned!" cried Antonia, rising up out of her chair. "That's my husband you're talking about, Mr. Niswanger, not some ordinary defendant. The father of my children."

"Children? You have only the son, am I right?"

She tensed up and drew herself into a severe, almost military posture, as she said, proudly, "I'm almost three months pregnant. And I'm going to see my husband. Fire me if you need to, or whatever you think you have to do, but I'm going to see Russell today—right now—without delay. Is this all you had for me? Are we finished here?"

"Ms. Belizza?" asked Niswanger. "Anything?"

"You've been warned," said the USA. "I urgently caution you to use your head, Antonia. Right now, you're upset. It would probably be wise for you to contact an attorney of your own choosing before taking any further action."

"It—it—" the impossible nature of her situation was becoming clear in Antonia's head. The lights went on in her brain. There were so many legal dynamics at work right now that she did feel like she needed to talk to someone. Their mentioning her son and her remembering that she was pregnant were raising a red flag. She owed her children her allegiance right now. They had to be all right before she took any other action that might result in— who could say? She made her decision then, in that instant.

"I'm going to talk to Russell's father. He's a lawyer and he'll have good advice for me." Then Antonia suddenly collapsed again into her seat. "Wait one," she said solemnly. "Am I—is there any—am I under investigation too?"

Belizza blanched. "We can't answer that, Antonia. That's why we've asked you to stay away from the office while all this gets sorted out."

Antonia slapped the table with her open hand. "No, dammit! Tell me the truth! Have I been the subject of any investigation along with my husband?"

The USA and her number one assistant looked at each other.

"Yes," they said in unison.

"My God," muttered Antonia. She stood and managed to move her body toward the door even though she was in shock.

Then she was gone, moving as if in a dream first to return to her office and grab her pack and purse and then on out to the elevators. She punched the DOWN button several times and kept punching it until the doors whooshed open.

Then she stepped inside and, seeing she was alone, placed her back against the steel wall and burst into tears.

"I'm only going to cry this one time," she managed to say through her tears. "And then I'm going to fight you bastards!" she exclaimed to the empty space around her.

The FBI agents, watching the video feed coming from Antonia's elevator and hearing her words, looked at each other.

"Well?" said the first.

"What, you expected her to slink away and go hide?" said the second. "Not gonna happen that way and I told you people that. She's a fighter and this is going to get messy."

They continued watching the video stream. Already the tearful moment was past. The woman was dabbing her eyes with a tissue and drawing in a deep breath. Then she said to the eye in the upper corner of the elevator, "I'm coming for you bastards. This isn't going to happen like this. Now put that in your fucking report!"

"Done," said the first agent.

"I expected no less," said the second.

They were satisfied with their work. Upon coming into the office, Antonia's bag had been checked. As it was gone through, the security officer placed a small bug inside the coin pocket. It looked like a dime but it wasn't a dime. It was capable of hearing through anything—including walls— and would keep the FBI agents advised of developments from then on.

They listened as she broke into tears again inside her Volvo and then began cursing.

Then they tracked her vehicle as the bug broadcast GPS data. Her car stopped and the bug moved laterally away from it. She had parked and was walking. They turned up the volume and sat back.

They were getting very close and soon would have a name for Slosser.

They were sure of it.

Chapter 10

S he floored it and her Volvo jolted away from the RFK
Building. She needed to talk. Russell's father was who
she needed to speak to. He would be able to tell her more
about Russell and about what she should do. She fought
back the tears; it was still difficult thinking in those terms—
that her husband was in jail—and it was going to take much
longer for her to be able to say it to herself without getting
all teary-eyed and horribly frightened. As for Rusty, her son,
she knew she had done nothing wrong, which meant he
wouldn't be taken away from her. Unless...unless they found
something in her life that embroiled her in whatever Russell
had done.

She slowed her Volvo at the next light and then acceler-
ated when it turned green, passing by the FBI building that
serviced the U.S. Attorney's Office. Inside was a mixture of
FBI and D.C. Police, the one to investigate violations of
federal law, the other to investigate violations of city law. It
was complicated and yet it wasn't. Antonia had started out
in the U.S. Attorney's Office working the city crimes with the
D.C. Police before graduating into the federal area. Now

that's all she did. Or used to do up until fifteen minutes ago. She smiled grimly; they had even had the nerve to tell her she would have to submit to a polygraph and drug testing before she eventually could return to her job. "Sure, I'm going to jump through your hoops," she told the rearview mirror. "You bastards aren't getting rid of me that easily!" Realizing her car was probably bugged too, she made her face into a mask of rigid calm and continued her drive. But then the feelings came roaring back and, with them, the tears. She had to admit, she was more scared than ever in her life.

She calmed herself and asked what should be her first step. She pulled out her cell phone and called Henry Xiang, Russell's father. Hearing her voice and the worry there, he said of course she could drop on by and he'd make time to see her immediately. Twenty minutes later she was pulling into the underground parking at Xiang and Partners, Attorneys at Law.

Henry Xiang was a fearsome litigator, a man in his mid-fifties who bench-pressed two hundred pounds without breaking a sweat and who could move juries to tears with his words at will. He worked out religiously, determined to still have some gas in the tank when he retired at sixty-five, and his courtroom arguments were prepared and curated by a psychologist whose practice serviced only lawyers who wanted to get a leg up on the other side. Henry Xiang was married, five kids, all of whom still gathered at the lawyer's house for Thanksgiving and Christmas, a relatively happy man in a good marriage to a woman who was a broker. He told his secretary to immediately bring Antonia into his office when his intercom buzzed.

He stood and came around his desk and hugged his favorite daughter-in-law.

"Look at you," he said, stepping back from his son's wife and taking her in. "Pregnancy makes you glow, Antonia."

She felt her face redden and she smiled. "Thank you, Dad. I'm feeling very good," she lied. She was having trouble with the pregnancy lately and hadn't told anyone. But Henry needn't know all that. That was for later.

"So sit down and let me get you something to drink—tea perhaps?"

"Nothing for me," she said, lowering herself into a visitors' chair. "But you go ahead."

He waved it off. "Now let's talk Rusty. I'm stunned at his arrest—and very worried. Russia is not known for recognizing constitutional rights for those who they arrest. What in the hell do we know so far?"

"I want to speak directly and openly. I want to ask you a few questions about Russell. Let me get this off my chest."

The man looked troubled. "Are you here as a prosecutor?"

She could feel him withdrawing. She hurried and added to her previous statement, "This is personal, what I want to ask. It's only about Russell and me. Well, that's not entirely true. There's a professional aspect to it too. I'll get to that in a minute."

"Okay. Go ahead, then."

"Does Russell—did Russ ever study Russian?"

"Did he ever study Russian? Like to speak it? I don't really know. He never mentioned anything like that. You know, his Ph.D. is in software engineering. I think he wrote his dissertation on algorithms. I don't think he had any Russian mixed in there. I mean, would he have?"

She shrugged. "That's what I'm trying to find out. The fact of the matter is, I heard him speaking Russian on the phone one night."

"Why didn't you just ask him about it? Don't you imagine it's just something to do with work?"

"I should've, but didn't. I love my husband and I want nothing but the best for him. Most important, I don't want him to think I suspect him of anything. That's one side of it. The other side is that I work for the government as a prosecutor. I might at some point have a duty to go to the authorities with any information I come into—something I'm not willing to do where Russell is involved. I wouldn't turn him in based on even overwhelming suspicions. But I also don't want to be in the middle if something's wrong."

"Very problematic where you might be married to a person under investigation."

She explained how she'd just been put on administrative leave and that she didn't know anymore than that; that he'd been arrested and indicted following an event in Russia and she didn't know anymore than that, either. As she spoke, her hands shook and her voice quaked. This from a woman Henry Xiang had always known to be tougher than nails, a woman who could hold her own and more with any man in any courtroom at any time. He was stunned and suddenly very fearful for his son. The Russians didn't prosecute anyone unless they were going to put them away for a long time. They seldom missed their mark, either, Henry Xiang knew from Rusty's stories.

She finished up, "What should I do, Henry? I don't know the first thing about defending Russian cases. Is there anyone you can direct me to? Anyone who's tough as nails and won't take any shit from these people?"

Henry sat back and took several names into consideration, men and women he had worked with whom he knew to be strong defense attorneys. Then it came to him; of course.

"Let me give you a name. With the pregnancy and your job and Russell's job and Russell's freedom and maybe even his life on the table, I'd like a lawyer I know to step in."

"Who is he?"

"My college roommate. His name is Michael Gresham."

"Can we call him this minute?"

"I shall," said the father-in-law as he lifted the phone from its cradle.

Chapter 11

M ichael Gresham

HENRY XIANG CALLS me a few days after Christmas. Henry was my college roommate; his son is an agent with the CIA; of course I'm not supposed to know that. But I do; Henry and I have stayed up too late a few times, swapping stories and bragging about our kids.

"Michael, Henry," he says, "Russell's in the Moscow City Jail. Under arrest by the KGB. Can you help him?"

"Henry, seriously? Russia? I know nothing about Russian law. I'm not admitted to practice in Russia and I don't speak the language."

"That makes you just who I'm looking for," my old roommate says in that dry way of his. "I need someone who isn't connected in any way. At this point the CIA has disavowed my kid. They're saying they've never heard of him."

"Why would they do that?"

"Near as we can figure it's because of the arms reduction

talks going on between us and the Russians. The government doesn't want the talks impacted by my son's mission."

"Which was?"

"To take out a Russian arms dealer, near as I can tell. Problem is, there was surveillance that no one knew about. Russell got nabbed and now he's facing a firing squad if convicted."

My heart falls. My old friend's kid is in some really deep trouble. The Russians play for keeps and, from what I know, their judicial system is totally rigged. "Justice" in Russia is just another word.

"Look, Henry, there are all kinds of American law firms with offices in Moscow. How about I do some checking and turn up someone you can trust? Believe me, you'll be much further down the road with a Moscow lawyer. Does that help?"

Long silence. I feel like I'm letting my old friend down. Plus, there is more than I want to face. An old wound between us. An old wound that has never healed and likely never will, and I was the one who was wrong. But I can't let that color my professional judgment. Sending me into a Russian court would mean certain death for Russell Xiang. There is no good ending in doing that, not that I can see.

"If you're absolutely certain you can't do it, Michael. I'm going to have to trust your take on this."

"You won't be sorry. As soon as I hang up, I'll start making calls."

"All right, Michael. Please get right back to me when you're done."

"Will do."

"Do you think that will be today?"

"It has to be," I say. "Russian jails are worse than the Gulags. I'll be back before sundown."

We hang up and I start hitting Google. There has to be an American criminal law firm in Moscow.

I have a sick feeling in my stomach as I wade through names and practice areas. One thing I know, Russian courts have little if anything to do with seeing justice done like we're used to in America. But in a way, after a little thought, that isn't going to scare me off. American courts are the same, up close and personal. Justice always takes a back seat to the players' pedigrees and how much influence they wield around town.

I punch the keyboard and keep searching. A man's life is at stake on one level, and the arms reduction talks of the world's two superpowers are at stake on another. Knowing Uncle Sam, Russell will get kicked to the curb in this if necessary; he's on his own.

I have to talk myself down after that consideration wanders through my mind.

Anyway, I won't be going to Russia and that is that.

Chapter 12

M ichael Gresham

SURE, that was that.

Henry knew my feelings for Russell and he knew I wouldn't be able to say no to going. It was a *fait accompli* before he even called me, actually. Especially after I made some calls and found little to zero interest from any lawyers. No one wanted to take on the Moscow court system. They all told me the same thing: the case is over before it even begins. I'm told to go over and try to cut the best deal I can for my friend's son. Maybe they're right: life in a prison camp is better than a firing squad. Isn't it?

In the end, I throw some things in a suitcase, kiss the kids goodbye, and leave them with their nanny and with their maternal grandmother, at my home in Evanston. Mikey is now in half-day pre-school and Dania is moving up in the grades; their lives have begun to take on new dimensions to the extent that my absence for a few days here and there just isn't a major thing to them. Which is all I can hope for, since the loss of their mother is still so new.

Speaking of their mother—her name was Danny. The woman I loved and worshipped. On the flight to Moscow, in those first hours, I grow lonelier and lonelier missing her. Looking out the window, watching the land mass below pass by mindlessly and without sensibility, I realize I am aching inside and that I miss being held. There is a great comfort in feeling another's arms around me. Even more so when that other is one I deeply love, even treasure. As I grapple with these powerful feelings, I inadvertently allow my mind and my feelings to slide back another forty years. Back to Russell's mother, to Henry, to our long days and nights during one summer session just before our senior year, and the drama that played out until graduation. Now I'm morose —dripping wet with it. I decide it's definitely time to have a drink and even a private cry before Moscow looms large in my window.

The airplane's wait staff brings me a scotch on the rocks —a rarity since I seldom indulge. I down it and am asked whether I'd like another. I take my emotional temperature. The alcohol has gone down hot and bold but it has left me feeling even lonelier as stronger feelings surface. So I wave off the second scotch and opt instead for coffee. Soon it arrives and I am sipping and very near tears as I realize nothing is going to soothe the ache I feel inside for my wife's loving arms—at least not today. I'm damned to an evening alone without loving-kindness and solace. Then I stiffen my spine. The lawyer and the male pride inside me abruptly surface. I scoff at myself for allowing my emotions to run off with my quiet time alone on the aircraft. What could have been a long respite from client calls and staff interruptions and the general clamor of running a law office had been allowed—by me—to drift away into a pity party. At least that's how I chide myself just now. And it works. I come out of my funk feeling energized and determined not to go to that emotionally anemic place again. Such is the male psyche and I am definitely one of that species. I switch on my tablet computer and begin reviewing what I have been able to learn about Russell Xiang.

Hours later, I come awake as we're in our final approach. I look out the window at a black sky with millions of lights shimmering up. The city is huge. We pull up to the jetway and hurry into the airport. Then I find my luggage and head for Aeroflot desk.

Russia is pungent in December. Everywhere are the smells of body odor, and of tobacco smoke curling through the air inside public buildings such as the Moscow airport. *It is too cold here to bathe,* I'm thinking, *that must be it.*

"Mr. Gresham," says the Aeroflot clerk in good English, "your return flight has been left open, as you requested. Is there anything else I can help you with?"

He hands me back the ticket I have asked him to check over. I slip the return ticket back inside its folder and tuck it into the breast pocket of my bomber jacket.

"I guess not, but thank you. Oh, wait. There is one more thing. Can you recommend a good hotel where they speak English?"

"Many of our passengers stay at the Moscow Marriott. It's located on Tverskaya, which is the Fifth Avenue of Moscow. The front desk has English speakers."

"How far from Red Square walking?" I ask.

He purses his lips. "Maybe fifteen minutes. Twenty if there's ice."

"Is there ice?"

His face lights up. "Mr. Gresham, there is always ice."

"It is Moscow."

"Even in July. No, just joking."

"I'm not so sure. Anyway, thank you, Denis."

I make my way downstairs to the taxicab loading zone. I shake the cobwebs out of my head in the freezing air outside. I'm here after a fourteen-hour flight from Chicago to Moscow with a stopover in Brussels. Flying business class, I had a fairly decent sleeping setup, but still, onboard any public transportation with people and staff coming and going at all hours of the day and night, sleep wasn't really sleep. I was exhausted when I stepped off the plane and ready for sleep.

The cabbie drives me to the Marriott and helps me unload.

After a shower and four hours tossing and turning in bed, I'm ready to locate Russell Xiang.

First, a cab ride of twenty minutes to the Moscow City Court. This court has original jurisdiction over all criminal cases involving a state secret. A very kindly old gentleman in some kind of gendarme uniform is the English speaker for the office. He helps me locate Russell's file and then translates for me. Long story short, Russell has been indicted and charged with murder in Count I and with obtaining documents containing a state secret in Count II. There is little else to be known just now, the gentleman assures me. I then learn where Russell is being held. So I tell him thank you, and take a cab to Lefortovo Prison, AKA the Moscow City Jail.

Just inside the entrance, the jail is a hopeless, depressing matter. Lime green walls, faded gray linoleum, and huge pictures on the welcome wall of Lenin and Putin. Braced beneath by Russian lettering, I have no doubt those leaders are probably not reciting the number of prisoners they have sent here to dry up and blow away. This prison has that kind of reputation.

I approach the counter and immediately find there is no English. I write Russell's name—in English—on a yellow sticky, the only writing material the entire spread of clerk's windows has to offer. I pass it through a small door in the Plexiglas separating me from the clerk. Obviously bullet-proof and assault-proof, the window between us; I wonder how stupid a Russian would have to be to try and break into this jail? The benefits that flow from attacking security clerks behind Plexiglas in a place like this escapes me. But it is what it is.

The clerk I've passed Russell's name to is back from her huddle with another couple of clerks and supervisors. She isn't smiling as she passes the sticky note back to me.

"*Nyet*," she says, then raises her eyes to the next behind me in the line.

"Wait a minute," I say roughly, "the City Court told me he is here. Please let me see him. Russell Xiang, that's his name."

She ignores me. Then she brushes me aside with her hand in the air. But I don't move.

I pass the sticky back beneath the glass partition. She pushes it back at me.

"I'm not leaving until someone here talks to me," I advise her.

Whereupon she hits a button with the heel of her hand and in an instant an armed guard is standing beside me, listening to her words. He then nods curtly and grasps me by my upper arm. I don't resist as I'm steered back outside the huge glass doors and pushed down the stairs and along the sidewalk I'm fifty paces from the entrance. The guard then looks me in the eye, smiles a friendly smile, and says, in Russian, words that I'm almost certain mean "Don't come back and if you do I will hurt you. Bad."

I nod and jam my hands into the pockets of my bomber jacket. I'm wearing polypro and wool beneath my jacket, and a hat with ear flaps, plus heavy gloves, but I'm freezing and immediately cut apart by the icy wind. So I step up to the curb and start waving at taxis.

When I'm back inside the warmth of my hotel room and reasonably thawed and enjoying my second coffee of the day, I realize that I'm in way over my head. So I place a call to Marcel, my investigator, and tell him to hop on his favorite airline and meet me in Moscow. Marcel, who has worked for Interpol and the New Scotland Yard, has command of several Slavic languages, Russian among them. At this point I can't remember what I was thinking when I came here without him anyway. Probably that Russia would be like Mexico, where you can always locate someone standing nearby who knows English. And where the pocket language book contains words that are pronounceable. Russia and Russian are nothing like Mexico and Spanish.

Absolutely nothing alike.

Рассел.

I've learned that's Russell's name in Russian.

Marcel can't arrive soon enough.

Chapter 13

Michael Gresham

MARCEL LANDS in Moscow at ten a.m. the next morning. He has been with me almost fifteen years, and we go back to when we got called up to go to Iraq during Bush Two's misadventure. I served ten months in-country in the JAG Corps; Marcel served two tours as General Dumont's logistics officer—meaning, basically, he was a bodyguard who didn't get to shoot anyone because he was guarding a four-star Army general. We both came out frustrated, but we had gotten to know each other at beer call, and we had hit it off. When we returned to the States, I had a law practice to resuscitate, and Marcel had no place to go so he tagged along, got his investigator's license, and began working up criminal cases for me. It worked out well, and here we are.

Like me, Marcel is unmarried. His hard-luck story includes a deceased wife—colon cancer. My story is a first wife who ran off with a younger man to have a baby late in life. Number two was a wife who was murdered. Oftentimes Marcel and I find ourselves alone, ready to commiserate, something we do at beer call on Wednesday nights. My limit is two beers; Marcel, who has graduated beyond beer, usually sips a JW on the rocks. I don't know his limit; like clockwork he's ordering a third about the time I'm heading home.

I spot him coming up the jetway. He is traveling light today—a single bag on rollers. We head to the hotel and go straight to my room after checking him into his own room. We look each other over and shake our heads.

"What were you thinking, Michael?"

"I have no idea. Maybe that someone in this city would know English."

"No, Russia isn't like other places where you have English speakers lurking. You're really out in the sticks here when it comes to languages."

"So I learned yesterday. The hard way. But look, Russell Xiang is supposedly at Moscow Jail and I need to confirm that. Then I need to figure out how to visit him. Are you up for that now or do you want to go to your room and grab a few winks?"

"I'm bright-eyed and bushy-tailed," he says, always game for whatever I've got going on. I'm grateful.

"That's terrific."

"Just let me hit the head and I'm good to go."

"Take your time."

Five minutes later I hear the bathroom plumbing in my bathroom moaning and registering that it has been flushed. Now it serves up sink water to its occupant. Marcel whistles as he goes about his business, then he is finished.

"All right, you ready?"

We take a cab back to Moscow jail.

At the counter, the same woman looks at me, trying to remember, maybe, where she's seen me before. But this time, when it's our turn, Marcel takes over and speaks to her in Russian. She says something back. Then they go on like that for three or four minutes. Finally he turns to me.

"Don't step out of line. She's saying he's not here. I've demanded to speak to her supervisor."

"I have this," I say, and produce my cell phone with a picture I took of the court's slim file on Xiang. "Does any of this say he's here?"

Marcel spreads the pictures into a larger size on the screen and studies them.

"Look here," he says to himself after flipping through four screens or five. "Here's proof our boy is right here."

The woman returns to her window with an older gentleman in tow. He is wearing a terribly ill-fitting suit of Russian clothes and has coffee stains on his necktie. He looks back and forth between us, then Marcel says something to him in Russian. Moments later, Marcel is holding up to him—and her—the papers I've stored on my phone that came directly from the City Court. They take the phone from him, turn it this way and that, then confer among themselves. Then they speak to Marcel. He nods and smiles and turns back to me.

"Your man is being held under the name the Russian court gave him. It's a bastardization of his actual name, making it into something Russian."

"So—where does that leave us?"

"They have confirmed Russell is here. But now they want to know by what authority you are here to visit him. Are you his lawyer? Do you have papers to prove you're a Russian lawyer?"

I sense the entire prospect of seeing Russell slipping

away from me again. I almost thought we had it there, but it looks otherwise now.

"Damn," I say. Behind us in line I can hear muttering and what evidently are complaints from others behind us.

"They are demanding to go ahead of us in line," Marcel tells me. "What should I do?"

"Tell her I'm an American lawyer and I'm going to the American Embassy and filing a complaint against her if she won't let me see Russell immediately."

Marcel looks me up and down. "You sure you want to do that?"

"Yes, I'm sure."

He turns back to the clerk and speaks to her in a strong voice. She begins nodding as he speaks, and then types something on her keyboard. She then speaks to Marcel and he turns to me, smiling.

"She says there's no need for that. We can meet with him at noon."

"Beautiful, Marcel. Tell her thank you. Tell her we'll be back at twelve sharp."

Marcel nods and relays my message to her. She doesn't smile or acknowledge my words, instead waving up to her window the next man behind us. He steps around us and begins jabbering at her in Russian. I assume it's Russian— what else would it be?

So Marcel and I find a cafe and order breakfast. It is half-past eleven by now; we're both starved. We shovel down what you might call a Continental breakfast with dense, bitter coffee and chase it all with yet another cup of the stuff with as much cream as we can get into our cups without overflowing.

"Here's to you, Michael. You did good at the jail."

I raise my cup to return to his salute. "No, it was all you. Thanks for coming."

~

AFTER WE EXPLAIN to Russell Xiang who we are, the next words out of his mouth are about Anna Petrov. Where is she? Are we there to help her, too? Is she okay?

"I really don't have those answers," I tell him. "Nobody has said anything to me about Anna Petrov. Is she even in this jail?"

It is a useless question and I know it. He doesn't know anymore about this place than Marcel and I. He shakes his head wearily and wraps his arms around his torso. He is wearing a thin cotton shirt with vertical stripes and lettering on the back. There are matching pants, equally thin, though it is freezing in the jail. Inmate comfort is obviously far down on the list of the Moscow penal bureaucrats.

"I haven't seen her. I was knocked unconscious at the green house and woke up in jail."

"The green house?" I ask.

We are sitting in a small, private, conference room. We have no doubt we're being recorded word-for-word, so I purposefully keep it very general.

Russell swipes his hand across the steel table separating us as if he is wiping it clean. "The green house is a Company safe house."

"Company as in—"

"Of course."

"So you were working for them?"

His eyes narrow at my question. "Don't tell me, Mr. Gresham. They're disavowing me?"

"They are. They're having nothing to do with you."

"Then who sent you here?"

"Well, your wife and your father. Your father called me and got me onboard."

"Poor dad and poor Antonia. I'm sure the Company is telling them nothing."

"That's the gist of it. Now, keeping in mind that this room is bugged and probably videotaped, what I'd like you to do is slide over here beside me on this bench and whisper in my ear how it happened that you were arrested."

He complies, coming around the table. I move down and Marcel gives up his seat and crosses to where Russell has been sitting. Marcel lowers himself onto the steel bench and begins speaking nonsense—nursery rhymes, lyrics to songs, any and everything to provide white noise over Russell's whispers.

As Marcel makes his noise cover for us, Russell goes over the days leading up to his arrest. He explains to me about Henrik, about the bill of lading from the arms shipment, about the murder of the Moscow Station chief, and about Anna's work with him. He also gives me information on how I can prove his connection to the CIA but warns me never to use that information without consulting him first and getting his okay. I agree, and he tells me the entire thing, including where all the bodies are buried. Literally, in some cases. He tells me that they took him to court that one time and that an English-speaking magistrate told him what he was charged with and what the possible penalties were.

"I was charged with stealing state secrets," he whispers.

"Possible penalties?"

"Death by firing squad."

I sit there and let that information run around in my head. It is terrible news and I feel like I won't ever have enough tools to successfully defend Russell as I can't speak the language, aren't a member of the court, and have no idea of Russian rules of evidence and procedure. He might as well have a high school senior helping him as me, I say.

"Then get someone else, Mr. Gresham," he says calmly. "My father will hire a Russian lawyer for co-counsel."

"I'm sure he will and that's exactly what I'm planning to recommend. Just as soon as I get back to the hotel I'm going to start making my calls and then make my rounds. Will you be okay here for a few more days until I can get you back into court and try to get conditions of release set?"

"If you call eating beet soup with bread twice-a-day getting along okay, then I guess I will be. At first I thought I was passing blood in my stool. Now I get it: beets."

"Never thought of that," says Marcel, now that we've resumed talking in normal volumes.

"It's anything but pretty," Russell says, forcing a smile for us. We smile along with him although we all three know it's the same as whistling past the cemetery. These are scary times and we need to lawyer-up and do what needs to be done.

Chapter 14

M ichael Gresham

"You're going to need a new identity," Marcel says that night in my hotel room. We're eating roast beef, potatoes, and scallions and chasing it all down with that same rank Russian coffee as this morning. But we're not complaining. We see a path ahead.

"I'm going to need a new identity because why?"

"Because you don't want repercussions back home. These are the kind of people who would come after your family."

"FSB would?"

He scoffs. "Just a few years ago they were the KGB under Putin, who now runs the FSB too. Very scary people, Boss."

"So who am I going to be?"

"Mikhail Sakharov."

"Sakharov."

"Sakharov the Bear. You're going to be Russian. Mikhail

Sakharov actually once existed and we're going to borrow his ID since he would be about the same age as you."

"Well they'll figure that out immediately, if I'm someone who once existed, won't they?"

"Not necessarily. Because nobody will be looking. This afternoon I rented a flat a mile off Red Square where you'll be anonymous."

"Hot water?"

"Yes, hot water. And furnished like some noir film out of the Forties."

"Perfect. I can practice my Sam Spade. With apologies to Bogart."

"Listen to me, Michael. You're going to be there alone. I can't be with you."

"Why not?"

"Because the FSB knows who I am and has a complete dossier on me. From many years ago."

"Oh," I say, the light coming on in my head. Of course, Marcel has been in Moscow before and God only knows what he did here.

"I'm a very wanted man. So you don't want to be seen with me or connected to me in any way. For the record, I didn't fly in here under my real name."

"Got it. So I just take a cab to this flat tomorrow and move my stuff in?"

"Pretty much. I'm making up some cards in Russian that explain you can't speak, that you're a stroke victim."

The next day, I pack up my bags, load everything into a taxi van, and give the driver my new home address. It's about a ten-minute drive from Red Square, including two accident backups and heavy snow. The neighborhood is old and gloomy, with a few churches on the corners of the streets approaching my new digs. No one seems to be out and about—too cold. As we turn onto Inkanov Street—my new address—the light is dim, the sky is heavily overcast and gray, and I suddenly realize I could be in any of a million neighborhoods across the upper Midwest of the United States. Same architecture, same buildings and houses, same everything. Except the signage is all unreadable and the cabbie speaks a language I don't comprehend even for a second. He drops me at my address and comes around and opens my door. Moments later I'm left standing on the sidewalk, my worldly goods dangling from my arms, wondering how I can traverse the ice from the recently-shoveled walk leading up to my new digs. Ultimately I just put my head down and start up the sidewalk to the porch, slipping a bit on the porch steps, and let myself inside without knocking, for I'm standing in a common area.

Up the stairs I go; the second floor is all mine. As promised, the key is above the lintel and I let myself inside. Home consists of the barest of furnishings, lace curtains laden with dust—I find out as I try to spread them open for outside light—and wallpaper that could have been rural Wisconsin farmhouse, c. 1955. The place smells ancient and musty and I assume there's mold everywhere inside the walls and under the sinks. I'm very mold-sensitive as I've had it attack my house in Evanston twice in fifteen years and it's very expensive to remove. In the single bedroom, I set my bags on the floor and flop back on the double bed. Springs in the mattress and an unstable frame that could give way at any moment. *No girls up here*, I find myself thinking. I'm home.

I have picked up a burner cell phone and retrieve it from my jeans pocket. There is Wi-Fi in the house, as promised, and my laptop connects right up without needing a password. Now I'm ready to get down to why I'm in Russia at all.

Online I find four law firms in Moscow that claim a proficiency in English. The first two I dial are closed for the day, evidently, as I get voice mail. Bypassing those, I try the third.

The male voice speaks Russian. I of course don't understand.

"I'm calling for legal help. Do you speak English?"

I'm thrilled when the voice says, "I do. How can I help you?"

"My name is Sakharov. I'm an American lawyer with an American client in the Moscow City Jail. I need to associate co-counsel and defend my man. Can you help?"

"I think I can, Mr. Sakharov."

"What's your name?"

"My name is Ivanovich but I prefer 'Van.'"

"Fair enough. When can I get in to see you?"

"Is this evening soon enough? I live above my office and late hours are fine for me."

"What time is it now?"

"Just after three."

"It looks like nine at night."

"We are pretty dark in the winter. What about six p.m.?"

"I'll be there. Your address is current on your website?"

"It is. Come to the door on the side of the building and ring the bell. It shouldn't be frozen, but I'll make sure."

"Will do. And thank you, Van."

"I will see you at six, Mr. Sakharov."

"Mikhail."

"Mikhail, then."

Almost three hours later I'm ringing his bell. The door opens and a swarthy Russian man invites me inside an office that contains several filing cabinets; I must turn sideways to pass them. Next comes a huge desk and two visitors' chairs. I take a seat in one of the chairs and look around. First off, directly behind me is a large photograph of the World Trade Center Towers before 9/11. They are totally out of place here in Moscow, Russia, I'm thinking, but then I remember my man here does speak good English and so there's probably some connection. I tuck that away for later.

He takes the squeaky executive chair across from me and lights a cigarette. He holds out the open end of the pack and I shake my head. "Surgeon General and all that," he says with a smile. He has definitely spent time in the U.S. and encountered the warnings on our cigarettes.

"Yes," I agree. "Surgeon General."

"So, tell me a bit about yourself, Mikhail. Your name is Russian; are you?"

"Look, I have no choice but to be open and direct with you. Is that safe to do?"

He looks around the room, choosing his words. "If you mean is this confidential, then yes. If you mean would I turn in an enemy of the state, the answer is no. But would I break down under torture and give you up? Then the answer is also no, your secrets are not safe with me because I'm a huge coward when it comes to pain. And believe me, Mikhail, when it comes to inflicting pain there is no agency better equipped for that than the Russian military police, the FSB. They rule the country with Putin's blessing and they are poisonous snakes with their bite."

I like him and feel comfortable after that, except for the part about FSB the snake. Anyway, he's my kind of man.

"All right, then I'm going to trust that the FSB never collects you up for torture. I'm going to trust you with everything, Van."

He taps his cigarette on the lip of a large crystal ashtray. "Good thinking. Now, tell me about yourself."

I do just that, bringing him up to speed on my history, my roommate connection to my client through his father, the fact he's being held on a state secrets beef, and my desperation in extricating him from his mess.

"Mess, indeed," Van says when I'm finished. "Your client can be shot by a firing squad if he is convicted, a very common outcome in these cases. President Putin does not treat kindly those who would compromise state secrets. Or those who would trade on state secrets, which your man was probably doing if he was CIA. I'm guessing he works for the CIA, Mikhail, am I correct in this?"

I sigh and decide I'm all in. I have no other choice.

"You are correct. CIA all day long."

"That isn't good. As you say in America, that's two strikes against him right there."

"Your connection to the U.S. is evident. May I ask how that is?"

"NYU Law, 1986. My father served in the Russian Consulate in New York."

"I thought it was probably something like that."

"Hence the Twin Towers. I spent my share of time in NYC catting around."

"As every college student should," I say, recalling my own time at Georgetown and our trips to Manhattan on long weekend forages for exciting women. We were salmon fighting upstream to mate with them. I can only imagine the NYU salmon were much the same.

"So. Questions?"

"Yes. What about bail for my—can I say 'our'—client?"

"You can say 'our' if you have five thousand USD to retain me."

"Consider it done."

"Then let me tell you. Our client won't be given bail.

There is no bail for this crime. It's a capital offense and capital offenses don't get bail."

"So he's stuck in jail while the wheels of justice grind away."

"I'm sorry, yes."

"Speaking of which, how long will this prosecution take, start to finish?"

He lights another cigarette off the embers of the first. A giant plume of smoke is released from his nostrils.

"Much faster than you anticipate. He will probably have his preliminary hearing this week and his trial in about thirty days."

"Thirty days? Seriously?"

"Yes. Russian defendants have rights guaranteed by the Constitution, but in reality they are cursory only. There is no discovery such as in American courts. There is no reason to delay. The state is anxious to make an example of our client. When can you pay me?"

"I can give you a check right now."

"Do you have American Express?"

I look at him. He is anxious to get paid. Can't blame him; probably a huge windfall having me stumble in here.

"I do," I say, and flip my American Express card onto his desk. He picks it up and examines it.

"Who is Michael Gresham?"

"It's his card. I have his permission."

"Sweet."

He swipes the card through an ancient card-reader and lights glow and something beeps and in less than a minute I have retained my co-counsel.

"Do you need a written fee agreement?" he asks.

I shake my head. "The less paper, the better."

"I agree. My office could be searched by the FSB at any

moment once I'm on the case. So could your own. I assume you're working out of home?"

"Yes."

"Word to the wise. Never give your home address to anyone. Make stuff up. Or use mine. Here's my card. Show them this."

"Thank you, Van. Ah, one question. What is your normal area of law practice?"

He smiles. "Zoning appeals."

"As in real estate?"

"As in real estate."

"Have you ever defended a criminal case in Russian court?"

"No, but neither have you. We will be limited only by our imaginations. So get ready to soar, comrade. The sky is ours!"

As I'm making my way back beyond the filing cabinets to the door, I'm only wondering one thing: What the hell have I gotten myself into? And, by implication, what have I gotten Russell Xiang into?

Out on the street it's only five minutes before I flag down a taxi. I give the driver one of the cards Marcel has prepared for me—I'm a stroke victim and cannot speak—and he reads off the address in a thick voice and nods at me in the rearview.

Then we're off into the dark night, the whizzing traffic of Moscow closing in around us while in my mind's eye I can see the FSB two cars directly behind.

Or is it three?

Chapter 15

M ichael Gresham

VAN CALLS. Russell has tried to escape and was captured and severely beaten. He is in the City Jail infirmary. The jail called Van because he had sent them notice that he was now counsel of record for Russell. He asks me what do I want to do? I tell him to meet me there in one-half hour.

It is snowing when I run outside and catch a cab. It is always snowing here. The streets are black with ash, used by the Moscow streets department in lieu of salting the roads.

I'm dropped in front of the jail and I go bounding up the steps two-at-a-time. Inside, I find Van and he tells me that the infirmary is back outside and down two buildings. So we head out and find the correct building and hustle inside. We feel like time is of the essence, but, in truth, no sooner are we inside and asking at the desk to see Russell than we are told that it will be at least a two hour wait as the infirmary is short on staff to monitor visits. So we take a number, literally, and head for the waiting area.

A TV is droning about this and that, while around us sit other visitors. Van decides to change the channel and looks around for the remote. It cannot be located, so he goes to the TV and reaches up to the channel button. Immediately a gruff voice calls out to him. Van replies to the man then calls back to me, "He says he wants to keep watching Putin's channel. Can you imagine this stupid hairy oaf?" The man, who Van referred to, then speaks up again as Van makes the change. Then he stands and begins approaching Van from behind. Without another word, Van turns around and faces down the perturbed visitor. His fists clench and remain clenched and the man sees this and stops his approach. Words are exchanged in loud, angry voices, ending up with Van pointing at me and then at the chair where the man was sitting and then the man turning and returning to his seat. He looks around meekly and picks up a discarded newspaper. Van returns to his seat beside mine.

"What did you tell him?" I ask.

"I told him you were FSB and you wanted the channel changed to sports."

I look at the man, then, and narrow my eyes as if in deprecative appraisal. In other words, I'm looking down my nose at him. He looks away, in fear for his safety; he has believed Van's lie.

I'm unsure I like playing the heavy and whisper to Van that I'd rather not be FSB again. He grins at me and clasps me on the back. "You just have that look," he says, "with the short-clipped hair and the proud posture you always maintain."

"I do?"

Just then Van stands. "Come on, Mikhail, they've called our number on the P.A."

It hasn't been anywhere near two hours, but who's complaining?

We are taken back to the last bed on the right. The bed is bolted to the floor and the patient is restrained by handcuffs and ankle chains. Russell no longer looks like Russell. His face is beaten to a pulp, both eyes are black, the right arm is in a cast and tubes enter his body from all angles. On the side of the bed there is a urine bottle and it is filling as we approach. The man manages to smile despite his battered face. His front teeth are chipped—they might have been before, though—and when he speaks there's a small whistle on the s's.

"So, you're my visitors? Mr. Gresham, you found a co-counsel?"

I take the seat closest to his head. I lay my hand against his hand and say, "I did. His name is Van."

He eyes Van and looks back at me.

"This gentleman's suit tells me he's Russian."

"Good catch," I say. "His name is Ivanovich. Very bright guy."

"Excellent. I'm feeling better already, though I probably don't look like it."

"Escape attempt, that right?"

"That's right, I—"

"Hold that thought, please. We'll talk about that later when we're away from other people and microphones."

"All right." He moans and tries turning just a bit to better see me. I slide my chair around and now we can watch each other's eyes and faces.

"So here's the deal. Van tells me the court doesn't even allow bail for cases involving state secrets or murder. These are capital crimes and there's no bail for capital crimes here."

"Figured. I might as well settle in for a long stay is what you're saying."

"I don't know how long it will be," Van suddenly pipes up. "You'll be at trial by the end of next month. No later, I can promise."

"That's seven weeks," Russell says and turns his eyes toward me. "Can we be ready?"

"We have no choice," I tell him. "Now, we're going to need a method of communication. Are you good with any languages?"

"I grew up with Mandarin in the house."

I turn to Van. "Van, do you do Mandarin?"

"Not hardly. I've got English and Russian. Enough French to get me the disdainful eye of most *maître d's* in Paris."

"My wife is fluent in Mandarin. Maybe she could help," Xiang says.

I look at Van. He shrugs.

"Let me talk to a friend," I say mysteriously, avoiding the mention of Marcel by name.

"All right."

"How about this." I jot down a note on my yellow legal pad. I pass it to him to read: "You write me a phony summary of all that went before that's in any way connected to the criminal charges. Be sure you make it look like you're from China and that you were here checking out investment opportunities. Give me names, dates, places—all made up. Write it in Mandarin and a man from my office will be by to collect it. Does that work, Van?"

Van is nodding. "The accused definitely has the right to full and unrestricted communication with his lawyer."

I say, "Which normally is eavesdropped by the jail personnel and fed to the FSB, who turn it over to the prosecution. Actually not all that different from how we do things back in the USSA."

Russell gets the point, the oblique reference to the Beatles' song. He nods, trying to smile but ending with a grimace as his lips crack and the bleeding starts up again. The nurse comes and applies something that smells pungent, like camphor, to Russell's lips. She speaks to Van in Russian, who explains to me, "Five minutes."

Then Van draws me aside. "Are you under the impression no one in FSB knows Mandarin Chinese?"

I smile and he studies my face. "Of course they know Chinese."

"Then why have him tell you the confidential things in Chinese?"

"Russell Xiang is Chinese and speaks only Chinese. His father has provided me with an address in China that will confirm Russell lives there with family that never left China. So he's Chinese, as far as the Russians know. That being the case, why would a Chinese visitor suddenly start working for the CIA? It's called plausible deniability. Study Richard Nixon, about 1972, for the whole story."

"I don't follow."

"It's an American tradition. Politicians have used it for fifty years. Now we will put it to good use in Russia. It's like this. When we defend criminal cases in the U.S. we begin with the police report. Our opportunity is the stuff between the lines. The stuff the report doesn't address. Many defense lawyers will then create the unsaid portions. That's how a defense is manufactured."

"Do you do that?"

I smile. "I do when I'm in Russia in the kangaroo court."

We are whispering as we speak back and forth. Russell is trying to listen in, but we are too quiet for that. We wouldn't want them to be able to drug him and procure our words from his mouth.

Finally Van begins nodding, now and then a large smile. "So we're going to deny he's American at all!"

"Welcome to the rodeo, Van. We just found our defense."

"What he can plausibly deny."

"Yes, because we have access to China and our vouchers there through Russell's father. The Russians do not. They are hated and feared there. They can test out nothing we say."

"I like you, Mikhail," he says, raising his hand and resting it on my shoulder. "You Americans are as amazing as they say."

"As amazing as who says?"

He shrugs and blinks. "Everyone says."

Chapter 16

M ichael Gresham

THE VESSEL WAS Norwegian and it sailed into the Port of Long Beach on a Sunday night. The ship was a Panamax class and it carried 4600 TEU's—containers.

The containers lashed atop its long flat deck were of all colors. They were secured on deck in cell guides; there had been no problems with cargo shifting at any point.

At half-past midnight, the longshoremen were busy moving the containers onto American soil—concrete, actually. By sunup the retrieved containers were piled high and yet the process was still underway. Less than half the load had been swung ashore at that point. Among those already brought to shore were numbers including NB322V-1993x - NB322V-1223x. They were the numbers Russell Xiang had committed to memory and they were the containers the FBI and DHS were frantically scrambling to find. Sitting there on the dock in Long Beach the containers looked no different than the other thousands upon thousands of containers up and down the huge docks and receiving areas. They were just one more shipment of thousands of the fungible units.

Contained within the "Henrik boxes" were Browning machine guns in .50 caliber, thousands of AK47 assault rifles capable of full auto, F2000 assault rifles, a full container of FIM 92 Stinger missiles, Sarin nerve gas, tens of thousands of rounds of ammunition, M72 rocket launchers, chlorine gas and three thousand M4 rifles with ammunition. These were the items from Henrik's bill of lading. Many of the containers with their nerve gas and ammunition were hazardous materials and volatile and should have been segregated on the trip over but were not, thanks to an exchange of US dollars at different ports of call.

But there was one minor glitch. The bill of lading for the load was inadvertently erased from the ship's computers. Actually this was an act of sabotage, but the crew was left to think it was just a mistake by one of them. The result? No one came for the shipping containers. So there they sat, in the brilliant Long Beach sunlight in January.

Couples strolled by on the docks; sightseers walked paths created by the containers. Local kids played hide-and-seek among them. While all along the docks, the FBI and DHS looked for them. Except they had no description and no numbers. It was so much more difficult without the numbers; there were more than a million other containers just like these along the docks.

Sometimes the best hiding place is the most obvious when you're playing child's games.

Sometimes it is even for adults, too.

Chapter 17

M ichael Gresham

THE NEXT MORNING I'm up before dawn and headed for the airport. I need to make a phone call—from Zurich.

Snow blows from all directions and wind gusts threaten to blow our Lada taxi off the side of the road. But my driver persists and takes his time and I'm delivered to the unloading curb at the airport with only my backpack and my laptop. I'm wearing jeans and a wool sweater and my bomber jacket. In the inside pocket is my smartphone. It contains a new contact, the wife of Russell Xiang, with her phone number. Russell tapped it into my phone using just one finger before we left him yesterday. Now I'm ready.

On the Boeing 777, I'm flying first class. In the back of the seat ahead of mine is a Swiss brochure. I read it and remind myself that I really need to do some sightseeing while I'm in Moscow. The wait staff comes along and offers me champagne. "Mr. Sakharov," she says, "can I interest you in a lovely French champagne before we take off?"

I tell her no and keep reading the brochure:

> *Moscow became the Russian capital in 1480. Like most tourists you should start exploring the city at the Kremlin. St. Basil's Cathedral is surely one of the world's most astonishing pieces of architecture, with its exquisite domes and vivid brickwork standing out as a highlight of the many architectural gems that are located around the world-famous Red Square. The Historic Museum is here, the Lenin Mausoleum right next to the Kremlin Wall and the Spasskaya Tower from the 16th century. The famous gems of the Czars are on display in the Kremlin. But don't forget to visit one of the hundred parks in Moscow, with Gorky Park being the most famous and central. Have a world class evening out and visit the famous Bolshoi Theatre for a ballet performance seen nowhere else.*

"INTERESTING," I mutter to the empty seat next to me, "but I'm leaving Moscow and going to Zurich. Where's the brochure on Zurich?"

I gaze down on Russian farms, forests, rivers and mountains once we are airborne and turning for Switzerland. The air at this level is very smooth as we are far above the clouds and mountains and their fierce weather. Finally, I lean back and dream about my wife and try to remember her last words to me before she died. Dozing and coming to several times along the way, I dream that she is reaching out a hand to me and trying to get my attention. I try to shut out the engine noise and the rattling of silverware as our meal is prepared, just to hear what it is she is trying to tell me. But it is no use. In Danny's place I receive a lemony chicken breast, wild rice, steamed vegetables, and two cups of coffee. I chase it all with several glasses of water and I'm thinking I'm thirsty because of the tears I've cried while alone in my seat, nobody watching, missing my beautiful wife. Then we are touching down and life begins again.

My return flight is three hours away. Why did I come to Zurich? I came here to make one telephone call. On my cell phone I locate Antonia Xiang's number and tap CALL. The phone does its thing, there's a pause, and then a voice answers.

"Hello?"

"Mrs. Xiang, this is Michael Gresham."

"Who?"

"I'm the lawyer your father-in-law sent to Russia to meet Russell."

"Oh, yes! Have you seen my husband? How is he?"

"I have seen him. He's had a bit of a rough go, but he's going to be okay."

"Are they treating him horribly?"

"He tried to escape and was beaten severely. He's now in the jail infirmary where it looks like he's going to make a full recovery."

"Oh, thank God. When do you think he'll be coming home?"

I'm sitting in a passenger waiting area that is completely empty as there is no plane outside the window getting ready to take on passengers. Which is why I'm perturbed when an olive-skinned woman wearing a hijab comes into the area and sits down behind me. We are back to back now, the only two people in the entire boarding area. So I stand and move away.

As I move off I'm stepping backwards, when she suddenly produces a smartphone and begins pointing it at me, obviously taking snaps.

I'm stunned by her bravado and her utter disregard for me. But why the hijab? Why would a Middle Eastern woman be working for the Russians? Then it comes to me: she's not working for the Russians, she's working for the Americans and they are sending me a message: I'm being watched.

This is unnerving and I'm not a guy who gets upset easily. But the idea that the CIA is going to harass me because I offer legal services to one of its own agents really pisses me off. The hackles go up on the back of my neck and I'm ready to run at the woman and scare the hell out of her. But I don't.

Instead, I consider my circumstance. Here I am, taking up the defense of a discarded CIA agent, whose work evidently has the possibility of being hugely embarrassing for the CIA and, indirectly, for the United States. And I couldn't care less. I have little respect for a government that disowns its own agents when it's politically expedient to do so. And right now, disowning Russell is chosen because the U.S. and Russia are engaged in very sensitive arms reduction talks and Russell's alleged murder of an FSB agent's son threatens the whole house of cards.

The court documents are very clear about this, alleging that Russell murdered Igor Tarayev's son during a home invasion just outside of Moscow. Further, the documents allege that Russell Xiang was working for the CIA when the murder occurred. They also allege that the killing was done at the behest of the American government. It is obvious this is why the CIA and U.S. have abandoned Russell. All because it is politically expedient to do so, they have thrown him to the wolves. Even knowing he could be facing a firing squad, they have turned their backs.

Now she stands and approaches me. She says, in perfect English, "Would you mind if I snap a selfie of me and you together?"

I step away. I'm very angry and afraid I might take a swing at her.

I shout, "Are you out of your mind? Are the Russians this brazen?"

"Russians? I'm an American. As American as you. I heard you talking on the phone. I'm guessing maybe Indiana or Illinois. Am I anywhere close?"

"Why do you want my picture?"

She smiles, then, and laughs in my face. "We're everywhere, Michael."

Then she turns and begins walking away.

"Who's everywhere?" I call to her.

Without a word, she waves over her shoulder to me.

Then I get back on the phone with Mrs. Xiang.

"Sorry about that, Mrs. Xiang. I was interrupted."

"Goodness, that sounded bizarre enough."

"Russell is looking at a jury trial. I'm told that will occur within about seven weeks. If we're successful, he should be home right after."

"And if you're not?"

"Then your husband is going to be staying in Russia for a very long time, Mrs. Xiang. Which is why I'm calling you. Your husband needs your help."

"How so?"

"He needs you to come to Moscow and lend us a hand."

"Let me make arrangements for our son and I'm on my way. I'm sure Russell's folks will keep him for me."

"When can you be here?"

"Tomorrow okay?"

"That would be great. Just dial this number when you land and I'll come find you."

"Will do. Mr. Gresham, will I be getting to see Russell?"

"Probably not. There's a chance we could convince them you're part of my staff, but probably not. These are very bright people."

"Well, it wouldn't hurt to try, would it?"

"No, it wouldn't hurt to try."

We spend another five minutes discussing non-case-related things, then hang up. I manage to steal a nap during my remaining time in the airport. Then I sleep all the way back to Moscow. When I finally climb into my own bed it feels like a little bit of heaven, bedsprings and all. Like the proverbial light, I'm out.

ANTONIA XIANG ARRIVES by Aeroflot the next night. She has flown all last night and most of the day to get here. She calls my phone and I go right to her at the Moscow airport.

Baggage claim is frantic with passengers grabbing luggage and porters slinging it onto carts and rumbling noisily away. Everyone is in a great hurry and I feel sluggish among them, still exhausted after my flights yesterday.

She is young—younger than Russell by maybe ten years, I'm guessing—yet she is composed and sure of herself as she hands me the baggage claim tickets and backs out of the travelers surrounding the conveyor belt. "Red bags, gold handles. Two total," she calls to me from behind. I'm caught up in the claimants' circle and we try to avoid stepping on each other as we lunge forward, pull handles, and jerk back away from the carousel. At one point I feel eyes crawling across my shoulder and look sharply to my right. There! The woman in the hijab. I believe it is her and I believe she is smiling toward me. Damn her! Damn the CIA, the damn cowards! Which makes me all the more determined to set Russell free, fly him back to the U.S., march him into the foreign news bureau at the *Times*, and lay out the whole, nasty story about CIA abandonment of agents and U.S. cover-ups. Will she be smiling when that happens?

My reverie is broken by Mrs. Xiang, who is tugging at my arm and exclaiming, "Michael, you've let my bags go around twice! I told you the red bags with the gold handles!"

"Got it."

And I do, next time around, I snap them expertly off the carousel and begin moving away from baggage claim, outside to the taxi stand. She follows behind, wrapping her arms around herself as we are slammed by the wintry blast of Moscow night wind and sleet. It slices through my leather coat and even pierces my polypro.

On the taxi ride back to my flat I update Russell's wife. I explain that Marcel has retrieved a written case summary from Russell that is waiting for Mrs. Xiang's translation. I tell her I'm hopeful her husband has taken full advantage of literary license and penned a whopper of a tale, something so bizarre it must be the truth. The Russians will have no idea what to do with it, if done properly.

We arrive at my flat and I make coffee. It is a Mr. Coffee style machine. I fill the receptacle with dark, almost black, Russian coffee that wasn't grown anywhere near Russia, I'm certain. But the smell of brewing coffee and the hissing of the radiators gives my little home the feel and smell of warmth and safety. While the one is obvious, the other is tenuous at best, for nowhere in Russia is anyone truly safe, even the innocent. Then I produce a loaf of bread that is like a sourdough but very dark, a knife and board, and a round of summer sausage and a wheel of cheese and I begin assembling two sandwiches. Mayonnaise is slathered on, Russian-style—the condiment is hugely popular here, made of sunflower seed oil. Mayonnaise was never meant to be used in such huge quantities, I explain to Mrs. Xiang, but the Russians adopted it from the French and have abused it ever since. She laughs at my silliness and seems to relax just a bit, which is what I was aiming for.

After we have eaten and drunk down our coffee, I produce her husband's case summary. It is written in his handwriting on white copy paper. The ink is blue and there is nothing about it to commend it as anything special.

She finds her glasses in her purse and sits back on the worn sofa. A cup of coffee is balanced on the sofa's arm and her hand turns it ever so slowly as she begins reading. The story unspools as she reads, aloud, and I hear what our defense is going to sound like.

In the end, Russell Xiang's story sounds like something out of a Harvard B-School case study. His is the story of a Chinese entrepreneur who journeyed to Russia in search of a source of travel photographs and prices for a reservations website he was putting together for Chinese citizens. He explained that ever since China had relaxed its strictures on out-of-country travel by its populace, Chinese citizens by the tens of thousands had been jetting around the world, looking for new playgrounds and entertainment centers. Especially among the young. Russell Xiang came to Moscow with an eye toward capturing some of that money for himself and his angel investors, when he was suddenly yanked into custody and charged with the murder of someone he'd never heard of. He recites in his tale of woe how he has tried to contact his father in China for help; that his father has retained Mikhail Sakharov and that Sakharov is now in Moscow preparing Xiang's defense. Xiang is married, his wife is still in China, and he is the father of two children, one of whom went to math camp at the age of five. His life was looking rosy and he was successful in all respects until the FSB whisked him away in the backseat of a police van and dumped him in Lefortovo Prison.

And this is all just the beginning. There will be embellishments and add-ons, no doubt. There will be sufficient human suffering to melt even the iciest Russian heart in the sad retelling of one businessman's trip to Russia gone bad. Well, "melting hearts" is a bit overstating Russian reactions.

The next day, I take Antonia to Van's office and we discuss what Russell has written.

After reading the summary, he says, "There will be enough to sway the right jury—if we even get a jury."

"Meaning?"

"Even where jury trials are allowed by law, there is no absolute right to a jury trial. Without a jury, the conviction rate in Russian criminal cases hovers at around 93%. With a jury, maybe 27% are found not guilty."

"So how do we guarantee a jury for Russell?"

Over the next hour, we find ourselves wracking our brains, trying to conceive of all the possible ways we can obtain a jury for Russell. But even when we are finished looking at all the laws and the rules and the normal routines of the court system, we still don't know where the court is going to come down on our request for a jury. By contrast, in the United States the *Sixth Amendment* guarantees the right to a fair and impartial public trial by jury in all criminal cases.

I tell Van, "Constitutional guarantees in the United States cannot be abridged."

He sadly shakes his head and studies the anguish in my face.

Then he says, in all seriousness, "In Russia, there are no guarantees."

"How do people live like that, with that uncertainty?" I ask him.

"Who said anything about living? In Russia we are merely surviving."

"So what can we do? Anything?"

He shakes his head. "This case is a hot political spectacle. There will be no jury. Unless—" his voice trails off.

"Unless what?"

"Unless we can manage to blow it up into something so huge that we can embarrass the court into giving us a jury. That is our only chance."

I'm already down the road thinking about that one. But then I realize I'm not in the U.S. where I ordinarily would hold a press conference to twist the tail of the lion. Here, there is no such thing as a press conference.

"So how do we embarrass the court?"

"I'm thinking about that, Mikhail. I might have an idea."

"Such as?"

He spreads his hands and looks stiffly at me. "Let me talk to some contacts I have in the court. Then I will get back to you with a plan, perhaps."

"Thank you, Van. I don't know what we'd do without you here."

He nods his head. "I don't either. That's why I accepted your case."

We sit in silence.

Then Van brightens and his voice lifts up a note as he says, "Oh, by the way, a call came for you, Mikhail." He holds up a pink note.

"Who would call me?"

"Verona Sakharov is the lady's name. She lives in Moscow and she says she's your wife."

I am stunned. "Wait," I manage to say, "she says she's the wife of Mikhail Sakharov?"

"So she says."

"Meaning I've taken the name of her deceased husband?"

"She doesn't say anything about you being deceased. In fact—"

"In fact what?"

He smiles and chuckles. "In fact, she wants to meet with you."

He hands over the note.

"That is her number. Please call her."

"But I don't speak Russian."

"She speaks English. In fact, she teaches English at university. Her husband was a lawyer."

"But—but—"

"Just call her, Mikhail. She certainly deserves to hear from her dead husband, wouldn't you think?"

ANTONIA XIANG IS STAYING at the Moscow Marriott, so I have our cabbie drop her there. We promise we will speak later in the day, after I have been to see how Russell's doing. She wanted to tag along but I told her it wouldn't work in the infirmary, that they are very careful who they let in and out. I assure her that only Russell's attorneys have access right now. Unlike normal hospitals there are no visiting hours for family. She accepts that and says she'll be waiting to hear from me. I tell her she shall.

Then it's back to my flat, where I make coffee and slip into some ill-fitting slippers I saw in the window of a shoe store and purchased. They are a type of moccasin, though Russia never had Indians to pass along the moccasin tradition. So I'm wondering how and why the country sells moccasins. But that's a question for another day, I decide as I pour myself a large cup of Russian coffee. It's time to call Marcel.

Marcel is in hiding at the country home of a friend from his earlier days here. That's all he'll tell me and I, of course, don't push it. He has his skeletons and I have mine— evidently, I tell him, explaining that Mikhail Sakharov's wife has called.

His tone is very measured. He is calculating. "How did she get your name? Where did she make any connection?"

"Evidently the story of Russell and his work for the CIA has become somewhat of a story in *Izvestia*."

"The Russian newspaper has picked up the story?"

"Yes, and my widow evidently saw the story, read it, and was shocked to find her deceased husband was up to his old tricks, defending criminals in Moscow City Court."

"Good grief. What have I done, Mikhail?"

"That's why I'm calling you, Marce. What have you done?"

Long silence. Then, "I think I might have really screwed the pooch on this one."

"No lie, Sherlock," I say with all the sarcasm I can muster. "Now you have my widow calling me."

"What does she want?"

"She wants to meet with me."

"What have you told her?"

"I haven't yet. I thought I'd call you first and see if you'd like to kill her, her family, and all of her friends to protect my cover-up."

"No need for sarcasm, Mikhail. I'm sorry this has happened."

"Apologies for the sarcasm, Marce. But I sure as hell didn't need this development. Next time be a little more careful when you're choosing a name for me, yes?"

Long silence. Again. "I don't think there will be a next time, Mikhail."

"Why is that?"

"My friend here has a nice investigation business with government ties. He would like me to join him in that."

"Marce, think of what you're saying! You don't want to live in Russia!"

"It wouldn't involve living in Russia. My work would take place mostly on the Continent. Plus some in the U.S."

"Well please don't accept any offers just yet. Let me make you a counter-offer first. Please?"

"I won't do anything until your work here is done, Mikhail. After that, we'll talk. But I'm strongly tending toward accepting."

"Just don't. Not until you've heard my counter."

"I promise that. I owe you that."

"All right, then."

"Mikhail, meet with the woman, tell her you're actually American and that somehow you and her deceased husband share the same name. That should placate her. She'll have no way of checking that out."

"All right, then. So be it."

I CALL the woman's number, get her voice mail, and leave a message that I'll be waiting to meet her in front of St. Basil's at three p.m. I don't have anything else to add, so I abruptly hang up.

At 2:58 p.m. I'm standing in ankle-deep snow in front of the cathedral, smoking a nervous cigarette. A nervous cigarette is one I occasionally smoke when I'm too nervous to function. Which I am right now, thinking that I'm about to meet a woman who might be furious and ready and able to turn me into the FSB as an imposter. The FSB could then combine my deceit with that of Russell's and make me look like another plant by the CIA come to help Russell. Stuff like that is running through my mind, some of it a real possibility, some of it specious as hell, but there you are. Like everyone else gathering on the walk around me and shooting pictures of the famous Moscow landmark behind me, I'm only human and I have a brain quite capable of running off with my calm, logical processes and leaving me twisting in the wind with the insanity of whatever my latest crackpot idea has turned up. Taking over a dead guy's identity might be just that and it serves me right for trusting Marcel without question and for not checking up on his work myself. But what's done is—a taxi pulls to the curb and a mid-fortyish woman climbs out of the backseat. She is wearing overshoes, a heavy navy coat from shoulders to just below the knees, and her hair is pulled over to the side in a very stylish cut. She passes some currency to the driver and steps around to the curb as he pulls away. Then she turns around, spots me, and gives me the most beautiful smile I have seen in a long, long time.

"Mikhail!" she cries, coming to me with her hands outstretched to take my hands in her own.

I comply, tentatively holding my hands out and she does, indeed, take them into her own gloved hands.

"Thanks for coming," I say.

"Oh, this is exciting."

"How so?" We are standing there, still holding hands.

"Well, I'm getting to see my long-dead husband come back to life. Naughty boy, dilly-dallying around in court without calling your wife as soon as you set foot back on earth. Tsk-tsk."

I can see it's going to be an interesting afternoon. I hail another cab, we climb in, and I ask Verona to tell him we need a coffee shop, something close by.

Then we're off.

She learns forward in her seat and turns to face me. She loosens the muffler around her throat. She shakes her hair free.

"Okay," she says without a hint of how she's feeling about me, "who are you really?"

She has me, no doubt. But I need time to put my story together.

"I'd rather wait until we're alone in the coffee shop, if that's all right."

She sees me indicate the driver with my eyes, as if I'm afraid he might be listening.

"Driver!" she snaps, "This man has a million dollars for you if you'll only toot your horn!"

Of course, there is no reaction. The driver is immutably immune to the English language, just like she knew he'd be.

"Still, please let's wait until we're alone," I try again. I sound like I'm whining and suddenly I don't much care for me. After all, I've betrayed this attractive woman and now I'm feeling like an ass.

"All right, Mikhail."

We are dropped in front of a small cafe with a green canopy and a greeter at the entrance. He opens the door and waves us through.

Then we are seated and coffee is ordered.

"Again," she asks without waiting, "who are you?"

"My name is Michael Gresham and I'm an American lawyer." The jig is up.

She pulls a curl of hair from her forehead. I love her hair —a hint of gray mixed in with blond—and I love her deep red lip gloss. Plus she smells wonderful, like the Tweed of my college days.

"Are you working for the CIA? Is that why you're in Russia, to help the CIA agent they caught?"

"No, I'm anything but CIA. I was hired by the man's father. My client is Russell Xiang and he is charged with acquiring state secrets. He's also charged with murder of an FSB agent. It doesn't look good."

"Why are you using my husband's name? Why have you stolen his identity? And why shouldn't I go straight to the FSB and report you?"

Thankfully, our coffees arrive and we use the cream and sugar, me in copious quantities; her, very little.

It gives me a few moments to formulate my response.

"I'm using your husband's name because my investigator put together a Russian identity for me to keep me insulated from the FSB. We don't want them to know my real name for my own safety. So that's the why of your question. And you shouldn't go to the FSB with this because they'll toss my dumb ass right in jail and throw away the key."

She smiles suddenly. "Pity, then I'd have to come visit you at Christmas."

"And my birthday."

She is still smiling. "Silly man."

It doesn't take her but a moment longer to see I'm very taken with her.

"So who are you?" I ask. "I've shown you mine, now you show me yours."

"I'm Verona Kristinova Sakharov, I'm fifty-one years of age, a widow, and I support myself by teaching at Moscow State University. I have no children, but four brothers and four sisters, all of whom live in and around Moscow, so I always have plenty of company around the holidays and there's always a niece or a nephew waiting for a birthday present from me. My favorite band is ABBA and my favorite painter is Gaugin. The greatest American writer is—"

"Hold it, please, why Gaugin?"

"Because, Mikhail, someday I would like to retire to the South Pacific and laze around in the sun on a sandy beach and have a man spread coconut oil on my shoulders. My particular fantasy. What is yours?"

"Pretty much the same thing, without the man."

We both laugh.

Her features turn contemplative. "So tell me, is your man guilty? Did he really kill an FSB agent and steal Russian secrets?"

She is staring right into me. She knows Russell is guilty of the things he is charged with; after all, there is a dead agent—it's been all over the news—and the CIA is denying involvement several times a day. She wants to see whether I will lie to her now.

"It isn't my job to decide guilt or innocence. My job is to defend my client regardless."

She reaches across the table and takes my wrist in her grip. She squeezes. "Come now, Michael. Surely you can do better than that."

"Let me say this, then—"—it is making me very uncomfortable—"I will be investigating the Russian government's factual basis for its claim against my client. Then I will know more."

"Fair enough. We shall shelve this discussion until then. But we will come back to it. Fair enough?" She releases my wrist as she says this.

"Yes, that's more than fair."

"Are you married?"

"I was. My wife was killed."

"How awful for you. How long has it been?"

"Too long and not long enough. Know what I mean?"

"I do. Mikhail hasn't been gone so long. He is missed by me and by his family."

"How did he die?"

"Boating accident, Colombia. They never recovered his body."

An idea comes to mind. "Excuse me for asking, but it's very important to me. You say they never recovered his body? Was there a death certificate?"

She studies me as if I know something she wasn't going to reveal.

"Actually, no. They didn't recover his body and the Colombian government needs a pronouncement of death by an official before it will issue a death certificate. Evidently Colombia has been the site of many insurance frauds by Americans who go there to die and don't die but have their spouses file life insurance claims. So now an official pronouncement is required. Incidentally, our Russian life insurance refused to pay for Mikhail's death without the certificate. If you're really a lawyer maybe you can sue them for me someday."

"I would—"

She touches my hand. "I'm only joking, dear man. Forgive me."

I smile at her. "So we've both lost someone dear to us. It's very difficult, especially around the holidays."

"Especially."

Then there is a quiet between us. We're both very comfortable with it. Just as suddenly, the spell is broken. She shuffles her feet and pushes her coffee cup and saucer away.

"I need to get back to university. I have a class."

"Totally understand. We'll grab a cab and I'll drop you off."

"No need. I'll catch my own cab. But I must say—I've enjoyed this, Michael."

It isn't lost on me that she's using my true name. Evidently that person has proven acceptable to her.

I take a chance. "We should do it again. What are your dinner plans?"

"Tomorrow night I have no plans. All other nights this week are spoken for."

"Tomorrow night is New Year's. Are you feeling celebratory?"

"I'm more interested in getting to know you better, in all honesty. What if you come by and we have dinner at my place?"

"I'd love to. What kind of wine can I bring?"

"No need. Mikhail left behind a huge wine cellar."

"All right. Seven o'clock okay?"

"It works. Here's my card. Let me jot my address on the backside."

She pulls out a red pen and writes her address in red ink. "Old habits," she says, chiding herself for the red pen of the writing teacher.

"Seven o'clock. I'll be there."

"See you then." A cab whips to the curb and she disap-pears inside.

Then she is gone.

"Mikhail Sakharov?" I whisper into the shuddering after-noon wind with its endless snow. "What the hell?"

Chapter 18

"**D**id you shoot bullets at my son?"
"I shot nothing."

Anna Petrov sits at a long steel table in a room without heat. She is wearing thin cotton pants and a thin cotton top. She is shaking with the cold and snot is running from her nose to her upper lip. She swipes it away again and again with her sleeve, but it's no use. The cold is going to drain her nose until there is nothing left to flush out. She knows this, vaguely, knows that she's a mess and at this moment no longer cares. She just wants to feel warm again. That's all, just warm.

Sitting across from her at the table are FSB chief Igor Tarayev and MI6 agent Henrik Nurayov, who, as usual, is assisting the Russians. Both men are wearing warm winter wear against the frigid room air. Their coats are thick and the men are wrapped in mufflers and gloves. While they are toasty and peaceful, their prey trembles in the cold air. Tonight they are pulling out all stops to prove the United States CIA killed Tarayev's son. Putin wants the case made yesterday—the pressure is intense and both men are feeling it. Petrov is a key figure; she was with Russell Xiang the night young Tarayev was gunned down; she might even be the one who pulled the trigger. There is a fifty-fifty chance it was her and not Xiang. So they pursue her.

"But you shot at the guards who came outside Henrik's home that night, did you not?"

"No! I never saw a gun that night!"

"Ms. Petrov, we know you cooperate with the CIA. They have acquired you as an asset because of your knowledge of Moscow environs and Russian politics. Plus, there are your well-known abilities with a gun. Russians once hailed you as their hero for winning the biathlon with its rifle shooting and skiing just last Olympics at Sochi. A gold medalist, a hero to her countrymen, and what? You sell out your homeland for American dollars? Isn't that what you've become, an American whore?"

"No, I have done no such thing. Please, I'm freezing in here."

Tarayev waves his thick arm around the room. Despite the oversized coat, his body mass is enormous, like that of a sea lion. "We are warm here and you can be warm too. Just tell us the truth. What about Xiang? You saw him shoot a gun that night?"

"Xiang? I know no one named Xiang."

"You deny you were with him at Mr. Nurayov's dacha on Christmas Eve?"

"I deny. I wasn't there. And I don't know anyone named Xiang."

"What about the man you were caught with at the green house? What was that man's name?"

"I don't know. He was already there when I arrived."

"What if two of our agents saw you traveling on a bus with this man? Does that help your memory?"

"I was traveling on a bus and sitting next to a complete stranger. I don't know what your people saw. Please, a jacket?"

She draws her sleeve across her upper lip and nose. The two lines of discharge from her nose are cleaned away. The shoulder of her sleeve glistens from the repeated wipes. Tarayev sees this and rolls his lips away from his teeth in disgust. Normally he feels nothing, but the sight of her and her wet upper sleeve are killing his appetite, making him a little queasy. He feels nothing but disgust.

Tarayev stands and lights a cigarette. He inhales deliciously and, when he is satisfied the prisoner isn't watching him, he suddenly thrusts a heavy hand across the table and catches her with a right cross, knocking her out of her chair. He then scuttles around the short table and catches her with his boot as she lies curled in a fetal position on the concrete floor. His kick catches her in the kidneys. She will piss blood and he knows it from long experience. He kicks again and this time catches her in the forehead. She lolls onto her back and her mouth falls open. With all the disdain he can muster, he flicks his cigarette ash into her open mouth. She coughs and waggles on the floor like a netted fish. He leans down and extinguishes his cigarette on her forearm, pinning it beneath his boot as he smashes the ash to nothing.

"No use screaming, Ms. Petrov," says Tarayev. "No one hears you. And even if they did, no one would care. Soon even you won't care if you continue to lie to us. Now let me try again. Who shot a gun that night while pointing it at the guards, hmmm?"

She thrusts her hips upward on the floor but makes no attempt to move otherwise.

"I—I—" she utters. But the words don't come and she passes out.

"Damn it, Henrik! Have I killed her?"

Henrik hasn't moved during all this. His time with young boys has shown him that physical abuse is relative. Some adjust and accept it; others, like the Petrov woman, resist and make the intensity level increase until, like now, they pass out or die. Her inability to defend herself reminds him of the boys. He grows excited. He stands and eases around the table. With a quick glance at Tarayev, who nods, he draws back his hiking boot and kicks the unconscious woman. She doesn't move. She doesn't acknowledge the blow. Nothing.

He retreats to his chair and sits there glaring at the far wall. He feels inadequate when his best elicits no response. It has happened before. Now he hates the woman so much more. He would like to see her pay the ultimate price tonight, but he knows she won't. No, she will be used by the FSB, placed in a courtroom where everyone swears she has the right to defend herself. Then they will cut her apart and vacuum the life right out of her body. And the point will be made: traitor.

Tarayev goes to the steel door. He kicks it with his boot. "Water!" he shouts. It is less than a minute until an arm reaches inside and presents Tarayev with a carafe of water. The door closes. Tarayev moves and stands over Anna Petrov. He unscrews the carafe's thick plastic plug. Then he pulls it out. Steam comes rolling out. He turns the carafe onto its side, holding the open hole over Petrov's face. A stream of steaming hot water swirls and splashes onto her face, wetting her eyes and going up her nose. She gasps. Her eyes blink open and she reaches and tries to shield her face from the continuing downpour. Tarayev kicks her arms aside with his boot and continues the downpour. She turns her head away, to the side, eyes closed, and begins weeping. "So cold and you tease me with hot water! Don't you even care?"

Henrik smiles. Her ability to process what's happening has become juvenile. She could just as easily be a boy lying there, crying out for solace while yet another blow falls across his buttocks. "No one cares, Anna. Least of all us. Listen to the man. Just tell the truth. Tell us you know Xiang. Tell us you fired guns at the guards. Tell us you murdered Mr. Tarayev's son that night."

Somehow—despite the cold, despite the kicks to the head, despite the punch to the side of the head—a thought filters through. *Tarayev's son died out there. My God,* she is thinking, *that's what this is about! We killed this man's son!*

Now she knows it will never stop.

She is going to die.

But he will never know her truth. He will never know that she shot the men on the right, the first one being the young man with the dyed blond hair. She recalls sighting in on him and putting the bead of the shotgun in the middle of his chest. She recalls seeing his chest explode and sail away across the snowy yard.

Tarayev's dead son died stupidly and without a fight. Of course they would award him a posthumous medal, maybe a ribbon or two. They would print his name on a document and present it to his mother, as well.

Sometimes even the very stupid make bank.

She manages to raise herself onto an elbow and says, looking under the table at the men's legs, "I saw your son and I saw his ribcage go flying across the snow. It was beautiful and ugly all at once. But most of all, it was stupid. Your son died a stupid man."

The two men bend forward at the waist and peer under the table. She smiles at them.

"Seriously? This is the best you have?"

Chapter 19

M ichael Gresham

I HAVE LEARNED that Moscow is one of the most—if not the most—expensive cities in the world. Yet, Verona has obtained enough meat to make a fine spaghetti sauce as we're eating Italian tonight. There is the gravy, made with peppers and sausages and hamburger, and there is grilled asparagus, and there is a fine French bread, lightly salted with a garlic spread. For dessert we eat Ptichye Moloko (Bird's Milk) until we are so full we have trouble sitting. And then comes the pièce de résistance: Verona has shopped at the Starbucks on Krasnopresnenskaya and picked up fresh ground French Roast. How she knew it was my favorite, I don't know. But we sweeten it with a drop of honey, add cream, and it's delicious.

This woman is beautiful, kind, and seems very intelligent. She is wearing a long purple skirt with a green top and a heavy silver necklace with native American squash blossoms. Her face is full of life, the eyes sparkling and the teeth bright and perfectly aligned, and when she smiles I feel as if a long-time friend is giving me approval and sending me warmth. Being with her leaves me glowing inside and I want to take her soft hair in my hand and pull her face to mine. Of course I don't let onto any of this—or so I think.

We go into the living room of her small apartment and sit at either end of a blue couch. There are three cushions, she has number one and I have number three. She suggests we remove our shoes and I do as she does.

After almost an hour of small talk, she shuffles uneasily on her cushion and says, "I need to stand and move around. Would you like to dance, Michael?"

I was hoping I would get to hold her tonight. Smiling takes over my face and I know I'm turning red as I stand and accept her invitation. She places her smartphone in a player and a serene Russian ballad fills the space between us.

She moves up to me and says, with a soft smile, "Hold me, my husband."

Instantly I have her in my arms, drawing her near, and we begin shuffling our feet in time to the music. As we dance I can feel her breath on my neck as her face is turned toward me. The song finishes and a second, much faster song cheers us along as we separate somewhat and begin doing something resembling a slow jitterbug. Helpless dancer that I am, I try to make it appear as if I'm very comfortable dancing but nothing could be further from the truth.

"I've missed you," she smiles. "You've been away far too long."

It dawns on me—maybe I'm only imagining this, but is she thinking I'm actually her husband?

Halfway through the third song—another slow,

romantic Russian ballad—she slows to a stop and looks into my eyes. "Please, kiss me," she says and I press my mouth on hers. She tastes sweet and—how can I say this—healthy. Perhaps not a romantic insight, but this is a woman who cares about herself and who has taken really good care over the years. Is that your normal turn on? It is for me.

Anyway, five minutes later we're shrugging out of our clothes although we're back to moving our feet to the music again as we do so.

"Dance with me nude," she says, and steps over to the light switch. Now it is dark except for the glow from a digital wall clock and the slight light from the face of her phone as it plays and plays. I fully embrace her then and she shudders against me. "This won't last long, she says, and allows her hand to trace down my spine to my buttocks. She leaves it there, softly caressing and at the same time humming into my ear.

Then she moves slightly away. "Who are you really?" she asks.

"I'm Michael Gresham. I really am."

"Well, if you need to pretend you are my husband, that is acceptable. But you will have to prove it to me first."

"How do I prove it?"

She steps back to me and throws her arms around me. "By taking me to bed. There are certain things only my husband would know. Let's find out if you're really him."

An hour later, as we are lying and embracing in her bed, her eyes flutter open and she pushes back from me. Now she is looking deep into my eyes.

"Mikhail, you have returned."

"Thank you," I say, happy that I passed whatever the test was about.

"I'm grading you an A-plus. You make love like a Mikhail

who has been away on a long trip and learned many new skills in your travels. Now come here."

I slide to her and place my free hand in the center of her back.

"I have been gone a long time. It won't happen again, Verona." I lightly brush her eyes with my lips. She shivers under my touch.

"You're forgiven," she says. "You may keep the name."

"Thank you."

Chapter 20

M ichael Gresham

WE COME INTO THE COURTROOM, Van and I, on the Monday following my arrival in Moscow. It is the day and time for Xiang's preliminary hearing. I have no idea what to expect and, like all events I've ever engaged in where the rules are unknown and the results can be disastrous, I'm afraid. But I suck in deep breaths and release them slowly through my nose. An inner calm is restored and allows me to continue to act as if.

The courtroom is large, rather like a ballroom. I look around for my clients—I'm accepting Petrov's case and representing her alongside of Russell. I don't see either one, so I turn to look. Along the rear wall is the defendants' glassed-in cell where, locked away, sit my clients, side-by-side on a wide bench. They evidently observe the proceedings from back there. I walk back toward them until I can reach out and touch the glass. Russell sits, heavily bandaged and still showing signs of the abuse following his escape attempt. And there is a young woman beside him who can only be Anna Petrov. I nod to them and force a fake smile. They only look at me. So I turn and go to find my table.

The courtroom is packed with deputies—women all—wearing navy pants, light blue short-sleeved shirts, and utility belts with guns inside holsters with flaps. On their heads are the equivalent of baseball caps with a silver star in the center forehead of each. The women are heavy, muscular, and extremely serious about keeping their jobs, so the courtroom is very efficient.

Spectators are herded into the first four rows of pews facing the judge's platform; media finds itself sitting in the next two rows. All cameras are banned and requests for filming are denied, Van explains. He tells me that we lawyers sit up front at a long table perpendicular to the judge's platform.

As Van and I take our seats we find ourselves facing the prosecution's staff: two men and two women, all wearing well-cut business suits with heavily starched white shirts and black ties. They remind me of the agents in *The Matrix*, except no one wears sunglasses. At least not inside the courtroom.

I hear my name, turn and spot Antonia Xiang. She stands when I nod at her and comes over before I can stop her. I don't want the court officials to see that we know each other, but it is too late.

"I tried to talk to him back there through the glass but the meter maids ran me off."

"Yes, it's very different here, I'm sure. Listen, I'd rather they didn't know we were connected but it's too late for that now. Can we speak after we're finished here?"

She ignores my request. "I went to see him last night.

Sunday night is visitors' night. They refused to let me see him, even with a fake name. 'He's accused of state secrets,' they said, whatever that means. They said state secrets defendants get no visits except from their lawyers. Do you think I might enter my appearance as one of his co-counsel?"

She has me there. Back in Washington, Antonia Xiang is a world class Assistant U.S. Attorney. She would likely prove invaluable to my team. Of course there is the fact her usual beat is terrorism. FSB might already have a line on her and violently object to her coming into the case.

"Let me talk that over with Van. Right now I'm tempted to say yes, come aboard, but safety first. Let me get Van's input and I'll get back to you."

"Call me at the hotel?"

"I promise. Later today."

She smiles and moves back to her seat in the pew. Another issue for us.

Van has explained to me what is happening in the case right now. The criminal investigation in Xiang's case is divided into two stages: an informal inquest performed by the police, and a formal preliminary investigation, usually conducted by a legally trained investigator who works for the Ministry of Internal Affairs.

A word about confessions, for they are rife in Russian courtrooms. Van has explained it to me on the taxi ride to court. To protect suspects against being coerced to confess to crimes, a constitutional right to counsel from the moment of arrest is on the books. In addition, the Russian Constitution guarantees the right not to testify against oneself. The Supreme Court has interpreted this to mean that the police must advise a suspect of the right to remain silent and of the right to counsel before commencing an interrogation.

Unfortunately, the police routinely coerce suspects into "waiving" their right to counsel. If suspects refuse to give a statement they are often tortured. He tells me that something like forty percent of all suspects are tortured, usually through beating, and by asphyxiation or electric shock. He also says the guards will give other inmates special privileges to beat, rape, and force suspects into confessing. We are assuming that Russell has made no such confession since we last met with him. Still, judging from his looks and wraps and bandages, our assumption could be totally wrong.

The judge strolls mechanically into the courtroom once the lawyers are seated and their papers spread before them. For some reason he is known as Chickenhawk, Van tells me with no small glee. When I ask where the nickname comes from he looks at me and shakes his head. "Perhaps we'll find that out this morning," he says.

The judge begins speaking. His words are interpreted in real time by an interpreter standing at the right side of the platform, standing and speaking the English interpretation as a counterpoint to the judge's continuing exposition. In other words, the judge speaks and the interpreter immediately is offering the English even as the judge moves onto his next comment.

The interpretation at the beginning is this: "Mr. Sakharov, you have filed papers asking for pre-trial release from detention."

Then he launches into the language of criminal bail law. "Most suspects against whom a preliminary investigation is initiated remain in custody in preventive detention facilities until trial. Detention is authorized if there is fear the defendant will not appear for trial, will destroy evidence, commit more crimes, or just because of the seriousness of the offense. Mr. Sakharov, this is your case on all points. One, if released on bail, Xiang will fail to appear for trial. Two, by doing so he will commit more crimes, even destroy evidence. Three, there is no more serious offense than acquiring state secrets. So defendant Xiang is remanded to the custody of the City Jail. Now we shall have our preliminary matters heard. Mr. Prosecutor, please proceed."

The prosecutor climbs to his feet. He is a thin man, sallow of complexion, who riffles nervously through his papers and constantly pushes his rimless glasses back on his nose. He looks up at the judge and speaks Russian urgently, all the while pointing at me and sometimes even jabbing a finger at me.

Van nudges me and I lean toward him. "This is Sergei Gliisky, the prosecutor. He is claiming that you are not who you say you are and that you are not qualified to appear in this court. He is asking the judge to order the militia to take you into custody until your background is sorted and your identity established. You are a fraud on the court."

The judge then reacts and the interpreter starts up again:

"Mr. Sakharov, the prosecutor has filed papers just now stating that your real name is Michael Gresham and that you are an agent of the American CIA. These are very serious allegations. My inclination is to hold you in custody until your true identity is known before making a decision on the prosecutor's motion that you be held in criminal contempt for attempting to illegally influence the outcome of a Russian judicial proceeding. You could go to jail for a minimum of ten years if these charges are proven against you."

I almost faint when I hear "ten years."

"What?" I whisper to Van, "Do something, man."

Van then stands and looks around, blinking. His opening remarks are halted and spoken in a tone that even I can interpret as apologetic. His speech lasts less than thirty seconds, then he sits back down.

"What?" I ask.

"I told the judge that you came to me and told me your name was Mikhail Sakharov. I told the judge that as far as I was concerned, that was your real name. Then I apologized if it turns out I made a mistake."

"Van, what the hell? I paid you to co-counsel with me! I didn't pay you to cover your own ass!"

Van moves away several inches, separating himself from me. "I thought you were being honest, Mr. Sakharov. I had no idea you might not be who you told me you are. Do you have family that could come before the judge and clear this up?"

My mind immediately goes to Verona Sakharov. Then I shut it off. I will absolutely not, under any circumstances, ask her to come into this courtroom and identify me as her husband. That would be a terrible abuse of our time together and would crush any trust she might have in me to even ask. Absolutely. Will. Not.

"I have no family to clear this up. I live alone."

Then the judge is speaking and Van's attention swings back to him. I listen as the interpreter again announces, "The court will order defense counsel Mikhail Sakharov taken into detention and held while his identity is proved. After that he shall be immediately released and allowed to continue with his defense of Russell Xiang. The court is in recess."

Immediately there's a great deal of clamor in the court-room, the judge disappears, I turn and see that Russell has been removed from the cage, Van is headed for the doors;

four armed Russian women swarm me and put the bracelets around my wrists. But they leave me with a glimmer of hope because they have cuffed me in front rather than behind.

As she passes me by, Antonia Xiang flashes me a sad look. Sad because she knows me as Michael Gresham and her face says it all: See you in ten years.

As for me, the worst that could happen has happened. Suspicions have been raised about my true identity. The ID that Marcel put together for me will leak like a sieve upon close inspection. My pulse hammers in my neck and my breathing becomes forced. I'm gasping for air and swallowing it down. My lungs feel like they want to burst as they burn and cry out for normal respiration. But I'm scared and I know it and the guards know it too, as they push me along from behind, up the aisle, out into a long dark hallway, and down toward what can only be the freight elevator. Everyone else is heading to the first floor by the main staircase that opens onto this floor. My eyes quickly memorize every inch of it as I approach. Its steps are polished with use and the handrails are worn down. In great distress, I look at the lucky souls leaving by the stairs. I'm pushed ever more insistently as I slow to watch them leaving and consider making my break to fly down through them and escape.

But where would I go? How and where would I hide if I suddenly ran out the front doors of the Moscow City Court? Handcuffed? No one is going to assist a handcuffed man. I know I wouldn't. So I put that notion out of my head.

The elevator well holds two doors. The door on the left opens and a green arrow points down. I'm pushed from behind and stumble inside as my face is pushed up against the wall. I hear voices outside the sliding door just before it closes and I realize not all four guards have entered with me. Slowly I edge around and am astonished to see that only one guard is now attending to me. Where did the others go? Will we see them again downstairs when our door opens? I don't know, which puts me at a great disadvantage. But one thing I do know is this: cops around the world carry handcuff keys. Usually inside the chest pocket of their uniform. It's common and I'm realizing that I can hang onto that fact and make it into something much larger.

For example, the woman guarding me is several steps away, looking up at the floor numbers changing as we proceed downward. I'm cuffed with my hands in front, which makes attacking her possible. So I have a heart attack. Right there on this downbound elevator I suddenly collapse into a heap, scaring the Russian woman to death. Her face is suddenly over me and she is shouting the same word at me over and over, and I make no attempt to respond. Then the elevator door slides open and, before anyone can come inside, she backs them off with a stern warning.

She stands over me and studies my face. She feels my pulse and then says something into her shoulder mike. Help is probably on the way, so it's now or never. I struggle to my feet and lunge for her; she is knocked back against the wall. I locate her holster. I claw its flap open and pull her gun into my hand. Then I point it at her chest. "Handcuffs," I pant at her. "Key!" She seems to understand, for she raises a hand as if to say I should stay calm, then reaches inside her shirt pocket—sure enough—and produces the tiny handcuff key. With a quick twist the cuffs come off and I fling them aside. I'm still pointing the gun at her. Only then do I realize a huge commotion has erupted just outside the door.

Without a second thought I push my way through the crowd that was waiting to board our elevator and come out the other side. I'm still holding the gun when I walk up to a heavyset Russian man and begin unzipping his coat and miming that he should remove it. He cooperates, raising his hands as if to ward off any shots I might fire at him.

As I'm shrugging into his coat, four Russian militiamen materialize on the steps outside and see me though the glass door, standing with a gun. They immediately pull their pistols and point them at me. I turn and look for a way out. But three more female guards have just stepped off the second elevator and are making their way toward me, guns drawn, their faces angry and determined. It is finished.

The first woman to me utters a loud command and I know what she means. She is going to shoot me unless I drop the gun. I bend down and place the gun on the marble floor. Then they are upon me and handcuffs are snapped onto wrists, this time pulled back behind me.

The man whose coat I stole comes up and speaks in an angry voice to the guards, who by now have been joined by the militiamen. Clearly he wants his coat returned. But he is told to stand aside, which he does, and I'm marched out the front doors and down the steps to a waiting van.

I'm pushed and pulled into the van and forced back against my manacled wrists. They hurt but I know no one will help so I remain silent.

The van has three rows of seats and it slowly dawns on me as I look around: Russell Xiang is in the middle seat just ahead of me. He says, without turning around, "Welcome, Mikhail. Now we shall have unlimited time to discuss my defense."

I want to laugh but don't. From the looks on their faces, these militiamen would be very upset to have their prisoner laughing. Maybe upset enough to rap him across the mouth.

So I maintain my silence.

The streets are a blur outside the window. I know nothing about Moscow streets and directions and have no idea where we are. Even if I had escaped I would have been quickly captured because I wouldn't have known where to run.

So we bump along over the streets rough with snow.

My fear begins to mount in my gut the farther we are from the courthouse. Because the farther we are from the courthouse, the closer we are to Moscow City Jail, and the stories I've heard about that place.

I silently pray those stories are not true.

Chapter 21

When she put her name to the confession, her left arm was broken in two places, her right wrist dislocated after being battered by a police baton, her right eye swollen shut from savage blows, three ribs cracked from powerful kicks, and two fractured teeth were embedded in the roof of her mouth from being sapped in the jaw. Anna Petrov saw two lines and two names being signed at once though there was really only one line and one name. Diplopia can indicate severe trauma to the optic nerve and Petrov, being sapped repeatedly in the face, now saw double everything.

She had been wearing no coat inside the green house when taken into custody and she is wearing no coat when they push her out the rear loading dock of the Moscow Jail down into snow up to her waist. She falls onto her back and lies there for several minutes, catching her breath and trying to stop the vomiting. Then she struggles to her feet and shakes off the powdery snow clinging to her backside. On her feet are green deck shoes and her lower garment is blue-jeans with torn knees while her upper garment is a wool turtleneck sweater with a cotton T-shirt beneath. She blows on her hands. She cups snow against her throbbing wrist. The dislocation is the worst, she decides, and she knows she needs medical attention. She also knows from the questions they've been asking her that she works for the government in some capacity, but she can't say what that is. She just can't recall those facts. They told her what name to put on the confession when she signed but for the life of her she has no memory of it. It just didn't ring a bell.

"It's short term memory loss," she tells herself in the dark alley while the wind howls all around. "It'll pass." Her words were words welded into her mind during training at the spy school in Maryland. Certain rote phrases and knowledge islands existed to help the brain-addled spy survive, courtesy of her employer, the Company.

She feels inside her pockets. There is crumpled up about six thousand rubles and a book of matches from a downtown Moscow lounge. Forcing herself to move and not just surrender to the snow, she trudges two hundred feet to the closest street and walks onto the curb, where she teeters, peering into the pelting sleet and snow. No traffic passes by for several minutes. She heads for the front of the building where she was incarcerated. In the yellow of the street lamp she makes out a double street sign that says, she is quite certain, Novoslobodskaya. Isn't that the street the jail fronts onto? She knows Moscow and thinks she is right: if her memory can be trusted. She waits, shivering and stamping her feet until a cab comes toward her before she steps into his lane and waves him down. He pulls to the curb. She staggers around to the driver's window and asks him, in her perfect Russian, if he will take her to a hospital.

"Which hospital?" he wants to know.

She asks him which one he recommends.

"Central Clinical Hospital and Polyclinic," he tells her. "That's the one I know best. They can help you."

"All right," she tells him, "take me there."

He drops her in a bladed driveway beneath an overhang at the emergency entrance of the hospital. She wanders inside and tries conversing with the intake receptionist. But she makes no sense and turns to walk back out. The receptionist, however, is a young woman who cares, and she catches up to Petrov and takes her by the arm, gently guiding her to a hospital gurney and helping her lie down. She then covers her with a light blanket and summons the ER nurse.

Her broken arm is cast from shoulder to hand and her dislocated wrist is put back into place—the worst of all the pain she has felt yet. Then they examine her eyes and teeth and commence an overall physical exam, making a plan of treatment. An ophthalmologist is caught as he is leaving the hospital for the night and he returns to his suite, where she is wheeled for evaluation. He thinks the visual disturbances are, at this point, likely due to edema from the trauma and he predicts that will resolve over the next forty-eight hours.

Next, she is admitted and taken upstairs.

In the morning, a staff physician removes the dental fragments from the roof of her mouth. A dental exam follows and temporary crowns epoxied in place.

By the third day, certain memories are beginning to return. First is her name and then her residence information and, by the fourth day, her employment details. Which shock her. She is a CIA operative working out of Moscow Station and it is imperative that she make her way to her employer immediately. Which she does, leaving the hospital AMA by way of the same ER door that delivered her inside three nights previous. The hospital has outfitted her with a second-hand coat from its County Aid stores and black leather gloves too large for her hands but that accommodate her swollen wrist.

She is dropped at the American Embassy that snowy noonday and by one o'clock she has passed all the ID tests —without any papers or pass cards—and she is back with her team. The last time there, the Moscow Station Chief Edward R. Henshaw was gunned down by a high-powered rifle, and in the chaos that followed she fled with Russell Xiang for the green house. That all seems like a dream to her now as she sits in the lounge and awaits new ID, keys to her flat, and money.

Then comes an intensive debriefing. She tells her manager the entire story, beginning with the raid on Henrik's house, the shootout, and finding the bill of lading for the weapons and munitions. They ask more questions and she tells them about the green house and the FSB raid where she and Russell were taken captive. She asks her manager how the FSB could have known she and Russell were hiding there and he looks at his chief and there is a moment of understanding, but then neither one answers her question. Then they ask her about jail, about court, about the beatings—especially whether the bruises and breaks and dental injuries were photographed and preserved and she answers yes, remembering that those things were done, especially the photographs. Of course, they all agree, yet because it is a Federation hospital those same artifacts proving the extent of her injuries could just as easily disappear if the FSB gives the word. Whereupon, a photographer and medical team are brought in and an *ad hoc* exam performed and photographs are taken for the CIA's files.

When it is all said and done, Anna Petrov wants only to go home and fall into Rodney's arms then draw a bath and sit in a tub of hot water and shut her eyes.

With her cast outside the tub, of course.

Chapter 22

Michael Gresham

THE GUARD MAKES HIMSELF UNDERSTOOD. He does this by making the universal hand sign for mouth talking, two mouths talking, two hands going back and forth. I have a visitor. Clever, I'm thinking. So I say, "Fine, take me to this visitor, please." If nothing else, it's a chance to get out of the part of the Moscow Jail that is unheated—the cells and holding tanks, and into the part that is heated—the administrative offices and the visitors' room.

He follows me as we make our way through corridors, at last coming to a door that is painted fire engine red and which has only buttons, no handle. The guard comes around me and clicks several numbers—five in all, I believe —and the door swings open on a pneumatic system. Warm air immediately blasts my face and I now leave the penal zone.

He continues guiding me along from behind, and I

quickly learn the Russian words for right and left and straight. Finally we make the last right and find ourselves in a small gymnasium type of room, with high ceilings and clerestory windows. Arranged one after another are booths that back up to the wall. He directs me to booth nine and pushes me inside. The setup is immediately obvious. Sit down, pick up the phone from its wall mount, start talking.

On the other side of the glass sprawls a man maybe in his early forties or late thirties, leaning his chair back on two legs. He greets me in English through the phone system.

"Hello, Mikhail. We'll be speaking English so the eaves-droppers can't understand."

"Hello. Who are you?"

"My name is Anatoly Palatov. I work for the Russian government."

"You have really good English for a Russian. If I didn't know better I'd guess Texas, maybe Arkansas."

"No, Leningrad by birth. Now, I'm here because the government wants to help you."

"The Russian government wants to help me?"

He smiles and I can see that his smile is anything but Russian: nice, neat teeth, the result of American orthodontia, certainly, without the metal fillings and shiny silver crowns so favored by the Russians. But, if he says he's Russian, so be it. Something deep inside tells me to give up that line of questioning. After all, FSB is on the line with us. A silent party, but there nonetheless.

"I'm glad your government wants to help me. Believe me, I have done nothing wrong."

"We know that. We've seen the error of our ways. So I'm going to post bail for you. You'll be going home today."

Tears come to my eyes, I'm so relieved. Right then if I could reach through the Plexiglas and kiss him I would.

Home! Away from the paralyzing cold, away from a shelf of concrete for a bed without bed covers—especially without any sort of blanket. Plus there are four of us in that six-by-nine cell, a ceramic hole in the floor for all body functions, and a window painted over with black paint and no light source at all. The only time we can see anything—and that is dimly—is when the door will suddenly fly open and the guards jolt us to attention. Then we have momentary light enter the door and we quickly look around to see with our eyes what we have previously have seen only with our hands, fingers, and feet. But now I'm going home.

"What time today will I go?"

"Within the hour. I've already posted the notice of bail, which has to be submitted one hour before the actual bail so objections can be made, if any. There won't be any objections because objections can only be made by the government and as far as these people are concerned I am the government. You're maybe a half hour to an hour from leaving. There will be a black government automobile parked out front to take you home. It has small Russian federation flags on the front bumpers. Just climb in the back. The driver already knows your address."

"Incredible. How can I thank you for this?"

"Really? Do a great job for your client. The government wants to see justice done. So go to bat for him and knock it out of the park."

Knock it out of the park? If that isn't down-home American, I don't know what is. Then it dawns on me. He's giving me clues with some of this.

"I'll be sure and knock it out of the park, Mr. Palatov. And I will do a great job for my client. That's all I've ever wanted to do. Now, will you be in touch with me again, or is this the end of it?"

"This is it. You're out, the court has been notified it is to give up all questions concerning your nationality and fitness to practice before it, and you will proceed from here with a clean slate. Congratulations, Mr. Sakharov, you win."

"I win," I say in wonder.

"Say, you're not Sakharov the Bear are you by any chance?"

"Not that I know of. Why?"

"Oh, its a legend that this Sakharov comes into Russia from the west every hundred years and destroys the enemies of the Russian people. You'd know if you were he."

I smile. "No, I have no intention of destroying anyone. I'm a peaceful man from Moscow."

"I'm sure you are, Mr. Sakharov. Well, that's all I came to say, so farewell, my friend. And good luck with Mr. Xiang."

With that, he stands, replaces his phone, and turns away, buttoning his overcoat as he leaves me there. A sudden rap on the door behind me startles me back to reality and the same guard pulls open the door. I follow him out into the hallway and this time, instead of turning back left from whence we came, we proceed straight ahead.

Then I know. I'm on my way home.

TWO HOURS later I'm discharged. There was a ton of paper-work and I have signed at least twenty forms, some of which required that I swear under the laws of perjury that I was who I said I was—Mikhail Sakharov. So be it, I thought, and continued signing my name.

The coat I had stolen from the man in the courthouse is returned to me. For the first time, I notice it is at least two sizes two small but I pull it on anyway. It will be below freezing outside and I will use whatever they give me.

Out the main doors I hurry, and stand and pause at the top of the stairs. The waiting vehicle is one of many in a long line at the curb. But it is the only vehicle with the small flags of state. So I head down there two steps at a time.

The back door swings open as I approach and I climb inside.

And to my great surprise there is my benefactor, Anatoly Palatov, who just bailed me out of jail. Wonder of wonders. He moves to the far side of the backseat, giving me room to unfold my six-foot frame.

"So," he says, evidently amused with himself, "we meet again."

"And why is that?"

"Drive on," he says to the man at the wheel. "And raise the privacy panel, please."

He waits until the panel is fully raised between us and the front seat.

"I'm an employee of the Russian government, as I told you, Michael Gresham. But I also moonlight for your government."

"Moonlight? As in—what?"

"You have certain agencies that require certain inside information in Russia. I try to help them procure that information."

"You're CIA, correct?" I blurt out.

He smiles and brushes air at me. "Silly man, no one in Russia is CIA. We deported all those cowards years ago. Only official Embassy state department people remain in the Russia of today."

"Just like the KGB left Washington? Is that it?"

He ignores my comment.

"Your government wants you to free Russell Xiang. Your government is available to help you do that with anything you need. Need additional counsel? Just say the word. Need money for an additional investigator or five? Just say the word. Need an office with full staff? Snap your fingers and it's done. Need bribe money—"

"Say the word. So here's what I need. I need you to bail my client out of jail. It is miserable as all hell in there and I need him outside where he can help me."

Anatoly purses his lips and begins shaking his head. "That is not so easy. This case is under the microscope. Every Russian citizen wants your client put to death for the killing of a Russian agent, even though he was an FSB agent. We're funny that way. Loyal to the extreme even when it's unhealthy for us."

"No excuses if you are who you say you are. Bail him out today or just stop this car and drop me right here. We'll go our separate ways if you won't help me."

His face contorts but then relaxes and his charming smile returns. "Let me make some calls. We'll see if the wolves have abated somewhat by now. Time and distance are great healers, yes, Michael?"

"And stop with the Michael. Call me Mikhail at all times. I don't want to do the jail thing again, not ever."

"Mikhail it is, then."

We drive on. His driver knows the way to my flat without a word from me.

Someone has been doing their homework.

Clearly it is time to move elsewhere.

Chapter 23

M ichael Gresham

THE CIA HAD a rule against employees associating in public. The need for the rule was obvious.

On January 2, four software engineers violated the CIA rule by eating breakfast together at the IHOP on Stafford Street, just twenty miles from the CIA's new location in Virginia. The four engineers comprised the CIA cyberwar team known as CyWar. They were there to celebrate a silent success. They had shut down Russia's ability to make war all of New Year's Day. To do so, they had reprogrammed Russian nuclear codes into unintelligible gibberish incapable of launching a nuclear strike. On that day, Russian nuclear capability had ceased to exist for twenty-two hours while the Russians unscrambled their software.

Waiting in their booth for a waitress to appear, the four engineers took a poll. Chances of being caught while associating were ten percent, said Stephen Taft, an expert in algorithms; Ainsley Burshtin, an expert in cyber-mathematics, set it at fifteen percent. Always the outlier, Samuel T. Washington, an expert in Russian cyber-warfare put it at negative ten—though only he seemed to know what that meant, exactly. Not to be outdone, Melody Winston, an electrical engineer, surprised them all with a well-reasoned one-in-four chance of being caught on their illegal outing, because the CIA, in the District of Columbia and its environs, had eyes everywhere. The city was scrutinized at every turn by video cameras that missed nothing. A seat of government required as much. When Melody shared her rationale, the three men involuntarily hunched forward and lowered their faces from view.

The waitress appeared wearing a Christmas corsage of bells and berries and holly. Melody took one look at her and said, "Don't tell me: you're the same waitress whose Christmas lights are still up in July." The humor passed unnoticed. Menus were handed out. The diners studied the tasty offerings. Two Garden Omelets and one Country Omelet for the men, while Melody ordered a fruit plate with yogurt. Coffee was poured, orange juice was chugged, and pancakes were delivered just minutes later. A Lazy Susan of syrups arrived and soon the blues and browns and purples of the sweet stuff ran together with real butter. All was well.

The team relaxed as they gobbled down the pancakes. No CIA agent had been killed in the United States in years, save for the Qazi shootout on January 25, 1993. But that was an anomaly. That attack was long thought to be a one-and-done. It took place outside the Central Intelligence Agency headquarters in Langley, when a gunman killed two CIA employees and wounded three others. The perpetrator was captured, put on trial, and was found guilty of capital murder. He was executed by lethal injection in 2002. The

FBI said his fate flashed out a warning to all who would hunt Agency employees and that was why there had not been a single instance since. But the CIA knew better: they had been lucky, was all.

The agents' breakfast was only expected to last thirty minutes. As they cleaned their plates and washed everything down with coffee, small talk invariably turned to their work. They discussed, over breakfast, the hack the day before. The cyberattack was payback for the Russians hacking into the certain American computers during the presidential campaign. The CIA meant to cripple Russia's nuclear war capabilities to make a point: Don't Tread on Me. The team's leader, Russell Xiang, had even traveled to Russia to silence a UK agent who, it was reported, was willing to sell the Russians the details of the upcoming cyberattack.

Blood sugars running high after the syrupy pancakes, the CIA employees fell into a kind of quiet torpor. Thoughts were mostly on New Years goals at the Agency. They failed to see the diner who followed them into the IHOP and chose the booth next to theirs. They failed to see that he ordered only coffee, which he then left untouched. His ID said his name was Gorkin. He brought into the restaurant, under his Burberry, a Remington 870 Police Magnum. The shotgun was fitted with the shortened barrel, complete with ATF tax stamp, just not in his real name. The waitress tried a second time to interest Gorkin in a breakfast menu; she needed a tip from his table but he waved her off. "Not for me," he said in halting English. "Maybe later you should try again, okay?"

Gorkin's cell phone pulsed. A text was waiting. He slipped the phone from his shirt pocket and read:

    ????

He texted back, *Four legs of the snake w/o its head.*

Proceed

Gorkin shot a look around the restaurant. Good, no police uniforms. Slowly sliding his hand inside his top coat, he flicked the gun's safety. He watched as the waitress delivered the CyWar team's bill inside a plastic credit card holder. A card was handed over. The waitress spun on her heel and headed for the register. Gorkin drew a deep breath and suddenly erupted up out of his booth, stepping up beside the foursome and at the same time swinging the shotgun up and out of his coat. He fired four magnum rounds. Faces and heads were blown away, flesh and brain and bone matter splattered up against the window, or what was left of it after the second blast blew it out into the parking lot. Clutching the shotgun in his right hand, he calmly headed to the entrance. Without looking back to assess any plainclothes pursuit, Gorkin made his way outside to a blue and white Suzuki GSR motorcycle and swung his leg up and over. The engine caught instantly and the Russian shot out of the parking lot onto Stafford.

Exactly two miles down the road from the IHOP was a strip mall with several small businesses and the Langley Athletic Club. Gorkin nosed the motorcycle into an open spot in front of Terry's Gold and Coins, and parked. He climbed off and, carrying the gym bag, scurried inside the Athletic Club, then slowed his walk so as to not draw attention. Back into the men's locker room he went, stopping in front of an upright locker—one of hundreds—and dialed in the combination. A change of clothes was neatly hung and waiting. Into the locker went the gym bag carrying the gun. Then he quickly changed the shooter's outfit for a black pinstriped suit, blue shirt, rap tie, and wingtips. He immediately closed the door and spun the combination, locking it once again. Back outside, he headed in a diagonal across the traffic lane. At the first row, he removed a ring of keys from his pocket and clicked the fob, unlocking the doors of a blue Toyota Corolla. He climbed inside and started the engine. On the windshield was a CIA campus parking/access sticker displaying the familiar eagle and starburst compass points below. It granted Level 1 Security Access to the vehicle, as did the ID card inside the wallet he retrieved from the console and slipped into his inner jacket pocket.

Now he drove north on Great Falls Street and then west on Dolley Madison Boulevard, where he turned onto the CIA campus with its warnings and checkpoints. Along the way he passed a line of protesters holding signs that said CLOSE GUANTANAMO and OBAMA PROMISED. He smiled and began making his way to his designated parking spot.

After parking his Toyota, Gorkin made his way inside the entrance and approached the building security zone. He removed his wallet from his coat and flashed his ID to the card scanner then placed his face against the optical scanner and allowed it to read his retinas.

The ID card said, simply, *Anatoly Palatov, Level 1.*

The optical software was satisfied, the card scanner was satisfied, and the security bar was raised.

"Morning, Dr. Palatov," said the duty guard. Anatoly Palatov returned the greeting with a smile.

Palatov headed for his office at the rear of the horizontal H that comprised the first of the new buildings.

He was back.

Chapter 24

The call had come fifteen minutes ago: four CIA CyWar spies gunned down. At an IHOP, of all places. *Anatoly Palatov had struck.* The president snorted and turned away from the toilet, confident the drip-drip-drip of the urethra was played out and his boxers would remain acceptably dry. Washing his hands in the sink, he studied the face staring back at him. White, Anglo-Saxon but not Protestant. Not anything, for that matter, though he had tried many times to convert to something—anything—and to remain committed. The mandatory Sunday morning shot of the president and family leaving their place of worship. But, alas, none of it had taken and now Sinclair was an unabashed agnostic. He had lots of answers, sure, as any president must. But answers about God—that's where he disembarked the answer train. For he had none and didn't like to guess. Guessing about the fate of his soul was better left to the religious and, increasingly, the quantum mechanists. "You don't even know about sixty minutes from now, much less your prospects for eternity," he chided his reflection in the mirror. "Better to say nothing and appear a fool than to speak up about such things and prove it," he said with his campaign smile, the smile that had wooed voters over his thirty year career in politics. The Colgate smile.

He returned to his bedroom, where Harald Stennis, his personal assistant, had yet another dark blue suit ready and waiting, with yet another white shirt and yet another red necktie. "Some things never change," he muttered at Harald, whose usual practice was to simply nod that he had heard such comments, which he did now. The president dressed quickly and expertly, all tucks and pleats in place, then departed his bedroom, picking up his first Secret Service bodyguard of the day. He entered the North Hall, where he took a right and passed by his own reading room, then the Yellow Oval Hall, to the elevators and stairwell. Today he chose the stairwell—all the better to steal even a hint of exercise in hopes of keeping the fool doctors at bay. He two-stepped downstairs and the agent followed in kind. At the bottom, another two agents joined the party and off the foursome headed for the Oval Office. Past the Office of the National Security Advisor, down several doors and to the right into the presidential lobby, ending up in the Oval Office. President Sinclair sank into his desk chair, swiveled around and stared out at the Rose Garden, then reined himself in and turned back around to focus on the day ahead.

It was 8:30 a.m. and the President's personal secretary, Andrea Gomirivi, was waiting. She took him over the day's schedule. He remained impassive while she stepped through his meetings and calls and photo ops and appearances. He then attended the daily handshake sessions—the first and second of six—and then met with his legislative advisers. Throughout, he was anxious to address the CIA killings, but managed to maintain an even demeanor and happy smile for the photographs and visitors, none of whom he'd remember by nightfall.

At 10 a.m. he received the Presidential Daily Briefing from the National Security Advisor. Fifteen minutes later, the CIA chief joined them.

Jed Buchholz was the NSA chief. He was a portly man, caught forever between middle years and middle later years thanks to his babyface and perfect skin. He had the hunter's sense of smell for a nearby foe and was reported to be a man who would awaken from a sound sleep at 3 a.m. and call for a hit on an Afghani warlord ten thousand miles away. At the other end, someone would die and no one would know exactly why, except for Buchholz, who operated the agency on a need-to-know basis. The murder of four CIA agents was hand-wringing time in most offices in Washington, but not so with Buchholz. He was ready to give chase to whomever had pumped the shotgun blasts into the CIA's brain trust and then fled the scene. Give chase and hang them by the neck without a trial. That was Buchholz's perfect result: justice without the bother of a trial. For this reason, this character trait, he fit perfectly into the role of NSA chief.

The CIA was headed up by a woman who had never been married, never given birth, and was said to be moving the agency lock-stock-and-barrel from SIGINT back to HUMINT. The reason: she found human intelligence assets much more forthcoming, productive, and reliable than the ciphers of SIGINT. The old CIA might be happy pulling down signals from the ether, but not Lucy Ya. Her Ph.D. in Chinese was Stanford, her undergrad in math was Harvard, and her ethnicity was Chinese-American from the Bay Area where her father was a vice-president at Apple. Some called her a lesbian; some called her straight;

whatever; she hadn't been caught up in the mundane sexuality of the species, concentrating her focus more on career than relationships. Ya hadn't gotten where she was by being friends. She had gotten where she was by producing hard evidence for her station chiefs in Berlin and Baghdad by virtue of the clandestine encounters she had with hundreds of men who sold bits and pieces about everything German and everything Iraqi for the American dollars she paid out in what seemed an unending supply. She had helped George W. Bush invade Iraq and had come home to America shortly after, where she began her rapid ascent inside the CIA's administrative offices. President Sinclair had chosen her to head up the agency his second day in office. She had remained there ever since and reliable intel had never been in greater supply since the agency's inception.

This morning's meeting was attended by Sinclair, Buchholz, and Ya only. Electronic counter-measures were in place inside the Oval Office. The meeting started off across a coffee table. On one side, Sinclair sat hunched forward on a sofa with his coffee mug, while Buchholz and Ya manned the opposite sofa. Buchholz balanced his can of Mountain Dew on one knee while Ya sipped her green tea out of a White House teacup on a gold-rimmed White House saucer. After brief hellos, the trio got right down to it. Buchholz went first, describing the murder of the agents. Then Ya recounted the success of the Agency's plan to cripple Russia's ability to call for a nuclear strike. The President appeared elated. He also marveled at Palatov's timing: before carrying out the President's order to take out the agents he'd let them shut down the Russians' nuclear strike capabilities. Maybe it was only for a day, but it was huge—at least to the President.

President Sinclair then led the discussion—as he always did. It was time to put on his dog and pony show.

"Bucky, let's do some basic detective work here. Who would know that our quartet was meeting for breakfast?"

Buchholz spread his hands. "We're working on that. All we know so far is that the team set up the breakfast while they were at the CIA campus. No calls were made from or to anyone's home; no evidence of any email trail. It's a very difficult concept for the world of spies, but I'm thinking it was nothing more complicated than meeting at someone's cubicle and agreeing to breakfast. No big deal."

"And Russell Xiang of course is in Moscow. Does that figure into this?"

"Of course, sir. We killed FSB officers; they put our people on trial for murder with threats of a firing squad. We cripple their ability to launch nukes for a whole day, they kill CIA agents."

The President appeared thoughtful. Then, "You folks tell me where we go from here? What's the next rock to get turned over?"

"Know what I think?" said Lucy Ya, the CIA chief. The men looked at her. "I think I've got a mole."

"What?"

"It's been known to happen."

"So what do you plan to do?"

"Security is already looking. We're beginning with proximity and digital."

"So while you're doing that, what kind of video have you pulled down from IHOP? I assume there was video?"

"There was. We've analyzed it and it's undergone facial recognition. The problem is, the shooter had a line on the video cameras. He never turned toward one so all we have is back-of-head."

"Amazing," said Sinclair. "They can actually do that?"

"What, avoid the camera? A good spy is trained extensively in avoidance techniques. It becomes second nature. The Russians are masters."

"And where does that leave us?"

CIA looked at NSA. Buchholz of NSA said, "With an even score."

"Meaning?"

"It's now four-to-four, Russia to the United States."

The President stood. He bent and settled his mug on the coffee table. The visitors were oblivious, just as he knew they would be. The real truth was his secret and his alone. Of course there was Palatov, but he was reliable always.

"One other thing, Dr. Ya," said Sinclair. "I don't want your mole taken into custody."

"I wasn't thinking custody."

"Good. The world will never know about him. The world will never know what became of him."

"Yessir," said Ya.

The President looked at his visitors. "What about the American lawyer who's now helping Xiang? Any update?"

"He's just been bailed out of jail."

"Jail? What the hell was he doing in jail?"

"His identity was being established. The Russian court had decided maybe he wasn't who he was claiming to be."

"Who was he claiming to be?"

"Mikhail Sakharov."

"How was he going to pull that off? Does he even speak the language?"

"He does not," said Ya. "No Russian. We've contacted him, Sir."

"And?"

"He's harmless. Just another American lawyer, nothing special, but I think if we help, he can get the job done."

"Oh?"

Ya brushed her hand through the air. "We want Xiang out where we can control him. If he gets convicted in a Russian court maybe he tells all to the Russians to save his skin. Then they have their reason to break off the nuke talks. So we help Gresham walk him out. It's the best guarantee your nuke talks will proceed."

The President knew that was the best way to handle Xiang. Which meant Gresham and his efforts were a key component. If Xiang came out a free man, Ya would control him. If they didn't get him home, the U.S. and Russian talks to reduce nuclear arms would suddenly break off because Xiang would have turned out to be a CIA officer who had killed an FSB officer.

"We've told Gresham we're going to help him with anything he needs," Ya said, reading the president's mind.

"If he needs witnesses, make it happen. Money, unlimited. Anything else, do it if he asks." said Sinclair.

The agency heads nodded in agreement. "Well played, sir," said Buchholz.

"And what about Anna Petrov?"

"Who?"

"The agent who assisted in killing four Russian guards."

"Same treatment as Xiang. Set her free and bring her home."

"Yes, sir."

"Good. Good. All right, then. We're finished here."

Chapter 25

Russell Xiang reads the note brought to him by the guard who has been paid a thousand of the ten-thousand rubles Michael Gresham put into his commissary account at the jail. It was a payoff, yes; everyone did it and it was expected if you wanted to receive mail from the outside.

Xiang puts the note aside and stares thoughtfully at the wall across from his bunk. Then he picks it up and reads it again.

"Russell," it begins, "please don't forget me. Anna Petrov. P.S.: Who is your lawyer? Will he help me too?"

For yet another thousand rubles, the guards bring Russell paper and pen. He wrote, "His name is Mikhail Sakharov. I will have him contact you."

She knew that the contact from Sakharov would come through the Embassy. That was standard operating procedure among the operators reporting to Moscow Station. Now she could only wait

Over the next three days she checks in with her handler thrice daily. Then, on the morning of the fourth day, she's told where to go to meet the lawyer and when.

Arriving early at Verona Sakharov's apartment, Petrov stands outside the door, weighing whether she should knock. What if it is a setup and the Russians are going to grab her again? What if they want to kill her this time? Her mind is in full retreat after all the beatings and blows to the skull and face; she has no answers. Still...she knocks; Verona herself opens the door.

"I'm Petrov," the young woman announces as she tries to see around the older woman.

"Then you must come right in. I believe Mikhail is hoping you would come."

This makes the younger woman feel better. Could these actually be friends?

She is led into the small living room. Michael Gresham rises up out of his chair and takes a step toward her. He extends his hand and they shake. Then he throws his arms open wide.

"I'm Anna Petrov," says the visitor.

"And I'm Sakharov the Bear," says Michael, drawing the young woman to him and embracing her. "How horrible it's been for you. I'm so sorry I couldn't do more to help while you were locked away."

"I—I'm sorry too."

"Let me try to make it up to you for that."

"How?"

"By setting you free, Anna."

"Yes. That would be good. I just want to go home now."

"And you shall. You have my word on it."

Michael retrieves his phone from his coat and sends off a text.

Help is on the way.

Chapter 26

M ichael Gresham

WHEN SHE REALIZES I mean what I say, that I'm going to help her go home again, she wants another hug.

Finally, she pushes away and Verona guides her down onto the sofa. It's clear our Petrov is in great pain and every movement takes its toll. We pass the time in small talk for the next thirty minutes while I tread water until help arrives. We are just moving on to Petrov's work duties when we hear the front door open and close and Verona looks at me, alarmed.

But it's Marcel, who has responded to my text. He is introduced to Verona and Petrov and he takes a seat beside the samovar where he places one leg over the other and looks around at his surroundings.

"Anna Petrov," I say to Marcel, who nods.

"I know."

Verona pours four cups of tea, passes them out, and

takes a seat beside Verona on the sofa. She balances her teacup and saucer in one hand.

"Marcel and I have been working on the defense of Russell Xiang. We cannot go into detail about that with you."

"I understand. They might torture me again and you don't want me—'

"Exactly," says Marcel. "At this point, we're not even sure who's who. So bear with us, please, while we get it all sorted."

"Will you defend me too?" the young woman asks as a plea more than a question. She still isn't sure, it appears.

"Of course," I tell her, "but I'm not sure yet how that will work. We pretty much have Russell's defense plotted out and we're lining up witnesses to corroborate his story. But you, your background is different and that makes it more difficult."

She nods. "Meaning I'm not Chinese and you can't create an alternate reality for me."

Marcel and I trade a look. He rolls his eyes. Yes, he seems to say, she's much smarter than either one of us was ready for. But why shouldn't she be? She's a CIA officer, after all.

"Okay, let's start with what we know," I tell her. "First, tell me about your employer following your release from jail. What's happened with them?"

"I showed up at the embassy without any ID. So that was a hassle but they finally were able to reconstruct my ID and I was passed through to Moscow Station.

"Who did you talk to there?"

"That's just it. Nobody would talk to me. They had low-level administrative people tell me no one could see me. It didn't take much of that before I understood I was being disavowed."

"So, another Russell?"

"Just like Russell. It's the nuclear arms talks, I get that. But there are so many resources! They could just ship me—"

She begins to weep and Verona puts her arm around her visitor and pulls her close. "Go on and cry," she says to the girl. "You're exhausted and in great pain. Just keep in mind we're all your friends and we're not going to disavow you. We're going to see you to safety."

Petrov fixes me with her blue eyes. "How will that happen? Will you smuggle me out of the country? Are you working with the CIA behind the scenes? Please, give me some assurances."

"No, I'm not working with the CIA. They have offered to help but I believe that was done more for the record. They wanted me to have to tell anyone who might hear this story down the road that they offered to do whatever they could to help you and Russell."

"So what will you do?"

Marcel says, "Mikhail? Should we talk first?"

I'm thinking, *Talk about what? We have no plans for Petrov. She thinks we do, but we don't.* Then it comes to me that if the shoe were on the other foot I would have no one to rely on but her for help in getting me to safety. It's obvious I can't let her down because the Russians will beat her to death if no one stands up for her now that she's made her plea to the CIA and been rejected. She becomes a wounded rabbit to them and they will be all over her. She will surely die. So I make a commitment.

"I will help you by taking you out of Russia myself."

Everyone turns to look at me. *What?* Their faces are asking.

Petrov speaks right up; she has rightly sized me up as anything but a smuggler of human beings. "Mikhail, I'm expert in exfiltration techniques. Maybe it would be better if I just did this without jeopardizing you. If you're caught helping me you will die too."

"Let her exfiltrate on her own, Mikhail," Marcel warns. "If you get caught, then Russell has no one."

"He has Van," I reply. A weak reply, but it's the best I can do.

"Van," scoffs Marcel. "A zoning lawyer or some such." He shakes his head in total disagreement with me and I know he's right. But still, I need to do whatever I can for this young woman. Plus, Henry Xiang would replace me if something happened to me, I have no doubt of it.

"You're thinking your friend Henry would just replace you," says Marcel. "But it actually wouldn't be that easy. If you get caught helping Ms. Petrov then Russell Xiang's jury gets advised of that fact. It will result in his certain conviction, which will result in his death. Make no doubt about it, Mikhail, there are two lives hanging in the balance. You are deciding about two lives—three, counting your own—if you go ahead and try to help."

"You have no idea how to help," says Verona. "You're the lawyer, not some spy who has resources. You have no way to help."

"How long to have papers made up for her?" I ask Marcel.

He shakes his head and stares arrows back at me.

"What?"

"Don't do this, Mikhail. You will likely fail."

"Someone has to try."

"Let me do it, then," Marcel says with exasperation. "I'll lead her out."

"No," I say, "you've got a record here from years ago. They'll have your fingerprints and who knows what else? If you get caught with her you'll certainly die. If I get caught with her there's a slim chance I'll survive it. But with you it's certain death. So it has to be me."

"Wait with that," Verona says. "Why do either of you have to go with her? Why can't she go alone? Better yet, maybe, why can't I go with her? I can pose as her mother."

"I was planning on posing as her father," I reply sharply, my patience all but evaporated. I don't want anyone else put at risk. Especially not Marcel and not Verona.

"Then we'll both go and we'll pose as her parents," says Verona.

"You're out of the equation," I tell Verona. "I will not let you get involved."

"You will fail without me. Now hear me out. If we are stopped and questioned or if we are detained I will make the case that our daughter—Anna Petrov—suffers from autism. Thus she is unable to speak or care for herself and we're taking her to Europe for treatment."

"What if they decide to test her to confirm she's really autistic?" I ask. I'm playing the devil's advocate at this point because, I must admit, she is making very good sense to me in what she's saying, much as I hate the idea of her becoming involved.

"If they decide to test her? They wanted to evaluate my real daughter at one point. But there were no tests. Today the tests that are done to differentiate between normal brains and autistic brains are capable of being performed accurately only by scientists with the proper background and training."

"And where is this testing done?"

"At UCLA."

I ponder this for several minutes. Then, "Has the same testing been done here in Russia?"

"No. The Russians are in the Stone Age on this. Even if they wanted to test her, they just don't have the means."

"So it's nothing simple like a blood test or a DNA test. Nothing like that?"

"That's right. If you'll hear me out, I can convince any Russian authority who is asking questions that this girl is someone other than who they're looking for."

"Marcel, what about a history of her birth to Mikhail and Verona Sakharov? Can you make that happen?"

"How much money do we have?"

"Try the U.S. Treasury. If they don't play ball with me, then I might suddenly start talking to the press about what I know."

"That one's easy. They'll simply take you out, Mikhail. That's not the way you want to go."

"Then Russell's father will fund it. Hell, I'll fund it myself if that's what it takes to get her the hell out of Russia. You have my accounts, now make it happen."

"Same name?" he asks me.

"Except for the last name. Ms. Petrov is now Ms. Sakharov."

"Done."

"How long?"

"We can have the papers by morning."

"Eight o'clock?"

"Yes."

"All right. We'll meet here at eight in the morning. Verona, put together a suitcase for you and Anna. I'll bring my own bag."

"Fine."

"Tonight—Anna, you stay with Verona tonight. I have to go back to the hotel and meet with Van and I'll be up late.

But I'll be here by eight tomorrow morning. Agreed everyone?"

All three in unison, "Agreed."

Except the next morning when I'm about to leave my hotel room, there is a note pushed beneath my door. It is in Marcel's handwriting. It informs me that Marcel and Verona and Petrov met early this morning and left without me. Marcel is now playing the role of father to the girl.

I'm stunned and feel terribly betrayed. I retreat back into my room, cursing and pounding the sofa. Then I cool off and order up a full room service breakfast. After I've eaten every last morsel I'm nowhere nearer to understanding how they all three could trick me than I was when I got their message.

I'm angry and I'm hurt. But I'm also thinking long and hard about the last line in Marcel's message to me.

Boss, you are all that's standing between Russell and a firing squad. Now get over my deceit and go win this thing for your kid.

Only then can I smile. Marcel is very thorough. He has learned a secret from my youth and I'm impressed. How did he do this? Probably with the help of Henry Xiang. This is why he has deceived me, because Marcel has my back. Which means he couldn't let me leave.

He couldn't let me leave, because Russell is my son and Marcel knows it.

Chapter 27

M ichael Gresham

THAT AFTERNOON, after Marcel and Verona and Anna are far
away from Moscow, I take a cab from the hotel to the
Moscow City Jail. It is overcast, windy and dark when I
arrive. Just as I step out of the cab and am paying the driver,
it begins sleeting, the whipping ice particles burning my
face and eyes. I scurry into the jail, out of the onslaught. I
have come to see my son. Who doesn't know he's my son.

By now they know me at the visitors' window and I'm
processed into an attorney-client conference room after a
wait of only one hour. I arrive in the room before Russell,
who comes in fifteen minutes after me. He looks haggard,
unshaven, and his eyes are bloodshot. I can smell the stink
on his breath across the table. He nods at me and lowers his
eyes.

"I know I stink. Personal hygiene is not on the top of the
list in here."

"Don't worry about it. I'm here to get you out. I'm not here to judge you in any way."

Tears come to his eyes and he wipes them away with a grimy hand. He shakes his head violently and his body shudders, obviously angry with himself for the emotional display. "I'm sorry. I find that I'm very weepy anymore. Just feeling sorry for myself."

"Are they feeding you any better?"

"Near as I can figure out, they purchase food in bulk. And it changes every few days, what they have for us. Right now we're eating some kind of cold cuts that are rancid and fatty like you wouldn't believe. We get that twice a day. Before that we were doing some kind of white cheese. I never could figure out what the hell it was but that went on for at least a week. Gave me and the guys in my cell the runs. We were shitting in the hole at least a half dozen times a day, each of us. Smelled like a cesspool in there day and night. Thank God they finally used up all of it. The cold cuts are a great relief after that."

His voice trails off and he still won't make eye contact with me. A part of me wants to hold him close and pat his back and give him comfort as a parent might with a child. But I know better than to do that. So I keep careful boundaries like I always have so far with him and am careful I don't move too close in anything I say. He does not know me as a parent and it will have to remain that way. An unspoken contract I have with Henry Xiang. It's an odd thing, I'm thinking as I'm sitting there making preliminary small talk with my son. Henry Xiang is Asian and has all the facial characteristics you would expect. And Russell has those characteristics—but to a much lesser degree. His mother— with whom I spent one night when we were in college—is also Asian. But I can see my own eyes in the boy, maybe much more.

"So," I say in my professional voice, "I understand you are a CIA agent. How did that happen?"

"Growing up, I was exposed to Mandarin Chinese. My dad's siblings, his parents—there were always people around who wanted me to speak it with them. So I began learning the language early on. By the time I was seven or eight I was quite comfortable conversing in Chinese. Then, in college, I minored in Chinese. Which, at Georgetown, is a real bitch. Very difficult major and I struggled before I began to excel. Then, in my senior year, I was called into my advisor's office at the university. Someone wanted to meet with me, someone who didn't want to contact me directly. So I showed up, my advisor led me into his conference room, and there was a man in a suit sitting at the table, his hands folded, with zero expression on his face. My first reaction was, Uh-oh, I'm in trouble."

"Were you in trouble? I doubt that."

"No. My advisor left us alone and the man introduced himself. We shook hands. He asked me whether I'd ever considered working for the government. I told him I hadn't considered working at all at that point, that I was accepted into law school."

"You were planning to join your father's law firm, I'm guessing."

"Actually, no. I was planning on moving to Hong Kong after law school and working in a commercial firm. I was ready for adventure, Mr. Gresham."

I look around nervously. Then I fiercely type a message on my iPad. "Call me Sakharov!"

"Who?" I ask, hoping that he twists the "Mr. Gresham" thing into something innocent.

"Gresham—that was the man's name, I believe. Anyway, I told him that I wanted adventure in a foreign country, Mr. Sakharov. At that point, he actually smiled. Then he showed me his ID. He said he was a recruiter for the Central Intelligence Agency. Well, I all but ran out of there."

"You wanted foreign adventure but not that kind of foreign adventure, I'm guessing."

"Exactly. All I knew about that stuff was James Bond and Jason Bourne movies. It didn't look like anything I wanted to wake up to every day. So I flat refused him and got up to leave the room. He told me to wait one minute until he finished. So I sat back down."

"So he sweetened the deal?"

"Yes and no. He went to work on my patriotism—what there was of it. He talked about nine-eleven and how much the government needed help. Especially, he said, help from young people who have language aptitude, language training. It was really something I'd never even considered. I had minored in Chinese because I thought it would be an easy minor. It wasn't; it was terribly difficult. But that's a story for another day."

As this young man talks and I get to know him a little better, I'm advancing through several stages of shock and surprise. The kid sounds at times exactly like me and many of his facial idiosyncrasies, as he connects with me, almost make me feel like I'm looking in a mirror. I keep forcing that stuff aside, trying to concentrate on doing my job as a professional, but it's very challenging. This is sure as hell my kid.

"At some point he must have convinced you that working for the CIA had its good points."

"He did. He asked me for twenty years of my life. After that, he said, I could retire and go back to school and study law if I still wanted or I could rock."

"Rock?"

"You know—rocking chair. Do nothing except sleep and eat and read. Whatever. Actually, that held a great appeal for me. I had thought someday I might like to try my hand at writing. That seemed like a real possibility, the way he made it sound. Plus, by then I would have incredible stories to tell."

"I'm sure you would."

"So, I said I was open to discussing it further. Then we talked about pay and benefits and so forth. By the time we were finished, he had me at least half-convinced it was a good thing. But I still wanted to talk to my dad. And I told this to the recruiter. He didn't comment on that but made a follow-up appointment with me in one week. This time I would meet him at Langley for a tour. I agreed."

"So you talked to your dad?"

"I did. I wasn't allowed to tell him who it was exactly, that I had been talking to. Only that a government agency had approached me and I was interested. Like always, he told me to do what was best for me. So I did. I visited Langley, liked what I saw, and signed up as a candidate. Beyond that, there's not much else I'm allowed to talk about."

"Sure, I get that. Now, let's talk about why you were in Russia when you were arrested."

"I can't really go into that. I'm sorry."

"There are certain parts of it you're just going to have to trust me with, Russell. As your lawyer, there are certain parts of your story that I must have."

"That's just not possible, Mr. Sakharov. This room is probably bugged anyway."

At that point I pulled out my counter-measures device. I sweep the room for electronics and, to my great surprise, the

room isn't bugged. I tell Russell so and show him my electronic tool. It looks like a common cellphone, but it's
capable of much more than making calls.

"Actually there are no cameras and no mikes in here. I'm
astonished, but I trust my equipment."

"Where'd you get that?"

"From an old Interpol agent who knows what he's doing.
We're clear in here."

"All right. Mr. Sakharov, I'll tell you what I can. But there
are parts I could be executed for if I gave them up to anyone.
I'm sorry."

"Why don't we just play it by ear and see where that gets us?"

"Fine. Ask away."

"Why were you in Russia? Is the Russian Federation your
normal assignment?"

"No. We stumbled across some noise when we were
working on something else. I came here to investigate."

"Noise?"

"Certain keywords. Catch phrases. Things that NSA
wants to know more about."

"So you were here to find out about those things. But
why you? Why not someone already here?"

"Because I happen to have served in the Middle East
with the person of interest this time out."

"That person's name?"

"Henrik Nurayov."

"Who is this person?"

"He's a British officer."

"As in—military? Help me, Russell."

"As in MI6. He's my counterpart."

"So you knew him from before?"

Russell stretches out his arms, rubbing his shoulders,

obviously considering how he wants this line of questioning to proceed.

"I knew him from before, I knew he was MI6, but I can't tell you what we suspected him of doing. That might compromise our own security."

I smile. "Russell, as your lawyer, what you tell me is confidential. It's not like I'm going to go out and repeat these things because I'm not."

His dark eyes bore in on me. "Maybe not voluntarily. But there are people out there who can get you to say anything, Mr. Sakharov. These people can learn anything you have in your head. Trust me on this."

"I do. All right, that makes sense. So we won't go into details of the mission. But you came to Russia to look into whatever and you wound up getting arrested. The court papers say you killed Russian citizens and that you absconded with government secrets. Let's take those one by one. First of all, have you actually killed anyone since you've been here?"

He nods solemnly. "I have."

"Who was that?"

"They, Mr. Sakharov. They."

"Was this on official business?"

"Since you put it that way, yes. I know what you're asking."

"Where did this happen?"

"At Henrik's dacha, just outside of town. North of Moscow."

"Can you describe the circumstances?"

"These people I shot were looking for me to shoot me. I happened to shoot first."

"Was anyone else with you?"

"I can't say. I can't compromise another officer. That's a crime punishable by death."

"Then don't. It's not that critical at this point anyway."

"Thank you. The people I killed were Russian FSB agents. I have been advised that one of them was the son of a high-ranking FSB official. I've created a huge uproar between our countries, Mr. Sakharov."

"Do you know this person's name?"

'No."

"Do you know the father's name?"

"Yes. The father is Igor Tarayev, the chief of the Moscow FSB."

"Oh, hell."

"Yes. Evidently his son was a junior G-Man and I put him down."

"How does this Henrik Nurayov figure into this?"

"Tarayev's son was providing security for Henrik Nurayov. Let's just say a deal was going down."

"What kind of deal?"

Russell looks around the room, his eyes darting from floor to ceiling and wall to wall. Then he returns his gaze to me.

"Military items were being sold. Military items that the United States was compelled to learn about."

"Military arms that someone was trying to bring into the U.S.?"

"Exactly," he says. I'm not sure he would have told me this if I hadn't guessed it. I believe we just crossed a line he wouldn't have crossed just to save himself.

"So is Nurayov selling British arms to the Russians?"

"Not quite. He's acting as a go-between. There is an arms dealer on one side of the world and there is the FSB on the other side. The FSB wants to see certain military matériel make its way into the United States so that acts of terrorism can be carried out. The FSB—Russia—is paying a huge sum of money for these items and Henrik Nurayov is walking off with more money that he could have made in a a hundred lifetimes as an MI6 officer. Or as a CIA officer."

"And the CIA—NSA, rather—got wind of this and sent you to investigate because you knew Nurayov from before?"

"Yes, but there's more."

"As in?"

"Nurayov's wife is my wife's sister. I met my wife through Nurayov when we were working the Middle East. There was a Christmas party, of all things, and Nurayov was posing as a low-level diplomat whose wife had accompanied him on his posting. Her sister came to town as cover so it appeared the Christmas holiday was a normal, family holiday. The sister turned out to be someone I fell in love with and married on returning to the States. Small world, Mr. Sakharov."

"So it must be extremely difficult for you to now find yourself on the other side of the fence from your brother-in-law."

"We were never close at all. There's always been something about Henrik that puts people off. He's oily and always working some agenda and people pick up on it. Henrik Nurayov has never been a well-liked person. Then about five years ago, he and my wife's sister separated for a year and then divorced. So at this time there is no connection and I had lost track of the man. But the CIA hadn't lost track of him and hadn't lost track of my connection to him. When he surfaced on their radar they immediately turned to me and here I am."

"Wow, some history there. Were you—were you here to kill Nurayov?"

"Yes."

"Were you going to carry that out?"

"Absolutely. It's only business. Plus he's trying to create a mass attack in the U.S. He deserves to die and I'm absolutely ready to make that happen."

"If I can get you out of here."

"If you can get me out of here."

"What about the disavowal? The CIA says it doesn't know you. Where does that leave you with them?"

He smiles cagily. "Please remember, Mr. Sakharov, we're only talking business here. I'm still a CIA agent and always will be until I retire. They will take me back as soon as I resurface in the States and I will be utilized somewhere. Once you're in, you're in for life. Never let anybody tell you any differently."

"Now, let's talk defense of your case. I'm going to prove you're Chinese, not American, and that you are in Russia to start a business."

"Understand. Have you been receiving my letters? I've written them in Chinese just as you directed."

"Three?"

"Yes, three of them. Good, so you've got them all."

"Yes, we have. Antonia interpreted them for me and I think you've done a good job presenting your nationality as Chinese. The backstory you've chosen works for me too. Now here's a puzzle I want to present you with."

"Go on."

"Moscow Station has records that would clearly link you to the CIA as an officer."

"Correct."

"I was visited by a man who identified himself to me as Anatoly Palatov. He is the man who bailed me out of jail. Does that name mean anything to you?"

He shakes his head. "Never heard the name."

Just then there is a knock on our door and suddenly it flies wide open. Two guards seize Russell and begin moving him out. Evidently our meeting is over. Which is fine. I got what I came for. Now I know what I want from the CIA. It just remains for me to pry it loose from them.

I walk out the jail's front door.

Goodbye, my son.

Soon I will return to take you home.

Chapter 28

M ichael Gresham

THE VOICE that calls my phone sounds like a load of gravel sliding out the back end of a dump truck. It is rough, gruff, and heavily accented so I have to listen closely. But, it's English being spoken and that's uncommon as hell.

"Yes, this is Mikhail Sakharov."

"Mr. Sakharov, this is Sergei Gliisky. I'm the lead prosecutor in the case against your client Russell Xiang."

"Thanks for calling. How can I help today?"

"I'm calling in order to make myself perfectly clear, Mr. Sakharov."

"Clarity is good."

"Two cases. One against you for lying to the court. One against your client for murder and state secrets."

I don't reply. There's no need for him to remind me of what keeps me up at nights.

"Mr. Sakharov, we are convinced your real name is

Michael Gresham. We are convinced you work for the CIA. As you know, this is very serious. You could go to jail for a minimum of ten years if these charges are proven against you."

"Just how do you plan to prove I'm CIA?"

"We have our methods, Mr. Sakharov. But here's one to consider. We know about your children in Evanston, Illinois. Do you still want to continue your deceit in our court?"

I nearly drop the phone. They have me. They know where I live and they know about my children. I will immediately call home and have my children moved to a safe place no one knows about. My eyes see flashes of terrible events unfolding and things too awful to even imagine taking place. But I have to act as if I'm unfazed, and I do.

"You've just lost me. I don't know anything about Illinois and this Evans place. You have the wrong man for that connection."

"Evanston. We will make this proof to the court in your client's case."

"Wait a minute. You're going to try to prove your case against *me* during the case I'm defending for Russell Xiang?"

"You heard me correctly. It is allowed and I plan to do it."

"I'll fight you on that."

He scoffs. Then he clears his throat and the gravel dumping continues.

"Second item on our list. I'm going to personally witness your client in front of the firing squad. I'm going to watch as he is gunned down. There will be no deals for him, no appeals, and the jury is going to hate him all the more because you are a liar and a CIA agent. They will know all of this when they retire to the jury room to deliberate. Sound inviting?"

"Is this what you called for? Just to intimidate me?"

"Not at all. I also wanted to tell you we now have in custody a woman who claims to be the wife of Mikhail Sakharov, a man who claims *he* is Mikhail Sakharov, and a young woman claiming to be Anna Sakharov. It was a chance you took, sending them on the train to escape, but it failed."

I can hardly breathe. A boulder has been lowered onto my chest. They have arrested Marcel, Verona, and Anna. Proving their case against me is now the essence of simplicity. Plus, there will be charges filed against people I encouraged to flee. I have no words.

"Make no mistake. There will be no deals for these people just like there will be no deals for you. We will not offer to reduce the charges in return for a plea to a lesser offense. While Westerners like your client and your investigator might be hoping there will be a last-minute deal, we don't offer deals. You will serve at least ten years. With this new ruse which we can prove you arranged, you are looking at twenty years additional. As for your friends, they are already languishing in jail. I'm told the younger woman is already offering to testify against you in return for leniency. And don't forget, we have her confession putting the blame for killing young Tarayev directly on your Mr. Xiang. A nice, neat package of American CIA agents all bundled up for the work camps."

"Is that all?"

"Isn't that enough? Now you have a pleasant evening, Mr. Sakharov. Or should I say, Mr. Gresham? Whatever, it really makes no difference at this point. You will serve twenty years at a Russian work camp in Siberia no matter the name you use, am I correct, sir?"

He is laughing as he hangs up.

In a sudden explosion I'm running for the toilet in my

hotel room. Head buried inside the porcelain bowl I unload everything. All the fear, the deceit, the powerlessness I've felt all along—it all comes roaring out.

Then I drag myself into the small sitting area of my suite and flop down on the bench couch. It is uncomfortable as it is long and flat and the back is a ninety-degree wall. *Of course it's uncomfortable, it's Russian*, I'm thinking. I empty the half-full water pitcher into a large crystal tumbler. Taking huge gulps of the liquid I wash the bad taste from my mouth and throat. Then I sit back and loosen my tie. It has been a long, terrible day.

It's their system. Only the government can win in the Russian system. It is made that way. I can imagine the judges are all personal friends and confidantes of Vladimir Putin. I can imagine that they report to him on a daily basis how many crooked citizens they sent to the Gulag that day.

In my mind's eye, there is a jury I have helped pick. They are not a jury of peers and they are not a jury found to be unbiased after much probing during jury selection. Instead I see only puppets, people whose words and actions are controlled by the puppeteers who sent them into the court-room to perform in the first place.

Then I visualize myself trying to convince them of Russell's innocence, of his status as a Chinese citizen, of his undeserved predicament where he should be turned loose. But then I see the jury look at him and then look at me and then look back at him. He doesn't look anything like Chinese, they are thinking. No, he looks like his lawyer, Michael Gresham. That's who he looks like. Xiang is about as much of a Chinese citizen as we are. Then I see them look away in disgust. They don't even bother to discuss when they retire to the jury room. They just sign the forms of verdict without voting: GUILTY.

I decide to call Van and talk it over with him. But he doesn't answer his phone. Can't say that I blame him. He's probably heard about the arrests of the others and sees it linked back to me. I wouldn't be at all surprised to see him withdraw from the case. Withdraw and leave me twisting in the wind.

Then another large boulder falls onto my chest. Marcel and his Russian record from years before. He had warned me that he couldn't afford to be identified by the Russian authorities. But now he has been. What could that mean? I groan and wish I had more water. The case only gets worse each time I chase someone down the rabbit hole. Even my lover Verona Sakharov will pay dearly before it's all said and done.

There is a knocking on the door to my room. Instantly I'm electrified for I can only predict they have come for me. With every bit of speed I can muster I search around for a sweatshirt—anything to keep me warm in that freezing cell where they will put me!

Now there is yelling outside my door and I hear my name being called.

With the ultimate resignation, knowing I will spend the rest of my natural life in a Russian forest at hard labor, I make my way to the door.

Ever the Catholic, I make the sign of the cross.

Then I twist the doorknob.

Chapter 29

Michael Gresham

STANDING THERE, holding out a cocktail napkin, is a messenger. He tucks the soft paper into my hand and turns away. I unfold the napkin and read, "Gorky Park - Vremena Goda, first table on the right. Tomorrow 10 a.m." The messenger is gone by the time I look up. I have no idea who wrote this and I have no idea if it presents any hope. It could be bad news or good news or it could even be the FSB trying to trap me into something—anything is possible. But this much I do know: I'm going to be there tomorrow at ten a.m. Every bullet I came here with has been fired. I have no choice but to follow up with this invitation or command or whatever it turns out to be.

The next morning at nine a.m. I climb into the first cab to roll down Tverskaya Street. Then we swing into traffic and I'm on my way.

At the entrance to Gorky Park, the Main Portal, we pull

into the lot and drive forward. When we are as close as we're going to get, I climb out. All around are skaters—singles and twosomes—on the frozen paths, Further beyond, skaters glide along the frozen river. It is dazzling in the rare morning light. Within the hour it will be gloomy again but just for now—just for this one instant—I close my eyes, turn my face up to the light, and imagine that I'm five again and that I'm going outside to sled. Then I open my eyes and that child is gone. That child who will save me, that child who, five years older, will possess all the skills I will ever need to succeed inside any courtroom anywhere. The interlude passes and it is gone. But I'm back.

I climb the stairs to the Main Portal and study the map there. An arrow points to the restaurant Vremena Goda, so I head that direction.

It is a short walk down an icy path. Skaters whiz along-side me as I go, shouting out in Russian as they approach from behind. I move to the far right and allow passage.

As soon as I pass inside the restaurant, the first thing I smell is cigar smoke. Someone at the second table is smoking a cigar, waving it around while he speaks animat-edly, then puffing and blowing out large clouds of foul-smelling stuff. But the first table on my right is empty and I help myself to it. Whoever I'm meeting hasn't arrived yet, so out of habit I pick up the menu the waitress drops before me as she passes by and I'm greeted with two pages of incom-prehensible Russian. Service is going to be very slow as she doesn't return to take my order for almost ten minutes. By now it is ten minutes before the hour when she stops at my table, shifts her weight to one leg, and speaks in Russian. "Coffee?" I ask. "Do you have coffee?"

She looks at me and shrugs. So I make a drinking motion as if I'm holding a cup with a handle. I can see the light come into her eyes and I'm thinking perhaps she has understood. At any rate, she leaves, folding my menu as she goes.

Which is when I see a familiar face come inside the entrance and look directly at me, there at the first table.

Antonia Xiang. Russell's wife. She removes her coat and shakes the snow out of her hair—yes, I can see it is snowing now outside the window. Then she approaches.

"You're here," she says with a smile and takes the chair across from me.

"Yes, I am. Who could resist your note? Mysterious, presented on a cocktail napkin—I felt like a spy receiving his orders from on high."

"I saw Rusty last night," she says. "He's wasting away. The food is horrible and there's not enough of it. I'm going to guess he's lost maybe twenty pounds already."

"I saw him too," I tell her. "But weight loss isn't the worst of his problems. Let me bring you up to speed on what's been happening."

I proceed to tell her all of it—the part about Marcel and Anna and Verona being caught as they were trying to leave Russia, the part about me being found out and my home in Evanston pinpointed and me charged with my own set of crimes; Petrov's confession and agreement to testify against Rusty; the story comes tumbling out and when I'm done I'm shaking and she is white-faced.

"My God, Michael, this is bad. Very bad."

"What about you?" I ask. "Have you been working with Van?"

"I have. And I have prepared Rusty's defense, you'll be happy to know."

I almost think I've misunderstood and I ask her to repeat herself.

"Yes, I said I've prepared Rusty's defense. I have witnesses, papers, photographs, the whole nine yards. We're ready to spring him free."

My coffee arrives and Antonia points to what I've been served and nods and points to herself. She'll have the same, she's indicating. The waitress nods solemnly and slowly moves off.

"Let's back up just a minute," I say. "How have you done all this?"

She leans back and fluffs her hair with her hand. It is damp from the snow and probably cold on her head. I offer her my muffler but she refuses.

"I've done all this with help from our friends at the Embassy. They have been sweetly reasonable after all."

"How did that happen?"

"You remember I work for the Department of Justice in Washington?"

"Yes."

"My job gives me access to certain government documents. In my work in counter-terrorism I have top secret clearance."

"Okay, I'm following."

"Well, with my security clearance I was able to access certain files on certain government employees, one of whom is my husband, who also works counter-terrorism at the CIA."

A light is going off in my head. I think I know what's coming next.

"From there, armed with my husband's records, it was quite easy to gain an audience with the Chief of the Moscow Station. I then threatened him with disclosing Rusty's true employment to the FSB if the CIA continued to refuse to help Rusty. So they suddenly decided to help."

"I'm impressed. So, what's been done?"

"Well, our friends at the Embassy have been busy. First, they have provided me with a witness with impeccable credentials. She's a respected surgeon and well-spoken. She's Rusty's mother from Beijing. She will testify that Rusty lived in Beijing until he came to Russia looking for business opportunities."

Old feelings pierce me when I hear his mother is coming. It's been forever.

"Incredible. Go on."

"I've also got all manner of paperwork. School records, passport, medical records, the Chinese equivalent of tax returns—we've got everything we need to prove Rusty is a Chinese citizen who came to Russia on business."

"Wait. He was taken into custody at the green house. He was in the company of Anna Petrov. What about that connection?"

She smiles easily. "Michael, I'm a lawyer and I'm known back home for being extremely thorough. I have the same records for Anna Petrov, whose cover is that she was an American journalist assigned by her news syndicate to China. She and Rusty were on a story. She was covering his trip to Russia for a magazine piece. She accompanied him to Moscow."

For the first time in weeks I can actually see a ray of hope. A tight knot down inside my gut loosens maybe a half inch. This is terrific work she's done.

"You are good," I tell her. "You are very good, Antonia."

She smiles graciously. "Thank you. I've been known to win my share."

"One question. How did Russell and Petrov come to be at the green house? My understanding is that's a CIA safe house."

"The green house is located on the property of Rudina Alaevsky, who sits on the Duma, the lower house in the Russian Federal Assembly. She is friendly to the U.S. and to its agents. I've spoken with her and she's happy to come in and testify that Rusty and Petrov were visiting her when they were suddenly arrested for no reason and trundled away in handcuffs."

"That would be very persuasive, having an important Russian politician come into court and vouch for Rusty and Anna Petrov. Very persuasive, indeed."

Antonia nods and flashes an understated smile when no one is looking. "There's even more."

"Please tell me."

"I have been busy talking with Henry, your old roommate."

"What does Henry have to do with any of this?"

"Very little. But he says you do, Michael."

"How so?"

"He says you're Rusty's biological father. I plan to use that in Rusty's defense."

I'm stunned. This was all so long ago. I believed that Henry would never mention any of what happened way back when.

"How so?"

"You're going to be my witness. You're going to testify you're Rusty's father and that's why he resembles you. He does, you know?"

"But if I'm his father why was he living in China?"

"You and his mother were never married. She was a student at Georgetown when you were there. She returned to Beijing in shame when she discovered she was pregnant. You're going to testify your son was living in China too."

"No one's going to believe that."

"Oh, yes, they certainly are."

"Why?"

"Because we're going to have DNA testing done to prove you are who you say you are, that you're Rusty's father. Then they have to believe you."

I'm dumbstruck. How did she find this out? She has probably always believed that Henry Xiang is Rusty's father. What would have made her start questioning that?

"How did you get this information?" I ask her.

"Henry and I had some very open talks. One night he just tossed it out there that you were actually my husband's biological father."

"I see." I'm all but speechless. Then I manage to say, "To say I'm impressed would be a gross understatement. This is brilliant, your workup."

"Michael, back in Washington I have never lost a trial. I'm not going to ruin my record by losing one here in Moscow."

I'm thinking. The ray of hope is growing brighter.

"What do we do about Marcel and Verona Sakharov? They're still in jail because of my stupidity."

"I'm working on that. I'm thinking arrangements can be made between the CIA and FSB that will spring them free."

"Such as?"

She raises a hand. "Slow down, Michael. I said I'm working on that. I didn't say I had answers yet. Let me talk to a certain man I know at the Embassy. We might have some leverage left yet."

"I want to hug you."

She looks around. "Please don't. At least not here." Her coffee has come and she takes a long sip then scowls. "This stuff. How do they drink this?"

"I was beginning to think it was only me. What I'd give for a decent cup of coffee about now."

"I know where there's a Starbucks. Next time we'll meet there."

"I think it's time we meet at Van's. We need to get him into the loop."

"I've got that covered. Van is going to assist you at trial. So am I."

"Are you sure about this?"

"Am I sure I want to call you as Rusty's father and further corroborate his story? Yes, I'm sure of that. I need to be there at counsel table in order to do that."

"I have to ask. Everything else has been covered except for one tiny detail: my own case. I told you that I've been charged with misrepresenting to the court who I am. Any ideas for me?"

"I'll talk to the prosecutor. We might have to wrap you up in the deal we make over Marcel, Verona, and Anna. You'll be just another pretty face."

"Now I know you're lying."

We laugh and then we grow quiet. We sip our coffee and watch the snow outside. At last she is finished and tells me that I must leave first. She will wait fifteen minutes and leave in a different direction.

"Will you be all right?" I ask her.

She gives me an utterly resolute look. "What, you've already forgotten who you're dealing with here? Is that it?"

We laugh, then, and I stand to go. Again, I want to hug her and thank her but I don't. Instead, I shrug into my coat and head for the door.

Then I'm outside on the icy walk and I'm headed back to the main portal where I entered the park. When I look back

I cannot see her through the window but I know she's just on the other side, watching me.

For the first time since coming to Russia I have a feeling of some small comfort, as if I'm no longer in this alone.

Then I'm slipping and sliding along on the path with its new snow cover and I'm wiping my coat sleeve across my eyes as I fight back a sudden flow of tears. There is much that occurred inside that restaurant, not the least of which was my fatherhood. It's finally going to come out for all the world to know.

I'm that kid's father and I will do anything for him.

Chapter 30

M ichael Gresham

FIRST DAY OF TRIAL. It's late March and the courtroom fills with spectators and press dressed in the clothes they wear in the deep of winter. There is no sign of spring or spring thaw; I don't even know if that ever happens in Russia. It is quite cold inside the courtroom and I'm sorry I have to remove my outer coat. I begin shivering when it's set aside.

I sit at counsel table in the Moscow City Court, waiting for them to bring Rusty to court so he can go on trial for murder and for stealing state secrets. Regardless of the charges, I'm resolute; one thing I know, when we're done here, Rusty will be going home with me. Anna, as well. I've promised them I'll make that happen and now I have to deliver. The only problem is, I don't have the foggiest idea how that's all going to work if I can't make the jury believe Rusty's really a businessman from China who just happened to get swept up by the FSB in a wide-flung net.

At the table across from me, a fifteen-inch tall partition between us, sits Sergei Gliisky, the man I know to be the prosecutor. My co-counsel, Van, is seated beside me, noisily clearing his throat and blowing his nose as he struggles with a late-winter onset of the flu bug that is attacking everyone in Moscow this March. He has a box of tissues set before him, a stack of books on either side, and a small waste basket on the floor between us that he fills and empties, fills and empties, with his used tissue. Antonia sits on my other side. She has prepared a complete trial notebook with red tabs for witnesses and yellow tabs for exhibits. She is the glue that will hold us together.

I don't want to turn around and look behind us because the hundred or so citizens sitting back there are people who might serve on our jury. I won't turn around because I don't want them to see how damn frightened I am right now, feeling like a canary in a coal mine. Anything is possible here, Van has explained to me, including sudden death.

Now I hear a commotion behind me and I have to turn to see. Rusty, and Anna Petrov, have been brought into the defendants' glass cage at the back of the courtroom. From there they peer up at me and the others like two apes in a zoo. I suddenly feel very sad for Rusty. Since he's been locked up, I've only been allowed to speak to him by telephone through Plexiglas. Same for Anna. She seems to be fading into a kind of shell the more I visit her, each time without bringing hope or something she can cling to. But I haven't been able to let on to either of them how I'm going to defend them for fear the FSB will somehow tease it out of them or beat it out of them or drug them and coax it out of them. There is too much at stake for me to have been worrying about their feelings these past six weeks as I've been working up their cases and visiting with them as often as I have—usually three times a week. Today they've dressed Rusty in dark slacks and a gray shirt with a Nehru collar. Anna is dressed similarly but her shirt is cream colored. Neither prisoner has even a dot of color in his or her face and both sit there morose, staring straight ahead, as if they are already defeated.

Milling around the courtroom are at least eight uniformed female and male officers wearing blue slacks and blue shirts, waffle-soled boots, and police hats with huge badges. On their hips are large pistols that they all carry high so they touch the diaphragm on their sides. They remind me of the courthouse guards I have observed during my time at the federal courthouse in Chicago. Armed, unsmiling, and ready for anything. I look in the direction of one and she stares daggers at me. I move my eyes off her and look elsewhere. These are not guards to be taken any way but seriously.

Now the volume in the court increases among the spectators and the press when a door behind the judge's platform opens and a gaunt, scrawny looking man wearing a black and red robe ascends to the highest seat in the room. He leans to the side and says something to a woman who must be his clerk and then he turns to a fat file that's awaiting him on his desk. He flips it open, scratches his chin, and begins reading. His name is Gregor Herzmink and I've had several run-ins with him already. While preparing for this day, Van and I have filed no less than eleven pre-trial motions and he has ruled against us on them one by one. Except one, the last one we filed seeking to exclude witnesses from the courtroom except when they are testifying. That one he allowed. Van told me later I shouldn't feel too happy about winning that one; it seems Russian criminal law requires the exclusion of witnesses anyway. Still, it felt good to have at least one thing go our way.

Already I know Judge Gregor Herzmink dislikes me intensely. Several times during the workup of this case he has let me know that if I'm convicted of falsely posing as a Russian citizen that I will spend the rest of my life at hard labor in a place where it's never warm and where the prisoners freeze to death before their sentences are served out. Believe me, he has my full attention and I have wracked my brain trying to conceive of a defense for myself. So far I have very little to offer, but I'm putting Rusty and Anna ahead of me these days. While I might go to a Gulag, they must be returned to America.

My own problems are matters for another day. The bottom line is that the judge doesn't like me, whether it's because I'm a phony or because I'm a defense attorney or both. It doesn't really matter; I have my work cut out for me and even doubled thanks to his hateful attitude. As he continues flipping through the file before him, my mind continues to cringe then regroup, fearful of the next blow from the bench.

At long last the judge looks up, closing the file before him. He speaks Russian to a woman sitting just off to his side. She is the translator, I have learned these past months and—oh happy day—she struggles with English. She replies back to him and he looks at me and glowers. Says the translator, "The judge would like to know, do you have excellent protection?"

That one goes right over my head. I whisper to Van, "Do I have protection? I don't quite follow that."

"He told her to ask if you have Russian co-counsel familiar with Russian trials, an expert."

"Oh," I say. "Well, tell him I've got Mr. Ivanovich here, who's been with me all the way so far. He's my expert."

She turns and rattles off a stream of Russian to His Honor. His scowl deepens and he almost says something in reply, but either thinks better of it or has become bored with a lawyer like me whose only role is to be present as the case is lost and the defendants sentenced to death. He then speaks for a minute or so and sits back. He crosses his arms on his chest while the translator turns his torrent into English. In short, the judge has told the jury venire that they are honorable people today. He tells them that they will be treated honorably by the court and the parties as befits their honorable station. There are occasional responses muttered behind me. I take the moment to turn around in my seat as if to smile at the prospective jury but really to check on Rusty. I don't even know whether any of what's going on in court is being piped into the glass cell he shares with Anna. My co-counsel Van—who's never attended a trial of any kind before—has told me he doesn't know but he guesses they are getting a feed of some kind. Antonia is sitting with her hands folded on the table before her, the picture of calm.

The judge nods at the clerk and she stands. She then begins calling out names and one-by-one members of the venire step forward. They take seats in the jury box where they look around and blink as if startled awake from a long dream. In the U.S. we would be allowed by the court at this point to qualify each juror with a series of questions asked by both attorneys. Evidently that's not the case here; once their names are drawn and they come forward, they have become jurors without further ado. This entire process takes less than ten minutes.

The translator barks out the name of the first witness

and I turn to see this person come into the courtroom and make the long walk down front. He is a bull of a man, the witness, with a thick, powerful neck and buzzed white hair. A long scar crosses his forehead in a flat "Z," giving him the look of someone you wouldn't want to tangle with outside the courtroom. At the witness stand he turns and raises his right hand. The oath is administered and he sits mightily in the chair that is too small for his great bulk. Now he casts his eyes around the courtroom, unsmiling, measuring, taking stock as one would who is accustomed to brawling on a second's notice. I watch all this and almost instantly realize the man is FSB.

The prosecutor's voice is strident as he poses the first question to the witness. The translator speaks out even as the witness is giving his answer and she is suddenly much better than I had first thought, translating the witness's words even as they are being spoken.

"Dimitry Vasilov," says the witness.

And we have his name.

Now we'll listen and see how much damage he can do to my son and his partner.

Chapter 31

M ichael Gresham

"Mr. Vasilov," the prosecutor begins, "tell us your rank and employment."

"I work for the Russian Federation. I'm an investigator. My rank is captain."

Nonsense, I'm thinking. He's an FSB agent, a spy, a trained killer. He's anything but an investigator.

"How long have you held that position?"

"Seventeen years."

"Who do you report to?"

"Colonel Igor Tarayev."

"Mr. Tarayev is the chief investigator for the government, is he not?"

"He is."

"Now, directing your attention to the night of December twenty-fourth just past. Please tell us what you were doing that night."

"I was on assignment for my job. I was providing security for a member of the British Embassy."

"That person's name?"

"Henrik Nurayov."

"What does Mr. Nurayov do?"

"He arranges commercial sales of British goods."

"What kinds of sales does he facilitate?"

"Oftentimes a government agency will have an excess of certain items. Such as automobiles, computers, flat screen TV's—the kind of stuff an embassy might use. That's what he was doing the night I had his protection."

"So he was involved in a sale of British goods on Christmas Eve?"

"He was. He had just completed a sale of those goods to the Russian Federation and the shipment had gone out that same day."

"This sounds innocent enough. Why would a British embassy employee need guards in this case?"

"Money. He was in possession of a large sum of money once the deal was struck. My orders were to see him back to the British embassy with his funds."

"Had you served in a similar capacity before?"

"Almost daily. We are a security service."

Right. They are the world's nastiest spy agency and group of cold-blooded killers on the face of the earth. Security service? Like the devil is just a naughty child.

"Directing your attention to the two defendants in the rear of the courtroom in the prisoner dock. Would you look at them, please?"

He does as instructed, then returns his gaze to the prosecutor.

"All right."

"Have you ever seen these people before?"

"Yes. I arrested them in Moscow."

"Why did you arrest them?"

"There were charges filed against them. My supervisor had received a tip that the two could be found on the premises of Rudina Alaevsky, who sits on the Duma."

"What did you do with this tip?"

"My team and I loaded into two SUV's and went to the location. We entered the guest house of the premises shortly before nine-thirty p.m."

"What happened there?"

"We put the two defendants under arrest. They are both charged with Homicide One and Theft of State Secrets."

"Who are these people?"

"They are known by us to be American CIA agents."

"Did you personally see them at Henrik Nurayov's dacha on Christmas Eve?"

"I did not. But I know they were there."

"How do you know they were there?"

"The woman, Anna Petrov, has admitted as much."

"Who did she admit this to?"

"To me."

"Was there a written confession made?"

"There was. You already have it."

"Was her admission freely and voluntarily given?"

"Yes. She has been helpful."

"What did she tell you they did that night?"

"She confessed they approached the dacha in the dark with weapons drawn. They then shot and killed several members of the Nurayov security contingent. This included Colonel Tarayev's son. A sad development for everyone."

"Why did they do this?"

"I suppose they were trying to rob Henrik Nurayov.

Really, you should ask them. But I doubt if they'll tell the truth."

I'm instantly on my feet. "Objection! Witness is commenting on the character of my clients!"

"Overruled. Please sit down, counsel."

"Judge, please. It's inappropriate for counsel—"

"That's enough, Mr. Sakharov. Your objection was denied. Not another word now."

I have more I want to say, but think better of it. Judge Herzmink has never been open to entertaining my legal arguments. It is an awkward moment and I have clearly been brushed aside by the judge as if I'm only some bothersome fly at a picnic. One juror is watching for my reaction and she smiles as I meekly re-take my seat. She shakes her head at me and I realize her smile was not a friendly one. She is scolding me with her facial expressions, telling me I got what I deserved.

But the show isn't over yet.

"Have you found the defendant Anna Petrov to be completely truthful?"

"I believe what she has told me has been the truth. I believe this because I have checked out those parts of her story. But completely truthful? I believe she has left out the majority of her actions from that night. She omitted a huge chunk of the story in an attempt to cover up all the criminal activities they engaged in."

"Did you observe any other actions of the defendants that night?"

"I actually left through the front with Mr. Nurayov and his guest, a young woman he was entertaining. So I didn't see anything after that."

"Why did you leave with Mr. Nurayov?"

"For his safety. We were protecting him."

"That is all I have. Thank you, Captain Vasilov."

He stands as if to leave but the prosecutor speaks up and he re-takes the witness chair. The judge looks at me and gives a curt nod.

"Mr. Vasilov, am I correct in saying you didn't really see the defendants at the dacha Christmas Eve?"

The translator converts my question to Russian. The witness waits patiently.

Then he answers, "Correct."

"So you don't know if they shot anyone that night or not, do you?"

"The Petrov woman says they did."

Ignoring him, "You don't even know for sure if they were even there that night, do you?"

"She says they were there."

"Let me ask you about her so-called confession. When she was released from the city jail after you were finished with her she was terribly injured."

"I wouldn't know."

"Really? You couldn't observe her left arm was broken in two places?"

"No."

"Or her right wrist was dislocated after being repeatedly struck by your nightstick?"

"No."

"She didn't tell you she had terrible pain in her ribs and three were broken?"

"No."

"You didn't see the teeth you had broken out?"

"I did no such thing."

"Who did these things then?"

He learns back in the witness chair and tugs at his black necktie. "I have no information regarding your allegations.

This is unknown by me."

"Yet you obtained her signature on her confession, did you not?"

"I did."

"And the reason we know it was you is because your signature is on the confession as a witness. Did you witness her signing the confession?"

"I did. She looked fine to me."

"So when she reported to the hospital and was kept in intensive care for three days after her release you're telling this jury that those injuries weren't of your doing?"

"I'm telling you—I say no."

"Now Mr. Vasilov, we've all heard about the terrible abuses the FSB commits at Russian jails and prisons. Do you know what I'm referring to, sir?"

"I don't know about this."

"Mr. Vasilov, look over at the jury and tell them you're speaking the truth. Look them all in the eye and tell them you're not lying."

"Objection!" cries the judge. "The witness will do no such thing. This man's word is gold in my courtroom, counsel. You will refrain from such ridiculous requests as that."

I'm on my feet. "What, judge, it's improper for me to ask the witness to look at the jury? To look at the jury and swear he's telling the truth? Where's the harm in that?"

"Sit down, counsel! Your attitude with this court is beyond contemptuous. It is criminal and if it happens again you will find yourself behind bars with your clients."

I can feel Van tugging at my sleeve. "Sit!" he commands me, just audible to me and maybe the prosecutor. "Do you want to go to jail?"

It comes back to me in a rush—the nightmare I've been living since coming here. I'm not in an American courtroom with all the rights and privileges and rules guaranteed by the U.S. Constitution. I'm in no-man's land where any kind of judicial whimsy is possible. He very well could throw me in jail. I consider this fact, and I decide that I'm not afraid of going to jail, the hell with it. But then in the next instant I remind myself that I'm defending my son and his partner and I have no right to abandon them to the court system just to prove my own petty point. So I sit down and stare at the table top. Then the judge speaks.

"Well?"

"No, sir. I don't want to go to jail. Please accept my apologies."

"Accepted. Were you finished with the witness?"

"I was finished."

"Very well, the witness is excused. Mr. Prosecutor, please call your next witness."

Chapter 32

M ichael Gresham

THE PROSECUTOR CALLS HENRIK NURAYOV. I stand up to stretch while the clerk goes out to fetch the witness. I shiver all over. It is still very cold inside the courtroom. The judge looks at me askance. He says, through the translator, "Mr. Sakharov, do you need to take a break?"

I'm surprised. This man hasn't given me a break, ever. Now he wants to know if I need anything? I look around before I make my response. Something has definitely buckled the mood in here. But I don't know and can't guess what it is. So I shake my head. "No," I say unconvincingly. "I'm fine, thanks."

The judge speaks again to the translator. She turns to me and holds her hands out palms up and shrugs. The universal, "I give up," sign. I only stare at her. This is how it goes; most of the time I have no idea what is being said or what someone's intentions are. It is a mistake for me to be here; a huge mistake, but there's no turning back. I look down at Antonia. She rolls her eyes and shrugs. Two shrugs and one eye roll. *For the love of God, someone tell me what all this means. Am I the only one who doesn't get it?*

Then Nurayov comes hurrying down the aisle and everyone turns to look. He is a key witness and the jury takes note. How do they know such things? Does my face betray the strong concern I have about this witness? Can these jurors read it in my eyes? I sit back down and busy myself at my table. My intention is to telegraph to the jury that I consider this new person inconsequential, someone I probably won't even bother with. Still, I'm afraid the jury perceives otherwise.

Nurayov is sworn and seats himself in the witness chair. He looks out at the jury and sends them a nod and brief smile. At least two of them nod back. One of them includes a smile with her nod. At which point I'm feeling frightened, that maybe there is more here than meets the eye. Then Nurayov tosses off a very friendly wave and smile to Antonia Xiang, his sister-in-law. She doesn't respond in any manner.

Questioning begins by prosecutor Gliisky. First he leads the witness through the preliminaries: name, address, employer (he works for the British Embassy, he claims), and the like. Then Gliisky moves the focus to Christmas Eve just past.

"What were you doing on Christmas Eve? Please start with your actions following work that day."

"Well, first I stopped off with a friend from work for a drink. I had two vodkas, quite watered down, over about a two hour period. Then we said good night and I went to my car."

"What were you driving?"

"A Volvo. Not a new car; something I've had for a dozen years."

"Where did you go?"

"I picked up a woman who was to join me at home that night for dinner. We then drove out to my dacha north of Moscow."

"Was anyone else there when you arrived?"

"Yes. The embassy had provided me with bodyguards because I was handling a large sum of money."

"How could the bodyguards help?"

"As you know, the kidnapping of diplomats and state department workers has become very prevalent around the world. The guards were there to keep me safe in that regard."

"Did any of them follow you home that night?"

"I think so but I'm never sure. They don't announce it to me or anything."

"Take us through the events that followed your arrival at home."

"Certainly. We pulled into my driveway and entered my house through the front door. Several guards greeted us and then gathered themselves in the family room, giving my guest and me space in the living room. My cook was cooking a stroganoff dish with vegetables and the place smelled delicious. Once we were in the living room, I poured drinks for us. She was drinking gin and tonic; I again had a vodka. I'm not much of a drinker so I usually use one-half the measure of vodka bartenders might typically pour. We then sipped our drinks and engaged in small talk. The woman worked at the embassy with me and we had no end of things to discuss."

"Such as?"

Nurayov smiles and almost chuckles. "Gossip, mostly. Office gossip—who's going out with who, do we expect pay raises in the new year—that sort of thing. We were going over the plans we had for vacation time from our work when suddenly one of the guards came into the living room and whispered that I should follow him, that someone was breaking into the house through the rear sliding door. I was stunned; no one had ever tried this and it happened without any warning or prior threats. With my guards standing there with their guns drawn, the intruders were about to step inside though the hole they'd made in the glass. Then they came into my home, Russell Xiang and Anna Petrov. I spoke with them and told them they would be arrested. Then two guards suddenly thought I shouldn't be in the same room and they grabbed my arms and hurried me down the hall to my bedroom. My guest accompanied us. They then left us there alone.

We waited for a good fifteen minutes or so, then we heard gunshots. At that point, my guest and I ran for the front door of my house, then outside we ran for my car. We spun the tires coming all the way around the circular drive and then we were gone. We then could hear many gunshots back behind us at the dacha. We had no way of knowing what was happening, of course, as we made our getaway from there."

"Where did you go?"

"One other thing. I saw the intruders' Lada parked inside a nut grove just down the road when we went by."

"All right. Where were you going when you left?"

"The only place we knew to go: the embassy. We showed our ID and went up in the elevator and adjourned to my office. Then we waited after I had notified the director that we were there."

"What happened next?"

"The embassy has short-term stay facilities. We finally both went to bed in separate rooms and slept until just before dawn, when the embassy officials awoke me. My house had been blown up, I learned. So I went to a hotel and my guest went to her home. I then remained at the hotel for the next two days while my nerves settled down and the investigation was carried out by the British officials. What a night; one I'll never forget."

"Have we left anything out?"

"No, it's all been told."

At which point I'm told I may cross-examine the witness. I stand and walk up to the lectern and position myself there so that the jury can see my face and my reactions to what is about to be said from the witness stand. I've always believed that the cross-examiner's role is not only to ask questions but also to react dramatically so as to guide the jury in their perception of what's been said. What has worked for me in America will hopefully work for me in Russia. At least that's my approach.

"Mr. Nurayov, you've told us that your guest was a woman. Are you sure it wasn't a young boy you had picked up from Saint Basil's parking lot?"

The implication was clear. St. Basil's parking lot, at night, is a hotbed of connections between willing flesh and needful flesh. A place where prostitutes male and female offer themselves to anyone.

"That wouldn't be the case. My guest was a female."

"So if a witness came here and said he saw you pick up a very young boy in your car on Christmas Eve he would be incorrect?"

"No, he would be lying. No such thing happened."

"Objection, Your Honor," says Gliisky, suddenly animated and jerking up to his feet. "There is no such witness who will say any such thing. Counsel is trying to imply something to the jury that no one is going to offer as testimony."

"Objection sustained. The jury will disregard all questions about some imaginary boy. Counsel, you are admonished. Stick to the facts, please."

"Your Honor—" I start to reply, but he holds up a cautioning finger to me. I know he is warning me that contempt and jail are in the offing for me should I continue the questions about the boy guest. So I break it off and shuffle my papers at the lectern.

"Mr. Nurayov, exactly what is your job title at the embassy?"

"Investigator."

"What is it you investigate?"

"Applications for replacement passports. People come to us at least once a day saying their passport has been lost and they need a replacement so they can go home to England. I service those claims."

"What do you do to investigate?"

"I have them collect up and present to me all forms of identification they have. I photograph them. I make calls and send photographs of the claimants to a central repository in London where facial recognition software is employed. A decision is then made and I send the people along to the next embassy agent, where they will be given a temporary passport so they can go home."

"Isn't it true you work for MI6, British foreign intelligence services?"

"Not at all. I applied to work there twenty years ago but they turned me down. They turn everyone down."

"You've never worked for MI6 in Russia?"

"Objection, asked and answered. Move that the court give counsel a warning."

"Sustained. Counsel—"—addressing me now—"You are again asking questions that are in no way supported by the evidence—"

"How so?" I cry out. "How am I doing that, Judge? If I don't ask my questions those things never *will* be in evidence. It's a Catch-22!"

"I have read your *Catch-22* book, counsel. That isn't the case here. You have been warned a second time. The third time there will be no warning but you will spend the night in our magnificent Moscow City Jail. You've given me the impression now that you're quite willing for this."

"One moment, Judge, may I consult with my co-counsel?"

"Go ahead. Sixty seconds."

I head back to my table and Van pulls me close. "This guy is going to send you to jail, Mikhail. Give up asking questions about things that weren't testified to in direct examination."

"Seriously?" I ask Van. "I thought cross-examination was unlimited in scope."

Van smiles. "Maybe you're thinking of U.S. courts, Mikhail. Not so, here. We are very limited on cross."

"Oh, my God."

I push away from the table and return to the lectern. Now even my co-counsel has abandoned me. My mind is racing. How am I ever going to punch holes in the state's case if I can't ask questions intended to trip up the witness, to show him for who he really is? I flip through my documents. I have a copy of the bill of lading taken by Xiang from Henrik's bedroom on Christmas Eve after he and Petrov searched. Dare I use it? Or will it only wind me up in jail if I bring up a matter so clearly outside the scope of the direct examination of Nurayov? I take a deep breath. I've never been one to be cowed by what some judge might do. My clients deserve more than my fear; they deserve fearless representation.

I step around the lectern and approach the clerk. In a hushed voice I ask her to mark the bill of lading from Ehrlyich International Shipping as evidence. The translator gives the Russian interpretation to her. She marks my paper and hands it back. Now I'm committed to using the document I have flaunted before the jury.

"Mr. Nurayov, I'm handing you an exhibit that the clerk has just marked. It's written in English so you, a British subject, should have no trouble reading it. Have you seen this before, sir?"

Nurayov studies the document. He flips it over and finds nothing on the back. He turns it back over. He turns it this way and that.

"No, I haven't seen this before."

"Objection! Again outside the scope of direct examination!"

"One more question, Your Honor," I reply. "If I don't connect it up with one more question then I will gladly go to your jail every night for the remainder of the trial."

The judge smiles, something he's never done before.

"I can't pass that up," he says, and nods at me.

So I continue. "Mr. Nurayov, directing your attention to the bottom of the document. There is a signature line with the initial 'HN.' Are those your initials sir?"

"What?"

"Did you put your initials on this document?"

"I don't—I don't remember."

"Well, with the court's permission I've had the document examined by an expert handwriting analyst. If you'd be so kind as to write out today's date on a separate piece of paper and sign it, we can have your handwriting compared to the initials on the bill of lading. Fair enough?"

"Wait," he says, chewing at the inside of his cheek. He is again studying the document. "Wait, I think those are my initials. I think this was a document from work that someone gave me to prove they were in Russia shipping goods but they were really British subjects. Yes, it's coming back, they had lost their passport. A certain man I'm beginning to recall now."

"Really? A man shipping military grade weapons?"

"Yes, it was definitely a man who'd lost his passport."

"And where did the weapons come from and where were they going?"

Nurayov has quickly collected himself and now smiles. "Oh, I didn't go into all that. I think I may have turned the document over to the British security service but that's the last I saw of it. The man got his passport replaced, too, you might be interested to know."

"These aren't weapons that you signed for? You didn't sign this bill of lading by initialing it as confirmation the weapons had been received for shipment?"

"Of course not. That would be ludicrous and I resent the implication."

"Your Honor, the defense moves this exhibit into evidence."

The judge listens to the translation. His fingers tap impatiently on his desk top while the translator drones on.

Then, "It's already in evidence. Please continue with your questions."

"Mr. Nurayov, the night of the shooting, did you see Russell Xiang on your premises?"

"Yes."

"Did you see Anna Petrov?"

"Yes. I already said I did."

"Were you there to witness any of the shooting you say took place on your premises?"

"I was gone by then. I've said as much previously."

"Isn't it true you knew the defendants before the night of Christmas Eve?"

"Not true. I didn't know them before; I still don't know them now."

"Do you know me, Mikhail Sakharov?"

"Know you?"

"Yes."

"No, I don't know you. I know of you, however."

The bell has been rung. I can't quit now.

"Really? What do you know of me?"

As soon as I ask it I wish I had my words back. But I was left with no choice once he said he knew of me.

"I know that you're a CIA agent, Mr. Sakharov. I also know your real name is Michael Gresham. I also know that you were involved in shooting four CIA agents in Virginia."

I'm stunned. I don't even know where to begin. I sneak a quick glance at the jury, most of whom are sitting pushed back, arms crossed on their chests, glaring at me. Suddenly I'm the enemy, the CIA, whom everyone around the world hates.

But I jump right back into it.

"Strong allegations, Mr. Nurayov, so let's take them one by one. What evidence do you have I'm a CIA agent?"

"I was shown your picture by an agent from MI6. He warned me about you."

"What did he warn you about? That I might cross-examine you?"

"Not hardly. He warned me that you might try to murder me to shut me up from testifying. I've been hiding out these past several weeks so you couldn't locate me."

The sand is shifting beneath my feet and I'm sinking in deeper and deeper. This man is not only brilliant but he's also been brilliantly coached. My esteem for the FSB suddenly skyrockets. I thank goodness when Van hustles to his feet behind me and requests a ten-minute recess, which the judge grants. He flies up to the lectern and takes me by the arm, steering me out into the hall and around the corner into a small conference room. He pushes me into a chair and locks the door.

"What the hell, Mikhail?" he gruffly shouts. "Are you *try*ing to lose this thing?"

I look down at my shaking hands. I've never been in so much trouble in a courtroom before, not with an adverse witness.

"It veered out of control and then it just exploded, Van," I lamely reply.

"Right now he has you viewed by the jury as an American CIA agent coming into their court and using a false name. What are your plans to climb out of this train wreck?"

"I really don't know." I'm shaken; it is very difficult to think clearly.

Van's voice is soothing. "Let's back up to where it went off the rails. You were asking him about the bill of lading. He denied everything, saying it was only a minor piece of evidence for his work as a passport examiner. May I suggest we begin by investigating this item further after the trial today?"

"Further? Such as?"

Van leans back in his chair. "How about we track down Ehrlyich International Shipping, who provided the bill of lading. See what we can pick up there?"

"How would we do that?"

Van purses his lips. "Listen, Mikhail. You are in very serious trouble inside that courtroom. You have been accused of being CIA. You have been accused of being an American who's using a phony Russian Federation identity. If you are convicted of these things you will definitely find yourself in a work camp for the rest of your life. Plus, there is the problem with Xiang and Petrov. If you go down, they go down too. So, in answer to your question about what we might try, let me suggest we try everything conceivable. Including breaking and entering to get to their records."

"That's not encouraging. I see huge problems there."

He shakes his head violently. "But look at the problems you've created inside the courtroom! It's a house of cards in there and it's collapsing! Desperate times call for desperate measures, Mikhail."

He continues staring at me as if gauging whether he's getting through to me with the reality of our case. He is. He is getting through. And he's right. We're going to need to take desperate steps. I'm suddenly wishing Marcel were here to help me, but he's not. This time the dirty work falls to me. There's no one else.

"All right," I finally say, "tonight we go."

"No, tonight *you* go. There's no 'we' in this."

There it is. Now I'm truly alone, caught up in a Russian snare in a country I don't know and all the rest of it.

We finish our little talk and return to the courtroom. I

request of the judge that we recess and allow me to finish up with Nurayov in the morning. To my great astonishment, the judge agrees. Then we are in recess for the night.

I take a taxi back to the hotel with Antonia riding along. My mind is racing as I go. I barely hear her "Goodnight."

The time has come for me to put up or shut up.

And I'm never one for shutting up.

Chapter 33

Michael Gresham

VAN CALLS me at nine o'clock that night. I'm sitting in my hotel room, dressed in black jeans, a black turtleneck, and black watchcap. My heavy black goose down coat is hung by the door, waiting.

"Okay, Mikhail," Van begins, "I've located Ehrlyich International Shipping. Their main office is at the North Pier on the Moskva River. That is a good distance away. My suggestion would be for you to rent a car—"

"Hold on, Van. I can't read Russian and their building sign will definitely be in Russian. How will I know when I've found it?"

"Hmm. Good point."

"Any suggestions?"

"All right, Mikhail, I'll drive you there. But I won't wait around. You'll have to get back to the hotel on your own."

"Nice, Van. We'll compromise. You wait several blocks away and I'll come to you when I'm done. How's that?"

"All right, all right."

"While we're at it, there's one other thing. The bill of lading is in English. Will I be looking for a file or folder that has English on the cover or Russian?"

"You better hope it's English, my friend, because I'm not going in with you."

"I figured as much. I'm not trying to get you to. I'm just trying to understand what I'm up against here."

"Mikhail, this might be your last night of freedom in Russia."

"What?"

"The judge could very well decide tomorrow that you're CIA and that you impersonated a Russian citizen and just throw you in jail."

"Without a jury verdict? He can just do that?"

Van sighs. "We're in Russia, remember?"

He's absolutely right. There is no *Bill of Rights* here—not even close. Anything can happen.

"I remember."

"One last thing. Do you have cash? American dollars?"

"I have about two thousand USD."

"Good. Bring it along. You might need to make a bribe."

"Good thinking. How long will it take you to get to my hotel, Van?"

"Funny thing is, I'm pulling under the portico right now. Hurry downstairs and we're off."

"So you were coming anyway. Good man."

"I knew I would have to find their offices for you. Least I can do."

"I'm on my way."

Together we drive several miles north along the Moskva River. The lights have thinned out along here and the riverbank is very dark, although buildings parallel it this side of the water. I notice there are very few vehicles. What there is of traffic is mostly tractor-trailer rigs lugging along under what appear to be huge loads bound for the river barges. We pull into a drugstore parking lot and Van dashes inside. He returns swinging a silver flashlight. It flashes on and off then he climbs back inside the car. He passes the light to me and I stuff it inside my coat pocket. We're off, headed back onto the highway.

Van explains as we drive along that the Moskva River, at the city of Kolomna, flows into the Oka River, itself a tributary of the Volga, which ultimately flows into the Caspian Sea. In this manner Moscow has access by water to the sea. As one might expect, the river traffic is heavy and runs 24/7. Even as we drive along we can see the barge lights playing up and out of the river, locating navigation points along the shore, and proceeding cautiously where the river isn't all that wide and deep. Then we are slowing and we inch along to the North Pier. Van is reading the signs on the buildings as go.

Then, "That's it! See, it says 'EIS'. And below that in smaller letters is the name, 'Ehrlyich International Shipping'. I'm going to drive by and park several blocks away. Then you're on your own, Mikhail."

My heart flip-flops in my chest. I almost need to pinch myself to be certain I'm not dreaming. I have never committed a burglary in my life. Yet, I'm about to. I wish upon all wishes that Marcel were with me tonight. I think of him, locked away in Moscow City Jail, probably cold and shivering like I was; my determination redoubles and I know I'm going to do this thing.

Three blocks further along, Van turns left and goes up

two blocks and then pulls over to the curb. We are beside a park and on the other side of the street are fairly large houses and streetlights.

"Luck," he says, as I open my door.

I step outside and am smacked by the bitterly cold air. For once it isn't snowing—which means I won't be leaving tracks in new snow and the old snow is too slushy and tracked up to follow me anyway. Or so I think. I trudge back the way we came one block and then head right along the road that parallels the front of Ehrlyich International Shipping. With any luck, the building will stretch all the way back to this road and I can reduce my exposure around the front or even along the side. The going is slushy and slippery in places, especially just off the curbs where the day's melt has re-frozen and threatens to cause me to slip and fall. But I don't. Chicagoans like me don't fall on ice because we always expect it, even year around, it seems, and we anticipate those spots where it lurks.

Two blocks up there is a stoplight and I'm walking directly toward it and the streetlight that illuminates the intersection. Just briefly the light shows the planes of my face clearly to anyone who might be watching. I pull my head down into my coat as far as the collar allows, but I'm still exposed. I can only pray that no one has eyes on me. Hurrying to the other side, I speed-walk to the shadows beyond the intersection and then I—with my black clothing and watchcap—am absorbed into the black night.

One more block to go. Just as I make mid-block, a dog loose in someone's front yard begins growling. Then a yap-yap sounds, then it erupts into all-out barking as I make my way along its fence. It's not until I reach the next corner and turn left that the barking stops. Up to the alley I go and there, at last, is the rear wall of my building. I turn left down the alley and walk along a couple of hundred feet. I'm casing the joint, as they say in the gangster movies. What I'm finding looks very unlikely, I might add. For there are no alley-level doors, no windows, no obvious means of ingress that I can spot. Which leaves me wondering how the hell I'm going to break in.

I walk back down to the loading dock—actually a triple-dock affair. Three articulating doors reach from the top of the opening down to the lip of the dock. They are heavy steel and don't look penetrable. But I notice each one has a pull handle positioned at its center almost all the way to the bottom. The doors are set back from the lip of the dock maybe eighteen inches. Who was it who said, "Give me a level long enough and a fulcrum to place it on and I shall move the earth?" Was that Archimedes? The problem, viewed in this light, seems solvable.

So I need a lever. Nothing jumps right out at me, so I begin policing the alleyway. Down to the far end I snoop around and still nothing. So I dash across the street and into the next alley. Then, lo and behold, it can only be a plumbing company, because, just over a six-foot chain link fence, are pipes of all lengths lying like toothpicks in a long rack. Checking all around me, I grip the fence in my hands and start to climb up out of the alley. Another large step up and I'm at the top, swinging my leg over the crest, now easing myself off and jumping down to the other side. Without much thought given to the problem, I grab a twelve-foot length of two-inch pipe and locate an old cement block. Both are tossed over the fence to the alley. I survey my work as I begin climbing, and see that the block has shattered. So, back down until I find another. This time, it's closer to the building and this time I move near and a motion detector senses me. A floodlight blinds me. I'm totally announced to the world by the horrible light. I freeze. Then I seize my cement block and run for the fence. This time I don't throw the block over; clutching it in my left hand, I use my right hand and my feet to scale the fence and then drop back down into the alley. By now the floodlight has blinked off and I wait several moments while my eyes again adjust to the dark. Then I grab my pipe and I'm off: the pipe up over my shoulder, the cement block flopping against my thigh as I jog back across the street.

Back to the three dock doors I fly, arriving winded and breathing heavily. I have no clue whether my approach is going to work and I have no clue whether the doors themselves are wired to an alarm system. I'm guessing they are, but there's nothing I can do about that. At this point, I'm out of choices. I can only move ahead with my weak plan. One thing in my favor: the building is very old, the bricks crumbling along the edges all around the three doors. Maybe, I'm hoping, they haven't wired these, thinking no one can get them open anyway.

Hoisting the cement block into place on the lip of the dock, just this side of the middle door, I stand back, lay my pipe across it, and dig the far end of the pipe in under the door's central handle. I pry down and test. The pipe stays locked under the handle. So I press down even more, bringing some of my weight to bear on the problem. Then I ease up and step up to the door handle I'm prying. Much to my great relief it doesn't appear to be bending upward. That would have been the end of my plan right there if the handle bent and gave way before the door moved up. But it hasn't bent and seems solid enough.

So I place my lever back across the block and this time apply much more weight. Now I'm almost lying across the pipe and allowing more and more of my weight to press downward. I'm about to go check the handle again when suddenly, with a loud crack like a starter's pistol, the door springs free of its lock and is wheeling upward. I cringe, shut my eyes, and wait for the alarms I'm almost certain will begin wailing. Several moments slide by and still I'm waiting. It slowly occurs to me that no noise alarm is going off. A silent alarm, perhaps. There's nothing I can do about that, so I lay my pipe lengthwise up against the wall of the dock so it appears to be a castoff lying there. I climb up onto the ramp, duck down beneath the door, and step inside the loading dock.

It is totally black. I turn and pull the door all the way back down. Then my flashlight is brought up out of my coat pocket and the switch slides. I find myself in a catch-all room with a wall of tools hung from pegboard, round rolls of copper tubing and white electrical wire, barrels of nails, and a long wooden workbench. There are work gloves scattered about, pliers and wrenches, different lengths of wire, and a metal vise. I have no idea what kind of business this room is adjoining, but it is typical back-room stuff for almost anything you might imagine. So, I still haven't arrived. I twist the knob and push open the inner door. I'm facing a rectangular room that must hold forty work cubicles. All manner of plants and balloons and giant dolls levitate above several of the cubes, giving the place a lived-in/worked-in look and feel. People spend a third of their lives here and in one of these drawers—or in the myriad of filing cabinets that take up almost every inch of outer wall space—the bill of lading file I have come here for might be found.

But where to begin?

For someone who has just walked in, there is no rhyme or reason to the place. There is not one clue about which employee might have helped expedite the sale of arms from Henrik Nurayov, the arms that moved into the shipper's holds on its barges outside in the river. But at least I know I'm in the right place. I know I've found the shipper, and I force myself to focus on what I came for.

I remember how American companies work, where the higher you go in their buildings the higher you go in their hierarchy. Sure enough, on the other side of the room is a bank of two elevators. I hurry over and punch the button between them. Doors fly open and I step inside the closest one. There are three floors above, as there are three numbered buttons above the first. I hit four and the elevator begins its climb.

The door opens. Inside the elevator car the automatic light is on. Outside in the hallway it is pitch black. I step out and look right and left. At the far distance in either direction are signs lettered in red neon. I'm guessing those indicate exits as they would in the U.S. Also, in America, there is a rush among corporate employees to climb the ladder and get that proverbial corner office. So why wouldn't the same be true here? Why does this matter? Because the higher-ranking officials are more likely to have their fingers in many pots at once, including the sale and shipment of weapons of war. Especially that.

I mentally flip a coin and head to my right. At the exact moment I take my first step I see the beam of a flashlight play against the far left-hand wall. Someone is coming into the far end of the hall from where it comes off the right. I back up against the first office door and twist the knob. Locked. I step across the hall and try another. Locked again. I'm literally in the dark and don't know what to do. So I quickly close the distance between me and the light on the wall. Then, when I'm almost there, I feel the wall open on my right. I step inside a rather large room with windows that face the night sky. I can actually see the reflection of street-lights below coming up through the mist and snow squalls that have begun again. I race across the room and step behind a waist high table with a modesty shield. I squat down behind it and slow my breathing. Then I can hear the footsteps coming and I can see the light outside now shining down the hallway I just left. The light shudders up and down and back and forth and the footsteps come nearer. The person behind the flashlight is whistling a tune, *Deep in the Heart of Texas*. When he reaches the line, *The sage in bloom is like perfume*, he stops, enters my room, and switches on the lights. Then all goes quiet.

My entire diaphragm struggles to exhale in a huge whoosh. I strain against the impulse, forcing myself to breathe shallowly and soundlessly. Footsteps can be heard pattering in my direction. When the person is perhaps ten feet away, the footsteps slow and then stop. A match can be heard scraping along its igniter and then flaring up. Within seconds I smell cigarette smoke and hear a man's voice exhaling with no small amount of satisfaction. Another puff, another exhalation, and I'm about to burst with anticipation.

Then the steps turn away and retreat back the way they came. The person again pauses at the entrance to my room. I can picture him looking around one last time before switching off the lights—and then the lights are indeed doused. Now I'm in the dark, my eyes aren't adjusted, and I don't dare move, for fear he has only feigned leaving the room. I decide to give it five minutes and begin counting slowly to three-hundred.

At four-hundred I stand upright. My knees are trembling and crying out to buckle, but I support myself with my hands on the desk as I stare directly at the opening into my room. At this point I know I'm in silhouette against the windows behind me and that makes me easily seen by anyone passing by. But the time has come to get what I came here for, so I cross to the entrance and stick my head into the hallway. All clear both ways—at least there is no flashlight beam.

Down the hall I slither, one hand on the wall to my right, my eyes trained on the door ahead of me that opens onto the corner office. I'm praying it isn't locked. But it is, I find when I reach it. Now what?

I'm standing there in the open, unable to proceed inside, without a hint of an idea how to get in.

My mind roams back over TV shows and movies. Wasn't there something about sliding a credit card inside the seams between frame and door and forcing the lock to give way? Stupid as it sounds, I try it. I try it because I'm all out of good ideas of my own.

Voila! The credit card opens the door!

And I'm inside in one quick step, closing the door behind me. I say a silent prayer that I'm in the right office.

While I'm in there, I decide I might as well go all the way. Checking that the window blinds are all full lowered and twisted shut, I remove my flashlight and switch it on.

It is a beautiful office, with a huge desk made of what I believe is mahogany, a plush executive chair covered in blue leather, wall hangings of gold and silver, with a myriad of personal pictures on the credenza. I plop down in the blue chair and start sliding desk drawers in and out. With no idea what I'm looking for insofar as what kind of folder or binder was used, I can only open, rummage around, and close. After a minute of this, nothing looks promising. There is neither folder nor binder nor paper-clipped stack of anything resembling shipping records or a bill of lading like mine.

So I stand and look around. There is a long two-drawer filing cabinet covered in matching mahogany over against the wall beneath the window on the side street side of the office. I go there, kneel down, and open the bottom drawer. Files are arranged left to right with their tabs all facing left. So I scoot around to my left to where I'm facing the tabs and start pawing through. Halfway in, I suddenly freeze. All the other file folders are tabbed in Russian. But not the one I've just located. This one is tabbed in English and says, simply, *Nurayov to Brotherhood.*

I jerk it out of the drawer and flip it open.

Then I read, for everything's in English. The original of my bill of lading is on top of everything else. Then I read the file memos and letters. Evidently Henrik Nurayov procured and sold to the Saudi Brotherhood the weapons and matériel listed on the bill of lading. Nurayov delivered the first shipment of goods via a tractor-trailer rig that unloaded right downstairs on the loading docks. The weapons were then catalogued and checked against Nurayov's receipt of sale, and then entered onto EIS's own bill of lading. Now EIS has given copies of the bill of lading to Nurayov, says the correspondence in the file, and to the Saudi Brotherhood, signed off by an Abu Degav al-Zawihiri. The bill of lading—the original I'm looking at—has inscribed on its face the initials HN. Henrik Nurayov. The rest of the file contains various correspondence to Nurayov and to al-Zawihiri and memos and photographs of the weapons shipped by EIS.

Quandary. If I steal the file and present it in court, I have revealed myself as the thief. On the other hand, will EIS come forward and claim its records from what I'm certain was an illegal sale and purchase of military grade weapons inside the country of Russia? Would they be so foolish? I decide to answer that in the negative. So I take the entire file and slip it up under my turtleneck, and zip up my goose-down coat. I have what I came here for.

Immediately, then, I switch off the flashlight and hurry back to the office door. Standing just inside, I place my ear against the door and listen. Hearing nothing, I ever so slowly open the door.

And there, standing eyeball to eyeball with me, is what can only be the same man whose flashlight beam and cigarette smoking I encountered earlier.

Before he can react, I whip off my belt from around my waist and open its inner zipper. In one quick movement I strip out two thousand dollars USD and hold them out to the man. He is stunned beyond belief and finally collects himself enough to draw a gun from his hip holster. He points the weapon at me; I notice his hand trembling. I push the money toward him again, indicating he should take it, that I want him to have it. "It's yours if you'll just let me go," I tell him, though I'm absolutely certain he understands none of it.

Then, to my utter amazement, he says in a strong voice, "Lone star state? Don't mess with Texas?"

"Yes," I cry out, "Yes, I love Texas! Lone star state!"

And I thrust the money at him again. But this time he reaches out and takes it from me.

"Green Bay Packers," he says as he receives my cash. "Aaron Rodgers."

"Yes, it might buy two seconds of Aaron's time, but that's about it. It's only two thousand."

"NFL."

"Yes, we all love the NFL."

"NBA."

"Let me past," I tell him with a smile. "I go to Texas!"

"Deep heart Texas!" he cries out, this time lowering and holstering his gun.

Davy Crockett would have been proud of me as I lead the two-man procession out of the Alamo, back downstairs to the loading dock, where I jump down into the alley two thousand USD poorer but ready to cross-examine the living shit out of one witness named Henrik Nurayov.

Chapter 34

M ichael Gresham

THE NEXT DAY starts early for me, before sunrise, when room service raps on my door. Breakfast is served at the foot of my bed, leaving behind a cart with two plates and covers, a carafe of coffee, butter patties, and a large glass of water. It's all necessary, as it's going to be a long day and I need to fuel up.

After breakfast comes a long, hot shower and shave. My face is scarred from a fire several years ago and the skin stings when I draw a razor across my beard. But I do it anyway. Today I want to look my best and be at the top of my game as it's make-or-break time. Nurayov either belongs to me or I go straight to jail.

Then I'm nervous as the reality of what the day holds in store settles over me like a cold blanket. But I think my way through the fear: I have the documents and I sure as hell have the questions I want to ask the guy. So far he's lied about everything he's said and today he's going to hit a brick wall head-on.

Just after eight, Van pulls under the hotel portico. He leans across and pushes open the passenger door. I climb inside and look across at him. He has a huge lump that runs from the outside of his eye up and over his eyebrow.

"What the hell?" I say.

He touches the lump gingerly. "Ouch!"

"What happened, Van?"

"A man paid a visit to my apartment last night."

"Who was it?"

"No names, no introductions. But I'm sure he was FSB."

"What would the Russia spy machine want with you, Van? You're not accused of being a CIA agent."

"He said I needed to stay home today. He said you would be going to jail and the trial would be over. He wanted me home so I couldn't take over the defense of our clients by myself."

I'm incredulous. This can't be.

"So what did you say to him?"

"I laughed. I said 'that's quite impossible.' Just as I was about to ask him to leave, he hit me with a leather sap. It must have had lead in the end because it caught me on the side of the head and I was knocked out cold. When I finally came to, my cat Rasputin was licking the blood off the side of my face. Her rough tongue felt like someone was rubbing me with sandpaper so it woke me up. I tried to sit up and fell back. The room was going around and around. So I rolled onto my side and slowly pushed myself up with one arm until I was sitting. Then I threw up all down my front. Finally I made it into the bathroom and climbed inside the shower with all my clothes on. I turned on the hot water and took everything off. I threw up again but this time it went straight down the drain. Then I went in and got in bed even though I was still wet. I was reeling, Mikhail. This morning I woke up, peeled my eyes open, and tried to see out of my right eye. It's still seeing double. Oh well. But here I am. If you're going to jail, I'm going to finish the trial. They're going to have to kill me first."

"Why the fire in the belly? What's gotten into you, Van?"

"When I was little I was bullied every day, until I learned I was smarter than the bullies. I would dream of ways of making their little lives horrible for a moment or two. Payback, we call it today. Same thing with this trial. No damn bully is going to run me off. I don't run. Didn't then, won't now."

"Wow. That's quite a story. I'm really sorry it happened to you."

He looks over from the steering wheel. "Which? Childhood or last night?"

"Actually, both."

"Let's go to court. After last night, I'm ready to skin this Nurayov alive."

Thirty minutes later, we're standing at counsel table. Antonia has joined us late. Now the judge ascends to the highest seat in the courtroom. He makes eye contact with no one, pours himself a glass of water from a golden pitcher, and rubs his hands together briskly. He switches on his microphone and taps it twice. The feedback over the crackly sound system tells him he'll be heard. Then his eyes bore into me.

"Mr. Sakharov, you were just finishing up with the witness Henrik Nurayov. Anything further, or can I dismiss the witness?"

"Just a few more questions, Your Honor," I say, intentionally to mislead Nurayov, who is back in the witness chair listening closely. He seems to relax just a bit when he hears "few more." He is just about free and his eyes light up with anticipation.

"Very well, proceed with your cross-examination, counsel."

The jury shifts in their seats and prepare for me to be further skewered by this witness who has proven way smarter—cagier?—than me. It promises to be quite a show followed by my all-but-guaranteed sentence to prison. Who knows? Maybe this will be the end of their service as jurors. Wouldn't that be great?

I step up to the lectern, boldly laying out EIS's file before me. Now the world can see it. But the truth is, it won't. It won't because EIS is never going to admit the records in that file are genuine and belong to EIS. They will want the greatest degree of separation possible from what's contained in that file.

"Mr. Nurayov," I begin, "yesterday you told the jury that I had been identified by an MI6 agent at the British Embassy. He told you I was a CIA spy. Do you remember saying those things?"

"Totally."

"And do you remember telling the jury that your job in the British Embassy was to investigate claims of passports being lost. Do you remember that?"

"Yes." He looks around grandly, very satisfied that I have yet been stupid enough to allow him to repeat his damnation of me. Several jurors actually nod at him approvingly.

"Ehrlyich International Shipping, Moscow, Russia. Ring a bell?"

He looks up at the judge. "Didn't we cover this?"

"You have," the judge proclaims. "Move it along, counsel. Or were you done?"

I ignore the judge and address Nurayov again.

"Let me show you a document I've had the clerk mark as Defendants' Exhibit Four. It is a letter written by Ehrlyich International Shipping and addressed to you. Do you recognize this letter?"

I hand him the letter. He reads and begins squirming. But he holds tight. "No. I didn't see this."

"Look at the address. Isn't that your home address?"

"Yes. Or it was."

"Now let me hand you Exhibit Five. What is this?'

He looks it over. He turns it over and glances at the back. Then he turns it over again.

"It looks like a letter from me to Ehrlyich International Shipping. But I didn't write this."

"That's not your signature at the bottom of the letter where you confirm to them you're making a shipment on November first?"

"No, not my signature."

This time we're ready. "Mr. Nurayov I've hired Danil Lemerov to study the signature and study your initials on the bill of lading. If he testifies you signed this letter, would he be incorrect?"

"Hold on. This must have been the furniture I shipped to my daughter. She's newly married."

"Look again, sir. The value of the goods shipped is listed as one hundred million USD. Your daughter must be living very well."

"Where is that? I don't see that."

"Third paragraph. Fourth line. Where it says, 'Seller represents shipment value is one hundred million dollars.' You missed that before?"

"Look here, counsel. That line four is the last line in the paragraph. I believe it was added after I sent this letter."

"So you believe there's a conspiracy to get you?"

He leans back and collects himself enough to smile at me.

"I think you're out to get me, Mr. Gresham. I think you added line four. You're a CIA agent and you'd like nothing better than to see me imprisoned. Or dead."

I've been waiting for this moment.

"Finally, let me show you this photograph. It depicts you standing with a shipment being loaded onto a barge. It's many shipping containers. Do you recognize them?"

"No. I was at the river watching my daughter's furniture going away on the barge. Someone must have snapped this."

"Except for one thing. Please look at the number on the shipping container you're standing next to. Can you read the number off that container?"

"Yes. It is NB322V-1993x."

"Thank you. Now read the jury the numbers from the bottom of the original bill of lading. Very bottom, Mr. Nurayov."

He reads slowly, "NB322V-1993x."

"Again, please. Mr. Ivanovich? Please load the first slide."

Van projects a blow-up of the barge picture with the container in plain sight, side-by-side with a blowup of the bill of lading. The jury is able to compare.

"Now read the numbers off the shipping container, sir."

"NB322V-1993x."

"Wouldn't you agree that the two numbers are the same?"

"They appear to be. I don't know who put the numbers on the bill of lading and I've told you those aren't my initials on it."

"Doctor Lemerov will talk to the jury about your initials on the bill of lading. And your signature on the letter. The noose is drawing tight, Mr. Nurayov, wouldn't you agree?"

"Objection! The only noose in this courtroom is the one around Mr. Gresham's neck!"

"Overruled. Please continue, counsel."

I'm stunned. He denied Gliisky's objection? Did I really just hear that?

But the problem is, there's only the one number on the original bill of lading. Where are the other numbers? I study the the bill of lading as I contemplate my next question. Then I see it, plain as day: at the top it says "1 of 2." I have only the first page of the original bill of lading with only one container number. The other numbers are on the second page. Quickly I shuffle through my stolen file. There is no second page. It's missing and I don't know why. So I do the only thing I can at that point, which is to take the witness down another path.

"You've brought up my pedigree, Mr. Nurayov, so let's talk about that."

"I'm certainly ready, Mr. Gresham."

"What's the name of the MI6 agent who told you I was CIA?"

"I don't recall."

"You don't recall because he doesn't exist, am I right?"

"No, you're wrong."

"All right, then. Describe him for the jury."

"He's large and—and—"

"How large? Six-feet-one?"

"I—I—yes, six feet one or two. Plus he's heavy."

"How much does he weigh?"

"I don't know."

"Hair color?"

"Dark."

"Eyes?"

"Dark."

"What was his name again? I would like to subpoena him to come testify."

"You know what? I'm wrong. It was actually a female agent and she's been sent back to London."

"Oh, so now it' a woman and she's no longer here?"

"That's right. It's coming back to me now."

"What's her name? I don't mind going to London and taking her statement."

"I don't know her name."

"Describe her, please."

"I don't—I don't—"

"Objection, Your Honor," says Gliisky, who has lurched to his feet. "Counsel is harassing the witness."

The judge raises a cautioning hand. "Not at all. I, too, would like to know this person's name. Without a name, I'm going to throw out all of his testimony. Please give us a name, Mr. Nurayov."

Nurayov swallows hard. He darts his eyes from Gliisky to the rear of the courtroom, to me, and then sits, eyes downcast, silent.

"I don't have a name, sir."

"Ladies and gentlemen of the jury, the court is going to instruct you to ignore and forget all testimony from this witness about Mr. Sakharov being a CIA agent. The court will ignore it as well. Proceed, counsel."

I'm too stunned to move on to my next question. I've just crossed the goal line and scored!

"That's all I have for now, Your Honor. Subject to recalling this witness in the defendants' case."

"Very well, the witness may step down. But you are not excused, Mr. Nurayov. Now you must wait in the hallway outside the courtroom until counsel decides whether he will recall you to the stand. Understand?"

Nurayov is very meek when he says, "I understand."

He steps down, head bowed, and hurries up the aisle. Then he disappears out into the hallway.

Chapter 35

M ichael Gresham

HE IS a bull of a man like an NFL nose guard: thick neck, sloping forehead, tiny eyes and a large nose that looks like it's been broken a time or two. Nothing to like there, and his voice matches his rough-and-ready looks. Vassily Lukin is a night guard at Moscow City Jail in D Wing, he tells the jury, and he knows my client, Russell Xiang.

"How did you come to know Mr. Xiang?" Prosecutor Gliisky asks, all innocence. There's a game underway here, and it consists of Gliisky playing like Lukin is someone reliable, an officer of the law, who's telling the truth and only the truth. But some of us know better. Lukin is a dupe, a setup, a rube. I watch as the game moves ahead.

"I met Mr. Xiang when I was on duty at night. He used to ask for cigarettes."

"Did you give him cigarettes?"

"Of course. He's a very nice man. Very hard to deny anything to him."

Plus, he paid you for them, I'm thinking. *If any of this actually happened, which I seriously doubt.*

"Did you have talks with Mr. Xiang?"

"Of course. All the guards and prisoners talk at night. It's lights out at seven p.m. No one can go to sleep that early so the only thing left is small talk."

"What kind of things did you talk about?"

"Family, home towns, growing up, work."

"Did he tell you about his work?"

"Of course he did. And I told him about my work."

"What did he tell you?"

The guard wrinkles his nose and shrugs.

"He told me he worked for the American CIA."

"Mr. Lukin, that's very hard to believe he would tell you that. Why would he admit to being a spy against the fatherland?"

"We were trading stories and I bet him my story was the better one of all four of us."

"So there was more than just you who heard this?"

"Sure, there were others."

"We'll come back to that. Did he talk about his work for the CIA?"

"Not really. He said there were secrets he couldn't tell."

"Did he talk to you about his night at Henrik Nurayov's dacha? The night several Russian guards were murdered?"

"He didn't talk about that. But I know he was there."

"Really? And how do you know that?"

"His cellmate told me that Xiang told him. Spilled the beans, he called it."

"His roommate is American too?"

"Yes. A man who got drunk and assaulted a police officer."

"What is his name?"

"Abraham Smerconish. Number 16-3344-D. He's in D Wing."

"Why would this man tell you something his cellmate confided to him?"

"He thought it would help him get out of jail if he squealed on his cellie."

"Did it help?"

"Of course not! Our jail is above reproach. We do not take bribes."

It's all I can do not to burst out laughing at this point. Such humongous lies and fairy tales. But I keep a straight face and listen as Lukin finishes up.

There is little I can do to cross-examine so I waive cross-examination and the next witness is called. She is the second guard who also heard Russell Xiang's supposed confession. Same story as Lukin's: Xiang is lonely, told his life story, begged cigarettes, made a call to his wife while in jail. Lukin again, with some embellishments. She also adds that Petrov corroborated the story where she spoke with Petrov under similar circumstances as Xiang. Nothing can be gained by hammering home the same story on cross-examination, so I waive.

But now they have made their case against Russell. As well as against Anna Petrov. *Prima facie* cases, but cases nonetheless.

In the late afternoon, after a long lunch and after the court has been in recess while it attended to other cases pending before it, Gliisky calls a forensics expert. His name is Martin Dinavy and he is a crime scene analyst for the FSB. He takes the witness stand, shifts uncomfortably in the hard wooden chair, and tugs at his necktie. His uniform is that of the Moscow City Police, but he testifies he is actually assigned to FSB investigations. Was he there on Christmas Eve or Christmas morning at Nurayov's dacha? He says he was.

Then, "My job was to collect up all evidence that might help us learn the invaders' identities."

"Tell the jury whether you were successful."

He swings his gaze over to the jury and expertly addresses them.

"Yes. I took molds of the bootprints left in the snow where the invaders came around the side of the house. I could track those bootprints all the way back up the service road into a small grove of nut trees. Their vehicle had evidently been left there while they attacked Mr. Nurayov's home."

"Were you ever able to match up those bootprints?"

"I was. After he was arrested, the officers brought several boots belonging to the defendant Russell Xiang into my laboratory. I took my measurements and made my examination under our microscopes."

"What did you conclude?"

"Defendant Xiang's boots matched the bootprints I found left behind in the snow."

Gliisky seizes a large clear plastic bag in which two large boots are enclosed. "Are these the boots?" He hands the bag to the witness.

"Yes, these are my initials on the bag. That's my handwriting."

"You're certain it was a match?"

"There is no doubt."

Gliisky sits down at his table and flips through his notepad. Then, "Nothing further, Your Honor."

The judge nods at me and I hurry to my feet and to the lectern. I want to give the impression I'm anxious to face this witness and I believe I'm successful.

"Mr. Lukin, what brand of boots are these?"

"Work-Joy by Ollas. These boots are made by the company in Leningrad."

"Are they popular?"

"Yes, very popular among the working class."

"Is Mr. Xiang a member of the working class?"

"I don't know."

"Well, Mr. Gliisky wants the jury to believe he's a spy. Are spies members of the working class?"

"I don't know. No, I suppose not."

"These boots could have belonged to any one of thousands of people, they are so popular, correct?"

"Correct. Maybe tens of thousands. Maybe hundreds of thousands. They're a men's size ten. Very common size, very common boot."

"In fact, you've examined similar boots in your lab before, in other cases?"

"That's right."

"How many times?"

"One dozen now."

"So please tell me how you were able to distinguish these boots from the perhaps hundreds of thousands of others that might be out there?"

"That would be impossible to say. There are marks, tool-marks, you might call them, on the soles. But even those are common enough."

"What kind of marks?"

"Well, the soles are rubber and rubber is easily scarred. Such soles pick up peculiar marks."

Now I'm holding my breath as I ask, "Did these boots have peculiar marks?"

"Not more than normal. I can't say they did."

It's not going to get any better than this, so I thank the witness and take my seat.

Then we are adjourned for the day.

AFTER DINNER that night I receive a call from the U.S. Embassy, Moscow. The caller identifies himself as Harry Samson, who says he's a foreign service officer with the State Department. I'm thinking yes, sure you are, and I am too. Spooks all around, coming and going all day in the courtroom where I'm defending, some recognizable by their facial features, haircuts, and clothes, some not so much. Anyway, I tell Harry hello and ask what it is I can do for him.

"I'm calling about the trial of Russell Xiang and Anna Petrov. You are their attorney and I hear you're doing a nice job for them."

"Nice? Just nice? Considering that I'm the little boy with his finger in the dike who's saving Holland I'd say I'm doing better than nice. How about fantastic, Mr. Samson?"

A stiff chuckle is allowed by Mr. Samson. Then he pushes on to his business.

"We've been working behind the scenes to help you, Mr. Gresham."

"Sakharov."

"Right. Anyway, we've obtained the agreement of Russell Xiang's mother. She will attend his trial this coming Monday."

"Today is Thursday. Tomorrow will probably finish up

the state's case against my clients. So Monday is excellent timing. It couldn't have worked out better."

Long pause. Then, "We know, Mr. Sakharov. That's our business to know these things and to act accordingly."

But I'm already floating away, losing myself in my dream state, a state of desperate love and longing from so many years ago I can't count them all.

We were young and time stood still when we were in college. Days were long, nights were even longer. My roommate was Henry Xiang. We were thrown together by lot our first year in college and it worked well enough that we stayed together until we graduated. But we did have our differences, one of them being Mai H. Yung, who would turn out to be Russell's mother. She played clarinet and Henry played clarinet. The opening day of marching band practice they found themselves together, marching and resonating with their instruments, marching and resonating with their bodies as they checked each other out that fall on the practice football field. They left practice and strolled over to the student union, where they had coffee and pie and talked all afternoon. He was Bay Area born and raised; she was from mainland China. He was studying pre-law; she was studying pre-med. They were inseparable until our senior year when Henry went into the hospital for an emergency appendectomy. Two nights he was gone from our dorm room. The dorm room that Mai had moved into and was living in with Henry—and with me. Of course, I made myself scarce during those key times when they needed their privacy, but they would always reward me with pizza and a six-pack when they were done and I returned. One thing: no lovemaking after nine p.m. because I always studied from nine until one a.m. It was my routine.

While Henry was in the hospital, things changed

between Mai and me. Maybe "changed" isn't such a good word as things "came to a head." We had lusted after each other for two years. We both knew it; neither of us acknowledged it. Lusted after each other in the way that college students will when relationship boundaries aren't marked off with marriage licenses but rather are fluid like moods. By this I mean Mai belonged to Henry and she didn't. They weren't married; they weren't even engaged—Henry's failing. Because they were only boyfriend-girlfriend, while Henry was in the hospital the second night, Mai and I wound up in bed together. Thirty days later she announced her pregnancy—to me only, because Henry couldn't have sex during the time of impregnation because of his surgery. Her parents were told and they forced her to return home to China. That was the last Henry or I ever saw of her. But our son, Russell, was shunted back and forth between Beijing and San Francisco, where, at nine, he finally wound up living with Henry, the man he knew as his father. Why wasn't it me? Because neither Mai nor I could stand to break Henry's heart with the truth of his son's conception. So we let it go, as youth will at that age.

Did I mention I was in love with Mai? Still am, probably, judging by my flip-flopping heart as Harry Samson from State explains to me that Mai will be arriving in Moscow on Sunday and that she'll be brought to my hotel room to prepare her for trial. And one last thing; she'll undergo DNA testing immediately on arrival at the same lab that tested me. We'll both be introduced to the jury at some point as Russell's bio-parents. I just haven't yet decided when that will be, but probably during Mai's testimony. That would make perfect sense.

"And by the way, Mr. Sakharov, Mai will also be staying at the Marriott where you're staying in case you need more time with her. Does this work for you, Mr. Sakharov?" Harry Samson wants to know.

I all but swallow the phone. But I force myself to take me out of the center of the picture and instead put Russell and Anna there where they belong. This is all about them; it isn't about me and I'm not going to make it about me. I'm sure Mai hasn't agreed to come here because of me: she's agreed to come here because her son is facing a firing squad. Her intention is to provide a pathway that sets her boy free.

We hang up and I begin changing clothes to return to the jail for my nightly visits with Verona and Marcel. I'm on record as their attorney and have an almost-unrestricted right to see them as often as I need. I have gained favor with the guards and am allowed to bring cigarettes to Marcel and cans of mixed nuts to Verona. Their requests. The guards look the other way, receive thanks for their cooperation in the form of American twenties, and everybody gets on.

Verona has feelings for me. She has told me so as we've shared through Plexiglas on phones that are no doubt bugged. Which is fine; we're still fueling the myth that we are in fact husband and wife and that Anna is Verona's daughter by another marriage. I've told her that I still am desperately in love with her, that I only want to get her home. And so reality perpetuates myth by necessity. And as myth, repeated, sometimes can bring about something real, I'm beginning to believe the truth of it. I'm beginning to believe that maybe I do love Verona. I don't know. One thing: times of extreme stress, such as we're experiencing here in Moscow, are never good times to make judgments about personal matters like love. So I avoid getting into the topic with myself even though it's tempting at night when I'm lonely and projecting my needs onto my future. This is a dangerous activity and I try to avoid it.

It is late when Harry Samson says goodbye. But first he tells me he'll bring Mai around to my room about noon on Sunday.

After we hang up I begin discussions with myself about what I'll be wearing when she arrives.

Sometimes one can't help but feed their myths.

Especially the ancient ones.

Chapter 36

M|ichael Gresham

GLIISKY SOFTLY CALLS, "ANNA PETROV," and he turns to watch the female guards extricate Anna from the glass defendants' booth. They remove the handcuffs in back and bring them around in front of her, then march her up to the front of the courtroom. I watch as she comes forward. As she moves she tries to hold her head up high, as if she's not surrendered to the bastards who have her locked away yet again.

But when she turns around and raises her hand to be sworn in, that's when we all see. The bruises on her face are just barely visible, but visible, through the pancake makeup they've coated her face with. The eye injuries hide behind mascara applied liberally. She attempts a small smile that flickers on and off. But during that brief moment, I can spot the rectangle where once there was an eyetooth. Quite recently, too. It is all I can do not to run to her and fold her into my arms and demand medical attention. But that would only get me locked up just like her—and just like my son. I resist the pull of decency; my clients need me free more than they need my medical advocacy.

"Tell us your name, dear," Gliisky says to her in his friendliest tone. "We all want to know you."

"Anna Petrov. American citizen. I demand to see a representative of my embassy."

"Petrov. That sounds Russian. Are you Russian?"

"American citizen. I demand to see a representative of my embassy."

"Ms. Petrov, your present incarceration is actually the second for you this winter, is it not?"

She is determined, looks neither right nor left, but stares at the back of the courtroom.

"American citizen. I demand to see a representative of my embassy."

"In fact," Gliisky glides along, the Hans Brinker of smooth courtroom skating, "you were present at Henrik Nurayov's dacha the night of the shooting. Am I correct?"

This time there is no response of any kind. She just stares straight ahead.

"And you have given the guards your written statement, correct?"

Stares and ignores.

"Let me ask you to review your written statement."

He lays it before her on the witness desk but she doesn't even look down. There is again no response.

"The court has previously admitted this statement into evidence," says Gliisky, "so I request that it be read aloud to the jury at this time by the clerk."

"Very well," says the judge, quick to agree. "The clerk will read the exhibit into the record."

The single-page is passed over to the clerk by Gliisky and he takes his seat. She begins reading.

"I, Anna Petrov, do swear the following statement is under oath and is factually correct in all respects. On December 24, 2016, while I was in the company of Russell Xiang, we proceeded to the home of Henrik Nurayov on the north side of Moscow. We hid our car down the road from Nurayov's residence and walked back up the road. We were both armed and intent on killing Nurayov. At that time and place we were both employees of the Central Intelligence Agency and were acting under the terms of our employment."

The clerk pauses and turns the page over. She sees there is nothing on the reverse side and proceeds again.

"As we approached Nurayov's house we made a plan to cut the glass out of his rear sliding door. We made the cut, removed the large piece of glass, and stepped inside. We were greeted by at least six armed men so we gave up our weapons without a fight. We were taken outside to be killed but instead we killed those guarding us. Soon, the others inside the house came out to see what was happening and we caught them in a barrage of gunfire that killed all six guards. We then ran inside the house for the purpose of locating and murdering Henrik Nurayov, but he had fled. So we searched the premises and then walked back up to our car where we got in, drove off and departed. Signed, Anna Petrov, CIA."

"Is that all?" Gliisky asks.

"It is," says the clerk, and she holds out the confession for Gliisky to take. He returns the confession to the stack of documents which are collecting on a table just below the judge. They are all waiting to be taken by the jury into the jury room for deliberations. At that time the jury can read and digest at their own speed.

"I have no other questions for this uncooperative witness," Gliisky tells the judge. He nods at me and raises his eyebrows in a question.

"Yes, I have questions. Ms. Petrov, is that your signature on the statement the clerk has just read?"

"Yes and no."

"What does that mean?"

"My wrist was broken in two places. I signed with a broken wrist so it isn't my normal signature."

"How did your wrist get broken?"

"The guards at the jail hit me with their batons. They kicked me while I was down on the floor. They made me undress and ridiculed me. They hurt my genitals with wire and pliers. They cut out a fingernail with a knife blade. Only after they had done all these things to me did I sign their paper."

"Well, about the things contained in the paper. Did you and Russell Xiang in fact go to the home of Mr. Nurayov on Christmas Eve or morning?"

"No."

"Did you shoot guns while at his house ever?"

"No."

"Did you kill any guards at his house?"

"No."

"Have you ever been to this house?"

"Never."

"Have you ever pursued him?"

"Never."

"Why did you sign the confession, then, saying you did these things?"

"I hurt. I was scared. I signed."

"Do you work for the CIA?"

"I work for the U.S. Embassy in Moscow. I'm a keyboard operator."

"What are your duties?"

"I keep a registry of U.S. citizens who enter Moscow."

"Why is this kept?"

"In case our government needs to evacuate its citizens."

"Why would that happen?"

"Well, say the Kremlin ordered all Americans to leave Russia. We would have a list."

"So it's a safety precaution, this registry?"

"Yes, as much as anything, it's for safety."

"Where were you when you were arrested?"

"Sleeping at my apartment. It was before dawn when the FSB broke in and handcuffed me and took me away."

"Were you frightened?"

She smiles. "No more than you were when the judge threw you in jail, Mr. Sakharov."

"Thank you. That is all."

"Nothing further," Gliisky grumbles. He knows he should be so lucky. He also knows she won't answer anything he asks.

"Ms. Petrov," the judge says, "you will remain in our beautiful downtown jail until you change your mind and answer our prosecutor's questions. Guards, remove this witness from my sight!"

They return her to the glass cage where no one can protect her.

I cannot even bear to watch.

Chapter 37

Michael Gresham

THEN IT IS Saturday and I have some time on my hands. I'm bored with the hotel room and don't yet have my key witness to prepare for Monday. So I decide to go out and visit Moscow. First up is a stroll around Red Square. As I move around the outer perimeter, I wonder if what I've heard about Putin's KGB/FSB is true. Might they be following a nobody like me? Is my room bugged? Are they video recording everything I do and say in there? I decide they are, and for that reason I will take Mai out of there when she arrives. We'll go someplace random, someplace where they can't set up and overhear the plans we make for her testimony. I decide to pay a visit on Marcel and see if he can help me with this. I take a cab to the jail, where the admitting staff knows me the minute I walk in and they ask, "Marcel? Anna? Verona? Russell?" I offer a polite smile and say Marcel's name. A burly guard dressed in blue trousers and jacket and wearing a gun on his hip motions me to follow him. He leads me through the corridors I have memorized, but at the last door I turn and face him. "Do you speak English?" I ask. "I really hope you do."

"Enough," he says while maintaining his poker face.

"Would it be possible for me to visit Marcel in his cell?"

"I don't think. He has other men with him."

"How about in the hallway outside his cell? You could watch us from a distance. I need to talk to him and not be recorded or overheard."

"One hundred, USD."

I dig into my money clip and extract a hundred-dollar bill. "Will this do?"

He eagerly seizes the note from me and pockets it. "Come with me, Mikhail."

Now he leads us along the final corridor, and all along on our right are cells that I count as we go. At twenty-two, we reach Marcel's cell. The guard calls into his shoulder mike for the cell to be unlocked and seconds later that ignominious sound of a jail cell unlocking buzzes loudly not two feet from me. It startles me and I jump. Now the guard smiles. He motions Marcel to join him. He wraps handcuffs around Marcel's wrists, pulled behind his torso, and then turns him around. "Come," he says, and leads us to the very end of that corridor. There, he opens a locked door with his keys and holds out his hand. We are motioned inside. We go in and the door immediately closes behind us. I switch on the wall switch. A broom and mop closet. There's a sink, the large commercial kind, several mop buckets, a good dozen mops hanging from a wall rack, and box after box of cleaning products. Marcel takes a seat on one such box and I do the same.

"You're a sight for tired old eyes," he says.

I shake my head. "Sorry I don't have you out of here yet. But I'm working on it."

"Don't bullshit an old bullshitter, Michael. Nothing short of a Presidential pardon is going to spring me out of here. I'm in deep shit and I know it. Now, why are you here?"

"My hotel room. I know it's bugged and videoed."

He snorts. "So what else is new? This is Russia, Ducky."

"Sure. Mai Yung is coming in Sunday. I'm to meet with her and prepare her for trial."

"Who is she?"

"Russell's birth mother."

"Oh, shit. What the hell did she come here for?"

"She's going to testify."

"About?"

I look around. This room was random. I'm going to chance it.

"She's going to testify that Russell was with her in China on Christmas Eve. She'll say he flew to Moscow the next day to make business arrangements for one of his companies."

"So you've got a voucher. Everyone has a mother who will lie for them. What else you got?"

"I told you that I'm Russell's father. It's a long story that starts from our college days."

"She was in college with you, there was a wild night, our CIA agent is the product of that magical union. Got it."

"Shit, Marcel. Have you really become that jaded in here?"

The corners of his mouth turn down. He scowls. "I've always been this jaded. You've just never noticed before. Or maybe I kept it from you out of regard for your tender feelings. Just fucking with you, Mikey. No, I'm not. I'm going nuts, Boss. You've gotta get me outta here. And soon."

"I'm working on it."

"Really? What's our play?"

"I haven't decided. But I have some things in mind for you. I really do."

"Such as?"

His eyes are boring into mine. It's time to come clean.

"All right. Here's the bottom line, Marcel. You're charged with crimes against the state from your days here as an Interpol agent. The court papers said you murdered two Ministry of Justice agents. I've asked around. I've had Van ask around. Either one of those gets you a lifetime in a work camp. Two of them get you two lifetimes. You following me?"

"So there's nothing?"

"Afraid not."

He lets out a long sigh and his shoulders slump. I see for the first time that his jail tunic is a couple of sizes too big for him. It wasn't, the first month or two he was in here. He's losing weight. Hopefully it's the diet causing the weight loss and not something more serious.

Just then a large black bug emerges from under Marcel's box. It crawls toward Marcel's flip-flops. I imagine he's going to stamp on it like the Marcel I know would be quick to do. But he doesn't. Instead he sadly shakes his head and looks into my eyes.

"I know the guy. He visits us in our cell. He comes and goes as he pleases, the bug. We let him live because we totally admire his freedom to come and go as he wishes. We all aspire to be this bug."

The bug bangs up against Marcel's flip-flop and Marcel slides the rubber sole out of the bug's path. The bug lurches on past and disappears under the next box.

What can I say? We're living in two totally different worlds now, and I have no idea how to help my friend. What started as a day with some possibilities for sightseeing and some good food has now turned into a day of regret. I'm sick at heart that I ever asked Marcel to come to Russia. Had I known then about his record with the Russian Federation I never would have asked. But he's now my responsibility and his trial is still two months away.

There's nothing good to tell him.

"Marcel, where would you take Mai if you were me and you needed to talk in private?"

"Simple. Always do the random thing. Climb on a bus, go to the back seat where you can barely hear due to the diesel engine beneath your butt, and have at it. It's random and it will cover up your conversation with the diesel's knocking and gears. That's your very best bet."

"All right. That's what I'll do."

I have what I came for. We both know I have nothing else to offer Marcel at this point, yet neither one of us moves. It's too damn painful just to walk out of here and rejoin the sunshine and fresh air and leave Marcel in this place. It's inhumane.

"Are they mistreating you?"

"Naw, they're too smart for that."

"What do you mean, they're too smart?"

"They know I just might kill myself if they play too rough. That ends the game right there."

"Why would they care?"

He sighs a long, hard sigh.

"Michael, did I ever tell you I was part of the team that investigated the death of Princess Diana?"

"Princess Di—of Great Britain?"

"Yes. Two young men of her entourage that night were from Moscow. In fact they were employed not ten blocks away from here."

"Where would that be?"

"KGB headquarters. Two of her entourage were KGB agents who were friends of her boy toy."

"You can't be serious!"

"Serious, yes. MI6 wanted them taken out after she was killed. Yours truly drew the short straw. I came here, did the job, and was preparing to board the Aeroflot flight back to London when I was arrested at the airport. At the last minute, I escaped, jumped on a BOAC flight, flashed my Interpol credentials at the flight crew, and made my getaway. That's the short version. The long version is cloak and daggers and hours and hours of waiting for targets to arrange themselves—all that nefarious kind of stuff you read about and see in the movies."

"Wow. This is amazing stuff."

"Actually, it's all a state secret. For what that's worth. There isn't a soul alive in London who wouldn't applaud what I did if the story ever got out. We all loved her, you know?"

"Sure. She was beautiful and charming and wonderful. So the FSB knows it was you who pulled the trigger on these guys?"

"Sliced their throats—but yes, same thing."

"Why didn't you tell me this before I asked you to come here?"

He smiles a bitter smile. "It was you, Michael. I came because it was you asking."

"Well, thanks for that. FML."

"I know you feel terrible, but don't. It was bound to happen sooner or later. That's why I changed my name to Marcel Rainford."

"Wait. Marcel Rainford isn't your real name?"

"No. Read my court papers in the original Russian. You'll see my Interpol name was something entirely different."

"How can we use that? Wrong person?"

"Again? Aren't we beating that old horse to death here?"

"Let me change the subject." I proceed to update Marcel regarding the bill of lading and Nurayov's involvement. Then I tell him about the fact the original bill's page one only lists the one shipping container number. I explain the page I stole was one of two. And that there's no page two. Then I tell him why we don't need page two with the numbers. "Russell has those up here," I say, touching the side of my head.

"So you obtained the original file including the bill of lading from EIS. Is that a nice way of saying there was a burglary?"

"Something like that. So what's my play? How do I put Russell's numbers to work?"

"Contact the embassy. I'll give you a name there. Tell them what you have. Prisoner trades are made constantly between our government and the Russian Federation."

"Doesn't ring a bell with me, Marcel. I didn't know about that."

"They never get picked up by the press. Very hush-hush. It's extremely common, though. Usually it's bodies being traded back and forth. But sometimes information is traded. Your case would be a matter of making the U.S. interested enough in us that they cut loose a Russian spy or three and trade us out of here."

"I see. Give me the name of your embassy contact."

"Try Charles Sidemayor. He's been there forever."

"CIA?"

"Definitely."

"I'm on it."

He leans forward and holds out his hands as if praying. I've never seen him like this.

"Get me out of here, Michael. Please."

"If they want to play, I'll play."

He nods solemnly. "They have no choice. Otherwise Chicago finds itself under a major attack from troops armed with military grade weapons. Or Los Angeles. Or Toledo. Who knows?"

We say our goodbyes and I open the door and stick my head out. Our guard is waiting right there, his back against the door, examining his new hundred-dollar bill. He smiles when I pull the door open.

"That's another one," he says, indicating his cash.

I go to my money. This time I hand him two more.

Who knows when I may need to do this again?

I then follow him back out to admissions, where I ask to see Anna Petrov. It is time to prepare her testimony next.

Chapter 38

M ichael Gresham

WHEN I STOP in at the embassy, I tell the receptionist my name, ask for Charles Sidemayor, and tell her to tell him I have shipping container numbers. I tell her he'll know what I mean, that the containers were offloaded in the U.S. by the Russian company known as EIS. She says because it's Saturday Mr. Sidemayor will be out of his office, that I'll have to wait until Monday. I tell her to just get ahold of him and give him the message, then we'll see. She grudgingly agrees to contact him and I remember again what it feels like to be obstructed by bureaucrats, Russian and American. But that's for another day.

I take a seat in the reception area, open to the public, and put my feet up on the coffee table after removing my boots. I'm tired and could actually take a nap. I close my eyes and within seconds I'm dreaming. There is a vision of a conflict between Verona Sakharov and Mai Yung to see who gets me. My laughter at the ridiculous image shocks me back to reality and I open my eyes. The receptionist is standing right there wearing a wide smile and asking me graciously, "Mr. Sakharov, would you like some American coffee to take with you?"

"Where am I going? Is he coming here?"

"Actually he wants to meet you at the Pushkin at one."

"Where's that?"

"The Pushkin Museum of Visual Art. Everyone calls it the Pushkin. He'll meet you in the cafe."

"How will I know him?"

She smiles. "How about that coffee?"

"American coffee would make my day. I'll ask again: how will I know him?"

"He'll know you, Mr. Sakharov. Not to worry."

At one o'clock on the dot I'm waiting in the Pushkin cafe when in walks my co-counsel, Van. He sits down across from me and looks all around. Wearing sunglasses and a black turtleneck he looks nothing like the neat and conservatively groomed Van I'm used to seeing in the courtroom with me.

"Van?" I say. "You're what—you just happen to be here?"

He extends his hand across the table as if to shake.

"Charles Sidemayor," he says, "Central Intelligence Agency."

"What—what? Van, I'm waiting for Charles Sidemayor. Don't tell me you're—"

"Charles Sidemayor. I'm telling you, Michael, there's more CIA in Moscow than there is FSB. We're everywhere."

"Wait a minute. I called a random phone number to hire a lawyer to act as my Russian co-counsel. You're saying I got you instead?"

"You did. We intercepted your call and they routed it to me."

I'm all but speechless. "You've known all along about Russell and Marcel?"

"And Verona and Anna. You've been doing a nice job with Russell, by the way. You were on the verge of losing that damn trial. Now it's up for grabs, Michael. Nice work."

"This is impossible. I don't believe—"

"Get over it, Michael. We don't have much time. We need shipping container numbers. Your friend Russell has those."

At just that moment, we are joined at the table by a third man. He looks familiar; I know I've seen him somewhere here in Russia before. He smiles and sticks out his hand, "Anatoly Palatov. I bailed you out when you were in jail in Moscow, remember?"

It all comes back to me. "I do. And thank you once again for that. But it also sticks in my mind that I asked you about Russell and you said you'd do what you could to help. Remember that?"

He smiles grimly. "I do. I'm afraid that's been very difficult."

"Meaning what? Do we have a swap to make for Russell and the others or don't we? I know Uncle Sam wants those shipping numbers. So what's the holdup?"

"We want Russell. We want Russell and Verona, Marcel, and Anna. We have four Russian prisoners we'll trade for them."

"Who would that be?"

"Remember when the government sent all those Russian embassy workers home after the last election was hacked?"

"I do."

"Four of them didn't get to go. They were held. President's orders."

"The four we're going to trade for my friends."

"That's right."

"Has the President approved the trade?"

Palatov looks at Van—Ivanovich. Both men nod. "He has no choice," says Van. "He cannot afford a terrorist attack like these weapons would unleash. It's a done deal."

"So what are we waiting for?"

"The Russians won't trade. They're waiting for you to lose the trial. Then they get to keep Russell and keep us from obtaining shipping numbers. If we lose, Russell will have to cooperate with the Russians to stay alive."

"So there's no choice but for me to win and get him out of Russia."

"If you don't," Van said, leaning close to me and speaking softly, "we'll have to eliminate your son ourselves. There's no losing, Michael, not if you want to keep your boy alive."

Both men are standing, making ready to leave.

"Why do you think he's my son?" I ask.

But they don't answer. They have turned their backs to me and they are leaving.

I sit back and close my eyes. So, that's the CIA's game. Either Rusty comes home or he dies very young. My hands are stuffed inside my coat pockets and I realize they're balled into hard fists. I want to hit someone, preferably someone who put my son in this terrible position. But I'm powerless; they're all phantoms and there's no one to strike. Except I'm not powerless in court. There's the bottom line for Rusty and me: the courtroom.

There is a line at the cash register. I decide to give Russian coffee another chance, and get in line. We move forward inch by inch until I'm up to the pastries case. I'm just choosing a glazed donut when gunshots erupt outside the museum. A guard comes in from the outer room hands raised. He's shouting in Russian. The people ahead of me in line visibly relax and continue waiting so I do too. Whatever the trouble was, it must have passed by now.

Ten minutes later I walk out the front doors of the museum. There, at the bottom of the stairs are several police cars and an evidence van. Photographers and TV cameras are all around and there, in the middle of a cordoned-off area, lie two men who have been shot to death. I pause before my next bite of donut. The hair of the nearer one resembles someone I—then I realize. It's them, Palatov and Ivanovich. Van and Palatov have been gunned down.

I drop my coffee and donut where I stand and put my head down and start running. Out to the sidewalk I go, where I skid on the ice and head right, back toward the city. I run until I can run no longer. Then I slow to a walk and turn to see oncoming traffic. It's a simple matter to flag a cab and climb on inside. The driver in front studies me in the rearview mirror. I'll have him drop me a good block away from the Marriott.

A long, snowy block from my hotel, I have the driver pull over at the Moscow Ritz. He understands my hand signs and swings the cab to the curb. I push a handful of Russian rubles at him and climb out.

Then he is off, puttering down the road, tailpipe puffing a long stream of exhaust, and me watching, waiting until he turns the corner and is gone.

Now I trudge through deep snow toward the Marriott. I'm alone and it is snowing and all sounds are muffled. For a moment I'm free again and just taking a walk on a winter's day.

Inside my room I remove my coat. I look down. My hands are shaking. I have to urinate in a huge way. So I hit the bathroom and let fly with a long yellow stream.

I close my eyes. I'm writing my name in the snow with my stream and I'm a child again and none of this is real.

I remove my suit and stretch out under the covers on my bed. The springs creak as I settle in.

Several times that day I hear steps outside my room and the doorknob to my room door being turned. I come fully awake and lie there, panting in my fear and praying the steps will keep going.

And they do. All four times.

IN THE LATE EVENING, Antonia comes up to my room. I invited her, to discuss her husband's case.

We sit at my dining table and I give her a hard look. She's a tough lady; I can tell it to her straight.

"Today, two CIA agents were shot outside the Pushkin. They had just finished talking to me and had just walked down the front stairs. We were discussing Rusty's case."

"Oh my God, does this mean Rusty's in danger in that GD jail?"

"I don't think so. They've already worked him over once for an escape attempt—one giant lie. They don't get a second chance without the U.S. Embassy lodging a complaint. That's negative PR that the Russians can't afford. These are tentative times, what with the arms reduction talks."

"What did they say about his case?"

"They said they were hoping for a prisoner swap."

"But what about the trial itself?"

"That never actually came up. I think they're counting pretty heavily on a swap to get Rusty out."

"But they've been murdered. Does that change everything?"

"Honestly, I don't know. Palatov and Van were the only contacts I had."

"Van? How so?"

"Long story. But it turns out that Van was CIA. Clever, huh?"

"So our plan at this point is to go ahead with the trial?"

"That's the only plan I have."

"Thank God for that. So tell me, Michael, what do you think of our chances?"

"Well, the government just rested its case. Now it's our turn. My key witness comes into town tomorrow and I get to sandpaper her then."

"Key witness? Who on earth would that be?"

"Mai Yung."

"Rusty's mom. Good, she's coming."

"All the way from China. She'll be in around noon tomorrow if you want to drop by and say hello."

"She'll be here in your room?"

"We'll be starting out here. We'll probably go someplace else to have our serious talk."

She looks down. A moment passes in silence. Then, "Michael, the agents who were killed today. Did they have a plan for Rusty?"

I honestly can't look her in the eye. How do you tell a wife her husband will be murdered if his trial is lost? So my answer to her is very vague.

"They were talking about making a trade. Russians for Americans. It sounded plausible enough. I don't know where their deaths leave us. My guess is, nothing will change at the White House. The prisoner swap will be going ahead."

She looks relieved. She pulls a long curl of hair away from her forehead and looks around. Then it's back to me after she's collected her thoughts.

"What about Nurayov? He walks away free?"

I sit back and swirl the ice in my Coke. "Let's think about that. We have Nurayov, who we know is a British subject, works for MI6 and sells British secrets to the Russians or, possibly, the Chinese. Maybe the Iranians. Now the CIA wants him, since the bill of lading was found."

She thinks very fast. "What if the U.S. tells Nurayov they'll pay for container numbers? Then they wouldn't need Rusty anymore and maybe there wouldn't be a prisoner swap."

"The Russians would get their payback if Nurayov turned on them. He'd be dead in six months and he knows it. No, he won't be selling numbers to the U.S."

"So they have to have Rusty?"

I hold up my hand as if swearing an oath. "Absolutely have to have Rusty."

Her eyes tear over. She reaches and touches my wrist. "Michael, the only man I've ever loved or ever will love is Russell Xiang."

"I know."

She shakes her head; she slowly collects herself. She stands and smooths her skirt. "What say I drop by at one o'clock tomorrow?"

"Works for me, Antonia. Come by and say hello to your mother-in-law."

"And to your old love."

Stunned, I look at her, my jaw on my chest. "What—"

"Relax. Henry Xiang loves telling it like a college prank. It's all good."

"Does Rusty know?"

"Not yet. I thought I'd leave that to you—Dad."

"Oh my God."

"Dad. That feels kinda good."

Then she's gone and I spend the rest of the afternoon by myself, reading novels on my tablet.

While I try to remember how to turn off my smile.

Chapter 39

Michael Gresham

THE NEXT DAY, Sunday, I shave at seven when I shower and again at eleven, just before she's due to arrive. She hated facial hair; that's something that's stuck in my brain all these decades. Useless information. Or is it?

I sweep the room with my bug detector. Nothing found.

At 12:05 there's loud rapping on my door. I hurry into the hallway area and swing the door wide open. There stands an enormous black man with wireframe eyeglasses who's biting at a fat stogie clamped in his pearly whites.

"Harry Samson," he says with a laugh. "I called the other night. I said I'd be bringing Mai by your room."

Then he moves his six-four frame to one side and there she stands. Without another word, Harry backs out of the room to leave.

Here is the most perfect porcelain face, a green silk tunic buttoned up to the chin, two red combs deep in her thick black hair, and caught in mid-smile, the beautiful girl from forty years ago, brought here by the beautiful woman she has become. I would never have missed her: I was right all these years. She *is* the most beautiful woman I've ever seen. She steps forward and I fold her into my arms. She hugs up very close and in her hair I smell it: Tweed. The pheromones never lie and the nose never forgets. Tweed enriching the skin's natural oils and fragrances after a long session of love-making. Who would ever forget? She has me, preverbal.

"Michael, you haven't changed a bit."

I'm speechless. Her English is perfect. It's as if she didn't spend the next forty years after college in mainland China. But she did.

I at last manage to say, "I need lunch. Would you join me?"

She laughs. "Always to the point. That's my Michael."

My Michael. Of course, she's right about that.

"That just came out, the thing about lunch. I'm actually so excited to see you I probably couldn't eat."

"We might eat. Let's see what we decide to do. But do you have tea? I'm ready for a strong Russian tea."

I call down and order a samovar. If she asked me for a house I would buy her one and move her in. And maybe me along with her.

I lead her into the sitting area of my suite. She takes the wingback; I take the love seat. We are close enough that the cuff of my pants brushes up against her leg. I swing my leg away, embarrassed.

"So what shall we talk about, Michael? Shall we get right into Russell's case or shall we talk about what you've been up to first?"

"We should talk about you," I say with a big smile.

"That's the most interesting of the three choices you gave me."

"There were two choices, Michael. And talking about me wasn't one of them. But anyway, here goes. Yes, I'm married. Thirty-five years now to the same man, a thoracic surgeon on a pediatric ward. He saves at least one child's life every day. How could you not love someone like that?"

"I'm sure you love him very much. And what about you, Mai? Did you go on to medical school?"

"I did. In China. I'm a board-certified thoracic surgeon, too. Except I operate on adults. We're what's commonly called chest-crackers, my husband and I."

"What about politics? You were pretty much anti-everything back in college. A political nihilist. Has that continued?"

"You know what? I mellowed. As kids will do, I mellowed out and learned to get along. Live and let live."

"Are you a communist?"

"Next question. No, what about your wife? How old, what's she do, do you still love her madly?"

"My wife died. Yes, I still love her madly."

"I'm sorry, Michael. I'm deeply sorry for your loss."

I swipe my hand across my eyes. This is an old friend. I can talk freely here.

"A day doesn't go by that I don't talk to her and have a few tears for her. She was my everything."

"What was her name?"

"Dania. We called her Danny."

"My husband's name is Zhang Wei. It means he's great. So he had a lot to live up to, given a name like that."

"But it sounds like he did, Mai. Which makes me very happy for you. How long can you stay over?"

"Tonight and tomorrow night. I fly out Tuesday."

"Then what do you say we get to work? We have lots of ground to cover."

Our tea arrives and we doctor it accordingly. Then we sip and just enjoy staring at each other. It's been a long time but in that moment it feels like it was only yesterday. I find myself wishing I'd never lost Mai. I find myself wishing that we are still together and we are in this room on vacation and sightseeing in the world's most expensive and most interesting city, Moscow. I sip my tea and let that one play out. But reality calls me up short. It's time to get ready for tomorrow.

Twenty minutes later we're on a bus, in the back, ready to talk. Then we go to work on her testimony. It is tedious and crammed with persuasive details. At the end of the bus line we climb off and find a small cafe with tea and pastries. We order, get our drinks and cookies, and launch into storytime.

Two hours later, I have her story made up and she has embellished it and we're ready for her testimony tomorrow. I have learned that she previously provided a DNA swab to the same lab that tested me and that the DNA witness will be ready to testify on Tuesday. We catch a cab and head back to our hotel.

Then I ask, "Look, why don't you go to your room when we get back, change into some walking-around clothes, and let's walk Red Square?"

She smiles, tossing her head back and laughing soundlessly.

"What's so funny?"

"Harry Samson lied to me."

"About what, Mai?"

"He said he had talked to you and you had said it was terrific, his words."

"What was terrific?"

"If I stayed with you both nights."

I reach over and take her hand. I slowly shake my head.

"Know what, Mai? As much as I would like nothing more than to hold you again, you're married. I can't do that to your husband or to you."

"Michael, kick back and relax. We have a very open marriage, Zhang and I. He sleeps with all his nurses; I sleep with whoever I want. My straying from the fold is rare; his is almost nightly. Or whatever. But Zhang already knows I'm coming to see you and already knows I plan to stay with you. He sends his blessing."

"Holy sh—I'm way upstream on that one. But it's amazing and I'm—I accept."

So we go up to my room and she begins tidying the table we left earlier, humming as she goes. Something strikes her funny. She laughs out loud, sloshes her tea, and I jump up with a linen napkin. Carefully I wipe tea from the back of her hand and, as I do, she turns, places the cup and saucer on the low table to her side, and reaches for my hand. She caresses my hand and then holds it to her cheek.

Looking deep into my eyes, my hand on her cheek, "I never stopped loving you, Michael. You do know that, don't you?"

"Then we're equal. I've never faltered in my love for you, either. If only."

"Let's not do if-only. Let's just stay in the now and grab what we can."

"All right. It's time I did that anyway."

"Please call down to concierge services. They're holding my luggage."

"I'll have it brought right up."

Thirty minutes later we finish what we had started and find ourselves together in the two-headed shower, hot water pounding our bodies and steam filling the room. All I know to do is hold on and not think about Tuesday when this will end. There is no Tuesday, not today.

It's a short cab ride to Red Square, where we have the cabbie let us out at Theater Square. "Look," Mai exclaims, "the Boldshoi Theater. How I'd love to buy tickets!"

Directly across the street is the fantastic facade of the Metropol Hotel, covered with multicolored mosaics and sculpted stone.

From there, we walk southwest on Okhotny Ryad to Manezh Square. Then it's on to the Resurrection Gate. Our guidebook has it that although this triumphal arch was built in the early 1990s, it is an exact replica of the original structure, which stood on this site from 1680 to the early 1930s. Now the stunning square opens up. On our immediate left is the tiny Kazan Cathedral, and on our immediate right— the north end of the square—is the State History Museum.

We walk along the east side of the square, window-shopping the State Department Store, better known as GUM. Then we duck inside and Mai finds a few souvenirs among the fancy boutiques. The mighty towers of the Kremlin are in silhouette in the late afternoon sunlight, dominating the west side of the square.

At the far end of Red Square, the colorful orbs of onion domes and tent peaks belong to the Cathedral of St. Basil the Blessed, the 16th-century church that is probably Moscow's most recognizable sight. We step inside only briefly, find it crowded with tourists, and go back outside to the walkway leading south to the Moscow River. At this point, Mai takes my hand in her own and we are two lovers off for a look on our Sunday afternoon. It isn't long before we hurry back to the Marriott and our room, where we disappear into our bed and make long, languorous love, coming up only for a room service delivery and a new pot of tea later on.

Chapter 40

Michael Gresham

INSIDE THE COURTROOM the next morning, just before eight, there is an unrehearsed moment of mother and son coming together and symbolically pressing their hands together through the heavy panes of glass that comprise the witness box. They cannot hear, but I'm sure they don't need words to communicate how happy they are to see each other. I continue on, up to the front of the courtroom, where I sit and make ready at our counsel table. When the judge comes in and assumes his lofty position at eight sharp, Mai knows that's her cue to step outside into the hallway and wait there until her name is called to testify.

First up is the explanation of Van's absence. Antonia is early; she looks hurt and I know it's because of Van. They had worked up the trial together and I know she had come to like him quite a lot.

Then the judge looks down at me and says, "Well?" I

simply tell the judge that I don't know where Van is, but I'm ready to move ahead without him. "He didn't call you?" he asks and I answer in the negative. "Well," he sniffs, as though snubbed by a suitor, but he decides to plunge ahead without my co-counsel. Then, the judge tells me I can begin the defendants' case.

"Defendants call Mai Yung," I say in my most confident courtroom voice, and we are off and running.

Mai comes forward wearing a plain black dress and an understated string of pearls, nothing too fancy. She looks neither right nor left as she comes forward, a friendly smile on her face. Then she turns in the witness stand, raises her hand, and is sworn. The same translator is in place and renders English to Russian and vice-versa.

"Please tell us your name," I say to her.

"Mai Yung."

"Ms. Yung, where to you live?"

"Beijing, China."

"What do you do there?"

"I'm a surgeon. I treat all manner of disease and injury to adult patients."

"Are you married?"

"I am. My husband is Zhang Wei."

"Are you the mother of Russell Xiang?"

"I am."

"And who is his father?"

"You are."

An excited stirring ripples over the jury as this information takes them by surprise. I can only imagine what Russell is going through right now as he discovers that his father, Henry, isn't also his biological father. It's a cruel way to apprise him of all this, but I wasn't allowed to see him this morning when I stopped by the jail to prepare him for these words. So I can only hope that he isn't swept away by this revelation and stops hearing what else his mother has come to say. He might have to confirm her words; and he might not: I haven't yet decided whether he will testify. I always make that decision about the defendant at the last minute of trial, just before I rest my case.

"Tell us where Russell lives, if you know."

"Certainly. Russell lives with his wife and two children in Chaoyang Park, an upscale district in Beijing. Many upwardly-mobile young business people and professionals make this part of Beijing their home."

"What kind of home does he have?"

"Property is very expensive in Beijing. My husband and I made him a loan for a downpayment on a condominium unit that is about sixteen hundred square feet with three bedrooms. It overlooks the park and is an excellent place to raise children; the schools are the best in China and STEM curricula prevail."

"How often do you visit with Russell in China?"

"At least every week, I'd say. Sometimes lunch with just him; sometimes a family dinner on a Friday or Saturday evening. We're pretty close and I keep close tabs on my offspring." This last part is said with an engaging smile that the jury returns. There are many parents among them, I see from their response. So far, so good.

"What does Russell do in China for work?"

"Rusty is a businessman. He always has been, since he started selling packages of vegetable seeds door-to-door when he was nine. He hasn't stopped selling and innovating since then."

"What kind of products does he sell?'

"With kids anymore everything is a share. Rusty is involved in trade agreements—housing sharing—between citizens of China and Russia. It's amazing how many people want to travel to one place or the other. They go for business reasons and they go to vacation and sightsee. There are similar companies doing this elsewhere, but Rusty insists his is the first among our two countries."

"Perhaps that's a contribution to continuing world peace in its own way, as well. People getting to know each other."

"Rusty is very much dedicated to giving his children a better world than the one he inherited. He hates the things that make countries close their borders to others. He believes in free trade among all countries and he believes in letting market forces effect the change that is natural rather that prescribed by tariffs and isolationist policies."

"Is Rusty political, then?"

"Not even a speck. Rusty is a humanitarian, for want of a better word. He believes in families and intermingling of all people. That's where his heart is its happiest, working to bring people closer together."

"So travel and lodging between countries just naturally interests him."

"I would say naturally inspires him, not just interests. It's his raison d'être."

"Mrs. Yung, is Christmas celebrated in China?"

"It is by some of us. We're Catholics, my family, so we celebrate."

"This past Christmas Eve. Did you see Russell on that evening?"

"I did. Russell and Mya spent Christmas Eve and Christmas day at our house with Zhang and myself. We all celebrated together. We even went to a Midnight Mass on Christmas Eve."

"The prosecutor in this case says otherwise. He's trying

to tell the jury that Russell Xiang was in Moscow on Christmas Eve. You disagree with that?"

"That's ridiculous. Rusty was with me, his wife, their children, and my husband. We've never had more fun together or come closer together in our worship and adoration of the Lord."

"I appreciate that. Would you happen to have any pictures of you and Russell on Christmas Eve?"

"I do. Right here on my camera."

She then produces her iPhone and begins displaying pictures to the jury. All provided by her CIA handlers.

"Here's Rusty and the kids in front of the tree. Rusty and his wife Mya. Me and Rusty. The only thing we're missing is a picture of you and Rusty, Mr. Sakharov."

"Maybe next year," I smile. "Your Honor, we have prints of these same pictures that I'd like to pass to the jury."

"Go ahead. Mr. Gliisky, there are no objections?"

"None, Your Honor. I would claim surprise, but I won't. The pictures are harmless."

Harmless, hell. They place Russell with these people on photographs imprinted with the date, December 24, 2016 and December 25, 2016 right on the face of the print. I didn't ask where these photographs came from, but I'm guessing CIA. Gliisky will never know and neither will I. Fault me if you will for this deceit; how is it any different from the government using guards to come in and say Russell confessed to them (which he would never do) or that Petrov confessed to them—only after she was beaten unconscious and tossed out into a snowbank with missing teeth? I've never been one to be the first to knowingly use tainted evidence in a trial. But once the other side does it, and the court allows it, then anything goes after that. This isn't church; it's court.

"Ms. Yung, has Russell Xiang ever been employed by or associated with an intelligence services?"

"Never."

"How do you know this?"

"I keep very close watch over my children. Russell is one of three. They watch each other, as well."

"Would it be in Russell's character to kill someone?"

"Russell? He once demonstrated against Japanese fishermen who catch live sharks, cut away their dorsal fins and kick them back into the ocean while they're still alive. Russell abhors cruelty among living things. He would never kill anyone. He hates guns, refused to serve in the military and instead opted for social services. It's just not in his nature to hurt others."

"So shooting Russian guards would be something he would never do?"

"That's ridiculous. No, he would never do such a thing."

"I believe that's all the questions I have for now. Thank you for coming."

"You're welcome. It's my duty as Russell's mother."

Prosecutor Gliisky then attempts to cross-examine but Mai Yung is too smart to allow him to punch holes in her story. Added to that is the fact he has no statements to point out prior inconsistencies, no police reports to show inconsistencies between what she said and what the police say—none of the normal tools of the cross-examiner. He finds—quickly—that he cannot trick her and that she will not yield an inch from her prior testimony. So he quits ten minutes after he begins, and Mai is dismissed from the courtroom.

I next call to the witness stand the proprietor of the DNA laboratory in Moscow who performed our DNA tests. He confirms that Mai and I are Russell's biological parents.

Short and sweet—nothing more is needed. There are no questions on cross-examination.

I'm now faced with the most difficult question the criminal defense lawyer ever faces: do I let the defendant testify? Most defendants are anxious to testify; most would slip the noose around their neck and step onto the gallows without encouragement if I allowed them to testify. That's how difficult it is to tell an intelligent, impenetrable story to a jury. And a word to the wise: let your defendant slip up and show he was misleading or lying on even the smallest point— even something as tiny as someone's hair color or their age —and the jury will immediately stop whatever it is they're doing and find him guilty on the spot. They do not tolerate untruths back in the jury room. Not even the innocent kind. So beware; you have been warned, I like to tell my new associates.

Over the lunch break I visit the prisoner holding cells and speak with Rusty. When I'm sure we're alone and I've scanned the cell with my scanner, I nod at him. He immediately erupts.

"I'm stunned, Mr. Gresham. You're my father? Really?"

"We all thought it was better left unsaid."

"Better for who? My whole life is a lie!"

"I can't apologize enough to you. But can we do this later? We don't have much time right now."

His professional side returns. "I'm sorry. Of course. Go ahead."

"You know, Rusty, the truth of the case is heavily slanted against you. And there is much the prosecutors and FSB have against you."

"But my mother she was—"

"Her testimony is fresh in your mind. Give that the weight it deserves at this moment. Let's look at it in context.

The forensics lab puts your boots at the scene. They took molds and compared them to your boots. That was very effective evidence against you. The guards who testified you confessed to them—that is very strong. Then there is Anna Petrov herself. She was forced to incriminate you with her confession even though we showed it was beaten out of her. You also have Nurayov himself. He was likable enough and he puts you inside his home after cutting the glass out of his sliding door. That was very damaging. And all the photographs: the glass in the snow, the cutaway sliding door, the bootprints in the snow, the ejected bullet casings, the tire tracks up at the nut trees, your arrest not long after at the green house. You were there at the green house and there were just too many witnesses to dispute that. No, I think at this point I would rather you stand down, Russell. I'm going to go in and tell Anna the same thing when I finish up with you."

"I will go with your feelings. You're the expert, Michael."

"Thank you. You might hate me for it but you might also love me for it. We'll just have to see."

"All right. Then we're done in there?"

"We're done."

We chat another few minutes then I have the guards let me out of Russell's holding cell and let me into Anna's holding cell.

We hug and she holds on tight.

"How are you holding up?"

She shrugs. "Not good. I cry a lot. My body hurts. The guards make fun of me. My cellmates want to have sex with me."

"The women you're in with?"

"Please, Michael."

"All right. It was a dumb thing for me to say. Anyway, what are your thoughts on taking the stand to testify?"

"I've already taken the stand and testified. I don't want to ever go through that again."

"I don't have a mother here to help you, you know?"

"Yes, and why is that?"

"You know why. Your mother is an FBI agent. It wouldn't work so well to bring her here."

"I know. I was being facetious, Michael."

"Oh. So, no testimony from Anna?"

"No," she says. "Not today. Maybe not ever."

"And you're good with that?"

"Sink or swim, I'm good with that."

And so we left it at that.

We report to the court at one o'clock that we are resting our case. The jury looks relieved. They have been attentive —even rapt—during Mai's testimony, but the DNA stuff bored them to death and they've been casting furtive glances at the courtroom doors ever since. So they're ready to vote and go home.

By one-thirty, the jury has the case and I'm waiting with Mai and Antonia in the hallway just outside the courtroom. We tell our stories and make our estimates of the jury for the first hour, then we fall silent, lost in our thoughts.

At three-thirty we are summoned back inside the court-room. The jury has sent out a question, the judge tells the parties. He tells us he's going to read it: "Are we allowed to set the punishment if we find the defendants guilty or does the court do it?"

"I'm going to send a message to them that advises them punishment is the province of the court and not of the jury's. That potential punishments have no place in their deliberations."

"Agreed," says Gliisky, who's all but rubbing his hands together gleefully from the question.

My heart has fallen but I know I have to answer. "I think the court can tell them that a possible punishment is death by firing squad. Another is life imprisonment at hard labor. At least tell them something substantive."

The judge explodes in laughter at my suggestion. He waves a hand at me, the brushoff, which he has done several times during our trial. I'm ready to shout something equally deprecating to him, but manage to hold my tongue. This is Russia, after all, I remind myself. This isn't Chicago where you pay a fine for contempt. This is Russia where you go to a work camp in Siberia.

"I will send my message, counsel. You can send yours in person once the trial is completed. Assuming you're still free," he says with an evil grimace.

Tell them what? There are no closing arguments in Russian trials. I never did get a chance to speak to the jury from the heart. They never did get a chance to know me or Russell. Maybe if I'd known ahead of time there would be no closing arguments I would have let Russell testify after all. But Van wasn't there to guide me through these intricacies and I realized too late that there would be no closing allowed. This was a crushing blow; I always need desperately to talk freely to the jury before they retire to deliberate. Closing arguments are why we go to law school, so we can be the great, verbal Daniel Websters of our time, the Clarence Darrows of the Twenty-First Century. But not this time, not in Russia.

I stride boldly to the rear of the courtroom once we're in recess again. I demand to be let inside the defendants' box to speak to my clients. The guard, who doesn't understand a word of my English demands, for some reason pulls out a key and unlocks the outer door. Once I'm in the airlock he enters a code into the keypad and the inner door opens wide.

"Sorry, guys, no closing argument," I tell them. "I really missed that opportunity."

"Why no closing argument?" Petrov asks.

"It's just not part of their legal system," I tell her. I don't know anything beyond that. I really don't.

"But they were asking about punishment," Russell says, his voice full of doom and gloom. "That's very bad."

I can only agree. "It isn't good, I agree. Frankly, I'm very frightened. I wish Van had lived long enough to accompany us through this final day."

"What did happen to him?" Petrov wants to know.

"Somebody shot him. Nobody's saying anything. I tried calling the military police but they had no English in their station so I got nowhere."

Just then there is a rap on the door. The same guard is pointing animatedly to the front of the courtroom. I look up and see the judge has returned, Gliisky is back at counsel table, and the judge is waving me forward. The guard quickly opens the door and pushes me from behind, shoving me toward the front of the courtroom. I turn to glare but he is already stone-faced, impassive, standing at attention and totally beyond anything I might have to say to him. So I proceed down the aisle and take my seat at the judge's feet.

"Gentlemen, we have a verdict, I'm told. The bailiff will return the jury to the courtroom and have them take their seats."

Minutes pass by and then the jurors start filing in one by one. I try to make eye contact but no one returns my pleading look. Not one of them looks at me.

The jury passes the verdict to the judge who holds it at almost arm's length, then suddenly draws it near and reads a second time, his face turning red. "This is your verdict?" he asks the jury.

They all answer the same way and the translator confirms: it is their unanimous verdict.

The judge's shoulders sag as he reads, "We find the defendants not guilty of all charges."

There is no reaction in the courtroom. That's another thing. You don't react in Russian courtrooms to anything that happens. You react only at risk of going straight to jail. Have you noticed? Everything here results in jail, possibly.

But I cannot suppress my grin. And my smile. I turn and see Russell and Anna standing and embracing and bouncing up and down together.

"Your Honor, when may my clients be released from custody?"

"Immediately," the judge replies. "Guards, turn those prisoners loose."

No waiting around to be processed out like in American courts. Just BAM! and you're free.

And they are. I meet them halfway up the aisle as they're coming toward me. We embrace. There are many tears and sobs. Mai comes across from the spectator rows and joins us. She wraps her son in her arms and cries, wracking cries, against his shoulder while he pats her back and soothes her. Then it's Antonia's turn, but she very wisely only shakes his hand. She is his lawyer in here, not his wife.

I take Anna in my arms and we both hold on and pray this isn't some kind of monstrous joke, that they're really going to get to leave this terrible, repressive place.

But it's no joke. An hour later we're all in my hotel room

after we crowded into a small Lada taxi and came here together.

I'm sure the CIA is marshaling its agents to come and take Russell and Anna in for debriefing, but for the next little while they're with us. I pass around the room service menu and Mai writes down their orders. I call it down. There are more tears and lots of laughter and shivering as we realize how close we've all come to the razor's edge.

Chapter 41

M ichael Gresham

WE HAVE EATEN and are hoisting glasses of champagne when a knock comes at the door. I look at Russell and Petrov. They nod at me. It is the CIA, their look says, come to collect them up. Russell says he'll get the door and he does. He returns minutes later. "We're needed, Anna," he tells his partner. She gathers their things and they leave together, but not until Russell says goodbye to his mother, who is leaving tomorrow. "I'll see you before then," he promises her. She acquiesces.

Then it is just the three of us: Antonia, Mai, and me. We talk for awhile. Antonia, maybe a half hour later, excuses herself saying she wants to return to her room to shower and change. "Time to ditch the suit," she says with a smile, but we all know. She's leaving Mai alone with me for whatever we need to do.

No sooner is the door closed than I have her in my arms.

"Leave China. Stay with me," I beg.

"I could never do that. I have other children, Michael. Grandchildren. And I have Zhang Wei. I could never hurt him like that."

"I know that. But I wanted to say it. I wanted you to know that I would spend the rest of my life with you in a second if you changed your mind."

She pushes me back. "I won't change my mind. Now let's take a walk. I want to talk about Russell and you."

It turns out she wants me to resist becoming a part of Russell's life. We are standing in front of the GUM store, avoiding being trampled by shoppers when she says this to me. I move us to the curb and hail a taxi. As I do, I realize there are tears in my eyes. Perhaps it's exhaustion, now that the trial is over and the real feelings of exhaustion and terror at what we've just been through can surface. Or perhaps it's the thought of Russell's mother asking me to stay out of his life. Or maybe it's all those things; I don't know. But my hand trembles as I reach for the cab and pull open the door.

We arrive back at the Marriott ten minutes later. Mai tells me she's going to the gift shop, that she has to take sweatshirts and the like to her children and grandchildren. She's even brought a bag to hold those things to be checked through on her flight.

So I return to my room and let myself in.

Which is when I'm shocked to find Marcel sitting at my dining table, eating a hamburger and humming.

He looks ravenous. His clothes are at least two sizes too big.

"What—what—"

"Relax, Mikey. There was a trade, warm bodies for warm

bodies. I just happened to be one of those. And Verona. She's at home waiting for your call."

"Oh, thank God! I've been sick with worry. But I called the Embassy and they told me something was in the works. Russell told me the same thing when he talked to them on the phone after being released. But I didn't know; I had no idea it would be so soon. My God, it's great to see you!"

He stands and gives me a hug. Which is totally not Marcel. He just isn't a hugger but this time makes an exception. I'm sure he's only doing it for me.

"So," I begin, "let's book some air back to the USA."

"No can do," he says. "I've made my decision. I'm stopping off in London, where I'm going to find a nice flat to call home."

"You're really leaving me?"

"Yes and no. I can still handle major cases. I'm only a phone call away, Mikey."

"Sure."

A sadness overtakes me. I have been afraid it might come to this and now it has. There has been way too much loss. However, every morning, early, I have called my children and caught up with them, and with their nanny and grandmother. All is well at home; I am needed there and I have two incredible kids who miss me and love me.

"Mai's going home in the morning. That had to be."

"Sure, she's a married woman with a family. You can't walk into that, Michael. By the way, Russell called the room and I answered. He and Anna were boarding a government jet and heading back to Washington. Antonia was allowed to go with them. So all is well with those three."

"I know Mai's married. Let's just leave it at that. And I'm really relieved to hear about Russell and Antonia and Anna.

It couldn't happen to nicer people. So here we sit, but you're going a different direction."

"But there's a certain Verona Sakharov hoping you'll come to her now that she's been freed. She didn't beat me over the head with it but I know she cares for you. A lot."

Then it comes to me. I glance around the room. Two suitcases.

"Will you do something for me, Marcel?"

"Yes. Anything."

"Will you book two tickets to Chicago, first flight out tomorrow?"

He looks puzzled. "No can do, Boss. I'm not going back. I told you that."

I grin at him. "Who said anything about you?"

I call down to the concierge. "Come get my bags, I'm not staying tonight but I'm not checking out tonight either."

A look crosses Marcel's face as it sinks in.

"I suppose you want me to have dinner with Mai Yung tonight and answer all the questions she has about you."

I look up from my suitcases, zippered shut now and ready to go.

"Yes. Tell her whatever you want about me. Just be sure to embellish it so she sees how much she's missing by not going home with me."

"She already knows that, Boss. We all do."

Then we hug again and a knock comes at the door.

"Ready?" Marcel says, smiling ear-to-ear.

"Ready. I love you, brother."

"Love you too, Boss. Give the little guys a hug from their godfather."

"Done. Tell Mai—no, don't tell her anything. Just tell her thanks for coming."

"Done."

"I'm gone."

"I know."

Ten minutes later, I'm in the backseat of a green-and-yellow taxi, wondering about Verona. Will the real Mrs. Sakharov travel to the U.S. with the temporary Mr. Sakharov? There will be sightseeing and the holding of hands, hopefully followed up with much talking, love-making, and delicious sleep. Who knows where that might go? Maybe it takes on a life of its own, or maybe it's done in a week and everyone goes home alone.

Sakharov the Bear has said his farewells to Danny, the love of his life, to Mai, the love of his youth, and to Russia, a heartless old woman with too many scars to ever be beautiful again.

Chapter 42

I t is a mild day in early January down at the Port of Long Beach when the Cadillac SUVs with the black windows come roaring up the quay, dodging pallets and containers as they come, red lights flashing, sirens wailing—four of them plus a half dozen black-and-white patrol cars. They screech to a stop at a collection of several dozen shipping containers that have waited for so long to be claimed that little sprigs of Johnson grass and yellow flowers have sprung up around them in the cracks and crevices of the platform. It was a long journey just coming here. Russell Xiang, in the end, provided the numbers on these containers only when he and Anna Petrov—with her Rodney— were safely back in the U.S. with their families.

The police and ATF and FBI and hazmat techs jump out of their vehicles and run to the containers. Power shears open the locks and the doors are swung wide.

It is time to begin. The inventory must be taken. First out:, hazardous materials. These are thermos bottles marked SARIN. The shipping container itself isn't marked at all, contrary to law.

Other containers are cracked open. KALISHNIKOV say the crates of automatic weapons.

And on it goes.

By nightfall a fence has been setup around the find, spotlights beam in on the containers while crime scene techs, ATF, and hazmat experts open everything and add every piece to their inventory. The feds want it so the FBI winds up in charge.

The containers are loaded onto huge flatbed trucks just after midnight.

By dawn the area is clear and policed. Hazmat crews have done their work and the area is considered safe. Not a shred of evidence remains to proclaim that a deadly civil war never got started, all for a lack of armaments.

Not even a stray nut, bolt, or staple.

Later that day it comes over the news: the United States and Russia are proceeding with arms reduction talks. Whatever differences they had are apparently resolved.

And in Washington, D.C. Antonia Xiang delivers a healthy baby boy. His name: Michael Gresham Xiang.

THE END

ALSO BY JOHN ELLSWORTH

THADDEUS MURFEE PREQUEL

A Young Lawyer's Story

THADDEUS MURFEE SERIES

The Defendants

Beyond a Reasonable Death

Attorney at Large

Chase, the Bad Baby

Defending Turquoise

The Mental Case

Unspeakable Prayers

The Girl Who Wrote The New York Times Bestseller

The Trial Lawyer (A Small Death)

The Near Death Experience

Flagstaff Station

SISTERS IN LAW SERIES

Frat Party: Sisters In Law

Hellfire: Sisters In Law

MICHAEL GRESHAM PREQUEL

Lies She Never Told Me

MICHAEL GRESHAM SERIES

The Lawyer

Secrets Girls Keep

The Law Partners

EMAIL SIGNUP

If you would like to be notified of new book publications, please sign up for my email list. You will receive news of new books, newsletters, and occasional drawings for prizes.
— John Ellsworth

ABOUT THE AUTHOR

For thirty years John defended criminal clients across the United States. He defended cases ranging from shoplifting to First Degree Murder to RICO to Tax Evasion, and has gone to jury trial on hundreds. His first book, *The Defendants*, was published in January, 2014. John is presently at work on his 25th thriller.

Reception to John's books has been phenomenal; more than 2,000,000 have been downloaded in 60 months. All are Amazon best-sellers. He is an Amazon All-Star every month and is a *U.S.A Today* bestseller.

John Ellsworth lives in Arizona in the mountains and in California on the beach. He has three dogs that ignore him but worship his wife, and bark day and night until another home must be abandoned in yet another move.

johnellsworthbooks.com
johnellsworthbooks@gmail.com

Printed in the USA
CPSIA information can be obtained
at www.ICGtesting.com
LVHW010537070224
771130LV00018B/785